THE MAN FROM THE EAST

~

THE MAN FROM THE EAST

Istimah Week

Vantage Press, Inc.
New York

FIRST EDITION

All rights reserved, including the right of reproduction in whole or in part in any form.

Copyright © 1996 by Istimah Week

Published by Vantage Press, Inc.
516 West 34th Street, New York, N.Y. 10001

Manufactured in the United States of America
ISBN: 0-533-11698-8

Library of Congress Catalog No: 95-90748

0 9 8 7 6 5 4 3 2 1

'It is a direct experience of the power of God available through a man from the East.'

— *In a letter from J.G. Bennett, August 1958, describing the spiritual exercise of Subud.*

Contents

Acknowledgements ix
Introduction xi

PART ONE

Chapter One	Before the Latihan	3
Chapter Two	Bapak Muhammad Subuh	17
Chapter Three	Bapak Explains Subud, USA	29
Chapter Four	Guests at a Difficult Time, Indonesia	49
Chapter Five	Intermission in New Zealand	65
Chapter Six	Life Near Bapak, Indonesia	77
Chapter Seven	Bapak's World Tour, 1970	91

PART TWO

Chapter Eight	An Unexpected Gift	115
Chapter Nine	'Ibu Is Within You'	121
Chapter Ten	The Spiritual and the Material	131
Chapter Eleven	Helpers and Being Helped	145
Chapter Twelve	Bapak's Last Years	173

Epilogue 185
Appendix 187
Glossary 189
References 191

Acknowledgements

THIS BOOK owes its existence to Bapak Muhammad Subuh, who inspired it; to my close friends and family, who encouraged me to write down my experiences; to my husband, Mark, who supported it with love and understanding; to Raymond van Sommers, who as co-author made it possible; and to Tess d'Alpuget, who was the perfect editor, combining artistry of her craft with generosity of spirit. Where the book finds favour, may any praise fall where it is due, and where the feeling or fact in anyway offends may I be forgiven.

I dedicate this book to my daughter Sandra, whose generation I pray will see the benefits to mankind of the *latihan*—the spiritual exercise of Subud.

Istimah Week

Introduction

THIS STORY IS a memoir of that part of my life which was close to Bapak Muhammad Subuh* during the twenty-eight years from 1959 to his death in 1987. I describe the man in action, in my life and in his mission, which was to pass on to others the spiritual exercise of Subud, the latihan.**

It is a selection of personal experiences. It is not a biography of Bapak and does not attempt to describe in detail the Subud† movement. It is in the main my account of what happened after I made contact with the possibility of following the Will of God within myself.

Where I feel explanation about Subud would be helpful, I quote from Bapak. For example, here is his clarification of the principles and purpose of the latihan kejiwaan of Subud, as given in his London talk in August 1959:

The spiritual exercise of Subud is in truth the worship of man towards God, awakened in us by the power of God at the moment this same power arrests the interference of our thinking minds, our hearts and our desires. ...

You ask why it is that Subud has only now come upon the earth, and not before? ... It has come now because now is the right time for man to receive it, since all mankind is now under very heavy pressure from worldly influences and cannot resist them. This pressure of the world upon man, and its hold over him, are so dreadful that he has by his own actions thrown the world situation into a state of chaos.

... God knows when the time is ripe for man to receive His gift in the right way. [2]

---

* Bapak Muhammad Subuh—for short Pak Subuh
(Bapak, or Pak, is Indonesian for Father or respected older man).

** Latihan: Indonesian word which literally translates as training or exercise.
Here it means the latihan kejiwaan of Subud—the spiritual exercise of Subud.

† Subud is an abbreviation of Susila Budhi Dharma. It symbolises the possibility of right living through the grace of God received in the latihan kejiwaan of Subud.
See also Appendix: The Meaning of Subud. [1]

Introduction

When I heard, in 1958, that the latihan—a direct receiving from the power of God—was available in this world, I was at once convinced of its reality and yet unable to believe my good fortune. After thirty-five years of following the latihan, these feelings have not changed. That the power of God can be received so simply and directly is still a marvel.

I felt for sure that I would never be lucky enough to meet Bapak, the man chosen to bring this contact to mankind. It was to be quite otherwise and without my design. I later went to live in Indonesia, at Bapak's invitation, and after several years spent close to him and Ibu, his wife, I travelled around the world with him visiting many countries and translating his talks into Spanish, my native language.

Bapak's personal attention encouraged and supported me through the process of change which I was to face after coming into Subud. And he treated me with exceeding kindness even when I went through a severe test of faith.

This book started out, through the encouragement of my friends, as a record of my experiences with Bapak, but as I wrote I realised I wanted to do it as a token of my gratitude. If it brings the latihan to the attention of others, it will come nearest to Bapak's greatest wish and to what may be the Will of God for mankind.

Istimah Week

The Man From The East

Part One

Chapter One
Before the Latihan

As with many of us, I started life with difficulties to solve inherited from my forebears. In addition there was family violence in my childhood. If nothing remarkable had happened, my life—as with anyone else's—would have been lived out compensating for these effects. But something extraordinary did happen. By the grace of God, I was helped to heal the wounding and begin to repair the ancestral damage. It is about this grace—the spiritual latihan of Subud—that I write, and the impact on my life of my experiences with Bapak Muhammad Subuh.

I was born in Punta Arenas, on the Straits of Magellan in southern Chile, into a conventional Catholic family. My father was from Yugoslavia and migrated to Buenos Aires as a young man. At that time he wanted to join the priesthood but was frustrated from doing so by his parents. My mother was also from Yugoslav parents and was born in Punta Arenas.

My mother, known to everyone as Mayko,* had five sisters and two brothers. My grandparents on my mother's side lived to an old age. As a result I was part of an extended family. I was closely attached to my mother and was very fond of my mother's youngest sister, Fanny, who was married to the charismatic Jose ('Pepe') Grimaldi, a well-known poet in Chile.

My feelings for my father, on the other hand, were extremely ambivalent. He could be very kind and generous, but from my early years, I mostly remember his fits of uncontrollable anger directed at my mother—and towards me, in order to intimidate her.

When I was one year old, in order for my father to obtain better work, we moved to Antofagasta on the Tropic of Capricorn in the desert region of northern Chile. He took a position as an accountant with an American mining company. My brother, Guido, was born there when I was five.

* Mayko is Yugoslav for mother.

Chapter One

In those days the immigrant communities in Chile were very distinct. I was first placed in a German school. My mother wanted me to have an education that would emancipate me from the dependency which her childhood had produced. She felt that it would be a help in my life if I learnt another language. However, docile as I was—usually accepting everything—I rebelled against the German school. I remember standing in the doorway refusing even to sit down. My parents had to take me away, and they decided to try the English school. Here I gave no trouble at all. I became a model student, getting good marks from the beginning.

As a young girl growing up in Chile, I was devoted to the Catholic Church. From my earliest years, I was taken every Sunday morning to Mass, usually by my mother. I loved it. The church was fifteen minutes' walk from our house. I was particularly fond of the services of El Mes de Maria, a celebration dedicated to the Virgin Mary held every year from November 8 to December 8.

When I was nine years old and still living in Antofagasta, I attended a special catechism class every afternoon as preparation for my first communion. This took place in the cathedral in the main town square. The priest was very strict, impressing high standards of behaviour on our group of twenty or so girls. We made our first confession the evening before the communion.

Once in the church, we young girls, dressed in white, were seated apart. Our parents sat at the back. The Mass was very beautiful, and then the great moment came. One by one we received our first communion. It was for me a very special spiritual experience. I was transported to a state of near ecstasy. All that day the feeling was beyond anything I had ever known in my life. It remained even though I continued the day normally, playing with a friend.

We left northern Chile when I was twelve, my father having become dissatisfied with his promotion opportunities, and moved to Valparaiso on the central coast, a picturesque city with steep narrow streets. It overlooked the Pacific Ocean and adjoined Vina del Mar, a beautiful seaside resort with a Mediterranean-type climate. Here, we bought a small two-storey boarding house for about five guests, which my mother had saved for and which she managed. Each morning I took a tramcar to attend an English establishment, the Griffin School for Girls, in Vina del Mar. I finished my general education at the age of sixteen. All my schooling was in English.

Later I went to secretarial school in Valparaiso and became qualified as a secretary in English and Spanish. I was still in this school when my teacher recommended me for a job. My boss was a wealthy man of the social elite who lived in Vina del Mar. He was encouraging and through him I established my confidence as a secretary.

My father had meantime, through his contacts in Punta Arenas, been able to start wholesale trading in frozen lambs. When the business was established, we moved from Valparaiso to Santiago, the capital of Chile. Soon after our arrival, a cousin came to visit us. She said she knew of a man, Don Eulogio Sanchez, who was looking for a private secretary and why didn't I apply? Now my destiny had been set, and I soon found that I was working for one of the most important men in Chile. He was a national hero. As leader of a national militia, he overcame an attempt by armed communist forces to take over the government of Chile in 1932. Later he insisted on free elections but refused to stand for political office.

Don Eulogio was the president of at least five big companies that he himself had established. During the years I was with him, he continued to create new companies until by the time I left the number of employees had tripled. He was a wonderful man to work for, respected by everyone, highly educated and extremely intelligent. At the same time, he was caring and charming. We got on very well together, and he gave me responsibility for many personal matters, private appointments, management of his personal cash, and so on. I shared his day to day enthusiasm for his businesses and often his light moments of personal delight—a new song or a surprise present for his wife.

As I worked for Eulogio, my life changed. I was away from home at the office five days a week and Saturday mornings. I very much enjoyed what I was doing and developed a new confidence in myself. I had the chance to meet many prominent people. I was sometimes invited to lunch by Eulogio's friends. They in turn introduced me to their wives who invited me to their houses.

My father too changed. He now had a demanding and fulfilling job. He was capable and worked hard at extending and improving the enterprise that was now his responsibility. He was much more at peace with himself. If there ever was a sporadic outburst, my brother was able to reason with him. Our relationship improved considerably. I suggested to him that we build a house together, using my savings and his. I was introduced to a well-known architect,

Chapter One

Don Andres Garafulic, who built us a beautiful house only thirty minutes from the city centre. It had a large garden and a wonderful view of the Andes.

Among Eulogio Sanchez's company expansions was a branch office in New York City, downtown in Wall Street. It was through this office that I had the opportunity to travel to the USA. I had never thought this could be possible. I stayed five months and loved the experience. I returned to Santiago with a promise to myself that I would one day come back to New York. I continued with Eulogio, but by 1950 I decided I wanted to retire from work for a while. Perhaps New York unsettled me, but anyway I had been launched on a working career straight from school and now wanted some time for myself.

It was customary in those days for a young woman to live at home if she was not yet married, and for the next two years, I spent my time there, with plenty of outside interests such as tennis, swimming, and skiing. My close friends included Germans, Italians, and Americans.

My father had become settled and secure in himself. My mother and I could now enjoy the good and often ebullient side of his character, which had been denied us in the years of my childhood.

My love of the Mass and the place of the Church in my life continued well into my twenties. I attended Mass every Sunday and often went to confession and communion. But one day in Santiago something occurred that troubled me deeply. In a Sunday service, the priest gave a sermon from the pulpit during which he asked for money. He did this at the same time as the Mass was taking place at the altar. This was terribly wrong, I felt. The incident had the effect of loosening my absolute commitment to Church authority. Was it also connected with the impending spiritual possibility outside the Church that was to change my life?

In 1954, I took a ship and sailed back to New York, where I was invited to work as a Spanish-English speaking secretary with an American company. Their offices were in the Empire State Building. Among the few people I knew in New York were an American couple, Yaro and Vera Smirnoff, whom I had met during the previous two years in Santiago.

It was this couple who introduced me to Erling Week, at a dinner at the Plaza Hotel. He sat across from me at the table. He was a handsome American, above average height and slim, with dark hair. He was very neatly dressed and extremely polite. I was surprised to learn that he had been in Chile.

His business, he said, had taken him several times to Santiago. Erling was then in his late thirties. At the end of an enjoyable evening, he offered to walk me home. On the way he told me that he was from California and that he was in New York waiting for his divorce to come through. I accepted invitations from him to movies, theatres, and dinners. He was alone and I was delighted to be taken around New York in such a friendly way.

Erling told me about his life. Although he was very involved in business, he took a great interest in esoteric matters, reading many books on the subject. He had had many strong spiritual experiences some of which seemed quite bizarre to me.

One night in 1952 in a half-dream state he had heard a loud voice say: "You know enough! Your time has come!" He said he thought this meant he was going to die. Then he experienced a sound like an explosion outside the house and a bright light lit up the room. He and his wife of those times jumped up from the bed. They took a flashlight and went looking around, but could find nothing. The next morning they talked to their neighbours and nobody had heard anything. They realised that the experience had to do only with Erling himself.

From then on, Erling said, his life was totally changed. He was clairvoyant and had gained many other extrasensory faculties. An inner locution at that time said, "When his flock begins to stir, the Shepherd cometh." (This was a reference he later connected with the prospect of the Second Coming.) He wound up his business responsibilities and travelled to Europe in search of "someone." There he was introduced to a personal friend of Pope Pius XII, Bernard Fay, who was able to shed light on his experiences. He had not long returned from this trip when I met him.

When I had come to New York, it was my intention to stay only a year. However, when the time came for me to return to Santiago, Erling asked me to marry him. He had been able to finalise his divorce, and we were married soon after.

In the year that followed, we travelled to California to meet Erling's family and friends. When I was expecting my first child, Erling suggested we fly to Chile, for him to meet my family. He liked Santiago so much that we decided to make a home there. We rented a house in Las Condes, a rural area just ten kilometres east from the edge of the city. The house was contemporary

Chapter One

American style, single-storey and spacious. Large windows overlooked the garden on one side and the main range of the Andes on the other. The mountains towered over us in the clear air, especially El Plomo, stark and impressive with its glistening glacier. The Rio Mapocho, two hundred metres away, murmured through the still nights, sometimes growing to a roar. The land was one hectare, with many fruit trees, mostly peach but also apricot and quince, and raspberry bushes. There was a swimming pool and in summer flowers bloomed in profusion.

My mother, father, and brother lived in the suburb of Avenida Colon, not as elevated as the hills of Las Condes, but nearer the city. It took me only fifteen minutes to drive down to their house.

David was born in the Clinica Santa Maria in Santiago on November 11, 1955. Erling had meticulously arranged everything for the birth and hired one of the nurses to live with us for the weeks that followed. We settled down happily, devoting ourselves to family life. David was a strong and contented baby, easy to take care of. He was quick to learn and could walk at nine months.

A year and a half later, Cathy was born. She was small and fair. Erling was delighted to have a girl. When she was just two weeks old, my father arranged her christening at the local church. Pepe and Fanny came up from Punta Arenas.

Meantime Clementina joined our extended family. It was early March 1956. I can picture it as if it were happening yesterday. I had a maid, but on her day off, Maria, who was about twenty, came to help me in her place. She was one of the girls who lived with their parents in the small caretaker's hut built on the empty lot next to ours. Mayko had come to the house. She had lost her maid and wanted me to ask the people at the back if they had a daughter who would like the job. I was very doubtful, because I felt that I knew all the girls and they already had jobs. However, I asked Maria to speak to her parents. To my surprise her mother came over with a daughter whom I had never met. Her name was Clementina. She was very, very shy, but Mayko decided to employ her.

As the days passed, the leaves of the fruit trees turned to red and gold. Snow came again to the Andes, heavy that year, mantling the great peaks in white splendour and sending cold winds coursing through the garden. The swimming pool became too cold to use and frost cloaked the grass at dawn. Mayko told me that she had had to teach Clementina everything, even how to hold a broom, but that, little by little, Clementina had become very efficient. "She is still shy," she said, "but she is very willing and respectful."

Before the Latihan

On September 17, 1957, my father died. Clementina was the last one to see him alive. She said he went off to work singing an Argentine tango, *"Adios Muchachos Compañeros de Mi Vida,"* which translates, "Goodbye to you, the companions of my life." He died a few hours later of a heart attack.

David, who was not quite two, had been especially fond of my father and my father adored him. Normally David did not like to leave us, but he would eagerly go to his grandfather whenever they met. David had got to know my father's green Chevrolet and when my father suddenly disappeared, he would point to all the green cars as we drove along, calling, "Nono ... Nono ..." My heart ached for him.

In early 1958, it became obvious that Erling's business interests in the USA were deteriorating without him and it was necessary that he return and take over the management again. David was two and a half years and Cathy almost one year old. We moved to Briarcliff Manor, Westchester County, a suburb of New York, near Erling's business in Ossining—Collett-Week Corporation, which produced natural concentrates for the pharmaceutical and food industries, notably Vitamins A, D, and E, and chlorophyll.

We settled into a beautiful home overlooking the Hudson River and furnished it with every comfort. A trip to New York City took forty-five minutes along parkways through the most lovely woodlands I have ever seen. Autumn in Westchester County is famous. Shops in the district were top quality and I brought my maid, Sonia, from Chile. I had a new car every two years and we took many vacations. In short, our life in Briarcliff could not have been more perfect. It was a Camelot into which there was soon to come a change more radical than anyone could have possibly imagined.

ONE OF THE TEACHINGS Erling had read about was the Gurdjieff Fourth Way, a method for the development of higher consciousness in man. Gurdjieff, a mysterious Caucasian who established an esoteric school in France between the wars, had devised a series of exercises to enable followers to awaken self-awareness and the possibility of more intense states of being.

John G. Bennett, a pupil of Ouspensky, who taught the Gurdjieff System, founded the Institute for the Harmonious Development of Man in Coombe Springs, Surrey, England, to carry on this teaching and in 1957 was working with some four hundred pupils, including some living in other countries.

Chapter One

My brother, who was very close to Erling, became interested in the Gurdjieff System. Because of this, he began corresponding from Chile with Mr Bennett.

It was in the summer of 1958, when I was living in Briarcliff Manor, that I started to feel that I wanted to find a source of inner spiritual growth or religious experience that was wider than my worship at church. I couldn't quite relate to Erling's inner experiences, and, although I knew of my brother's connection with John Bennett's Fourth Way teaching, I had no personal interest in that.

One day in early June, I received a letter that changed everything, inwardly and outwardly. Erling was away on a short business trip. The mailman came and I picked up a few letters. One was from my brother in Chile. As I read it, I felt "This is the most important moment of my life!"

Guido said that he had been informed in a letter from Mr. Bennett that his studies of Gurdjieff were no longer necessary. Something new had come. "It is," Bennett had told him, "a direct experience of the power of God available through a man from the East. It requires no teaching and there is no dogma."

Mr. Bennett had gone on to say that he himself had received this contact and that it was indeed a force that was so pure that it could enter directly into the soul of any man or woman who asked for it simply by passing from one person who had already received it to another who sought it. Once you have it, no more intermediaries are needed. At the same time, it is compatible with all religions.

I stood in the living room, staring at the letter. I was alone. The children were in the garden with the maid. I felt as if I had received a revelation. I knew, without doubt, that I wanted this more than anything else in the world.

When Erling phoned me later in the day, I told him that I had something very important to tell him and implored him to hurry home.

For the next six days, as I waited for Erling, I felt charged up. I could do nothing in a normal way anymore. I couldn't sleep properly. When Erling arrived, I was at the door to meet him, holding the letter from my brother. He read it and I asked: "Is this what you have been waiting for?"

"Yes," he said.

Erling had already told me that he had come to believe, from his spiritual experiences, that there would be great changes in the world during his lifetime and that these changes would be brought about by what he interpreted to be

Before the Latihan

"the coming of a new expression of Christianity." Later experiences led him to expect that divine help would come through someone from the East.

I wrote the next day to Mr. Bennett, asking for information about this remarkable contact. He sent me the name of one of the three women in New York who had received the latihan of Subud—as the receiving of this grace of God was called.

The latihan kejiwaan of Subud, he explained, was a spiritual exercise (the word *latihan* in Indonesian means exercise or training and *kejiwaan* means spiritual). It is received through an attitude of surrender to God while standing with someone who already has practised the latihan. The first latihan is called receiving the contact and a person who has received it is said to be opened.*

The person standing by surrenders to God and follows his or her own latihan. Women do the latihan only with women and men with men.

Erling and I immediately became members of a group of forty to fifty men and women who met every two weeks to ask questions about Subud. We were told there was a waiting period of three months. Three months to the day I received the latihan.

My opening was conducted in a hall with normal lighting. I was asked to take off my shoes and any jewellery that I might feel a hindrance to free movement. Together with about six other women I stood with the three women who had already been opened and who were authorised by Pak Subuh to pass the contact to other people. One of the women then said a few words from Pak Subuh, which explained the conduct of the opening. It said that those passing on the contact were only witnesses to my sincere wish to worship God. And, as God is Almighty, it was not appropriate to try to use self-willed desires and thoughts. For this reason, I was not to concentrate my thoughts, but to open my feelings, truly surrender and submit to the will of God, and to be patient and sincere before Almighty God.**

When the woman had spoken these words, she asked me to close my eyes so that I would not be distracted by the other people, to relax and follow any movements that arose. She then said, "Begin." . . .

---

* Opened: The word in Subud means the release or the relief of the pressure of the desires, thoughts, and emotions of the person who wants to receive contact with the power of God.

** Later it became the custom that those being opened were asked before the opening to repeat a declaration of faith that they believed in God and that they wished to worship only God.

Chapter One

After half an hour, she said, "Finish."

During the half hour, the three women simply did their own latihan, surrendering to the will of God. I could feel that there was no influence from them. I received the latihan and had no doubt that it was directly from the power of God. I felt a deep state of peace and noticed my body swayed slightly of itself.

Meanwhile, up until the end of our three-months waiting period, there had been no man with the contact in New York City, so there was no one to open the men probationers. However, that week a man came from England on business and Erling was able to receive the latihan in another room at the same time as I did. What I did not know was that coincidentally on that same night my brother was being opened in London, where he had gone from Chile.

From then on I went regularly to the latihan, twice a week, rain, shine or snow, getting sitters to stay with the children. I became more and more certain, directly from my own experience, that this latihan of Subud was the true worship of God. I experienced it as an inflowing of divine grace, a contact with the power of God. I came away in a state of deep inner peace.

It is not easy to describe what happens in the latihan as a result of this surrender to God. The thinking, desires and emotions subside, and one finds oneself in a deeper part of one's spiritual being. In this state of surrender, the inner feeling is filled with belief and the worship of God. Gradually a vibration of energy is felt. This is the beginning of experiencing a new life of the inner self.*

Pak Subuh has explained it this way:

It no longer seems strange to you that, after a latihan, you should feel the stirring of a new life within you that was not there before. This stirring of life means that the soul is awakening and being liberated from its bondage to the power of worldly influences. [3]

As a devout Catholic, I continued to attended Mass every Sunday. My Catholic faith remained a quiet certainty in the background, setting the standards of my outer life while the latihan brought about a direct inner state of worship.

---

* Inner self: The eternal part of one's self. When the inner self has reached the human level, it has its own consciousness and (higher) wisdom.

Before the Latihan

Soon after I was opened, one morning during the children's school holidays, I felt a strong need to be alone. I asked Erling to take the children to his office, and as soon as he left, I did the latihan in the living room. It was an intense experience and I found myself lying on the floor. I heard a voice as if entering the top of my head. It was loud, yet with no outer sound, and said: 'Put your trust in God and not in man!' With it I felt touched by a mysterious mixture of love and closeness to God, which stayed with me for several days.

Later I came to realise how important this message had been in preparing me to deal with the enormous changes in my life that followed. The latihan had started to become a source of guidance.

Pak Subuh was later to explain:

This latihan that you have received is instruction from God, not instruction from man to man. The proof of this will arise by itself within each of you. You yourself will be astonished and amazed, because what is in your inner feeling will arise by itself. [4]

One night at the Subud House, I had another experience that impressed on me this sense of inner guidance. About eight of us were standing together in a dimly-lit room, preparing to start our latihan, when I heard a voice, as if from above, that said to me, "You will receive a gift!" In that case, I thought, this gift will come while I am doing the latihan, because to me nothing in this world was higher than the latihan. However, the latihan finished and nothing happened.

Afterwards, we sat on chairs together, quietly. Unexpectedly, over there to the left of me, I sensed there was something powerful. It was a force—as if from God himself. Instinctively, I looked in that direction. Then a voice said to me, "The love that you are yearning for will be given to you." I knew then this meant that I would find the love of God.

I was to understand much later that my father's threatening behaviour towards me as a little child had wounded my faith in God's love towards me. This was unknown to me until I was faced with its purification. When that finally happened, I became like Job, protesting to God, 'Why do you treat me like this?' Worse, I felt myself going into a darkness of despair wherein God was no more. In that darkness (that my father knew, but could not escape), faith in God's love was essential. My faith in love was finally healed by the process of the latihan. During that process Pak Subuh was for me the exemplar of impersonal love, kindness, and consideration.

Chapter One

Meantime in the months that followed my opening, I was experiencing the effects of the latihan in more immediate ways. Even if I arrived at the latihan worried about something, by the end of the thirty minutes, I would be at peace whether the problem had been resolved or not.

When I had a spiritual experience outside the latihan, it usually came as an indication of what the latihan could bring more permanently, showing me a possibility of living differently. Once I experienced an important change of consciousness in a simple situation. I was hanging out the washing when suddenly I had the experience of a new life in my hands as they were doing their work. With this I became an observer of myself and what I was doing. This was a job that I normally did automatically, wanting to finish it as soon as possible. This experience gave me a glimpse of a new dimension of inner life and it happened without the heart's interference.

Another time I became aware that I could be given a change of inner state. The experience started with an early morning dream. I was told to draw the face of St Francis of Assisi. I followed the instructions and drew an image of his head and face. When I awoke, the latihan was flowing through me strongly. I had no idea what it was all about. I had not been an especially strong devotee of St Francis. Later in the morning, I went to the garden to check some newly-planted flowers. As I bent down, I noticed, not far away, a little bird. I knew it was strange that the bird was willing to be so close to me, because it was a wild bird. When I stood up, it flew to the nearest tree. I went over and started to stroke its back, which it confidently let me do. For those moments the quality of St Francis had been made alive in me.

In those early days, I also experienced a spontaneous change in my relationship with my daughter, aged three. She was more demanding than my first-born. Suddenly I had a new perception of her vulnerability, and with it I felt a special love, more according to her needs. I did not have to try to do this; it came by itself.

I began to see what a great blessing purification by the latihan in this way could be. If I had never received the latihan, I would have been stuck, perpetuating the same mistakes. These dispositions to error I would then pass on to my children, and they in turn to their children, down the family line. As it was, the latihan was cutting across my patented attitudes, which otherwise might well have gone unchanged.

Before the Latihan

Meantime we had been opened about two months when John Bennett invited Erling to come to England to visit him. My brother was still there. Erling went and discussed plans for John Bennett to come to New York in early 1959, and for Pak Subuh to visit New York in April 1959. John Bennett asked Erling to take over as Chairman of Subud New York. On his return to New York, Erling devoted much of his time to the needs of the group, leasing and refurbishing large latihan premises, and making arrangements for Pak Subuh's impending visit.

Soon after this my brother came to New York. As we sat chatting in the living room, I could hardly recognise him. He was like a stranger, this man sitting in front of me, who had received the latihan for only a few months in England at the age of thirty. Here he was talking about God in virtually every sentence. Previously he never went to church. I had never heard him refer to God. What could have happened to him? Could the latihan have done all this?

AS PLANNED, John Bennett and Pak Subuh came to New York, invited by our group, and were lodged in the home of a member in Manhattan. With Pak Subuh, who was called Bapak by all Subud members, were his wife, Ibu, her daughter Rochanawati, his Indonesian translator, Dr Anwar Zakir, and Dr Zakir's wife, Ratna.

I was soon to meet 'the man from the East,' who had been chosen to bring the latihan of Subud to the world.

Chapter Two
Bapak Muhammad Subuh

I FIRST MET BAPAK when he came to our house in Briarcliff Manor, USA, in May 1959. Erling had invited him to lunch and he arrived accompanied by Dr Anwar Zakir. The house, which the maid always kept immaculate, was looking beautiful with fresh flowers beside the view windows. The dining table was laid with our best silver. I knew from experience that I had everything adequately prepared. Yet I was nervous. No, it wasn't the practical things; I'd done them all before. It was the excitement that welled up inside me. To me this was the person chosen to bring a direct contact with the power of God to mankind!

As Bapak entered the living room, I saw a strong well-built man with a kind face. He was in his late fifties. I had never seen an Indonesian before. His skin was golden brown, and he had perfect white and even teeth. His hair had been dark and now was beginning to grey. He stood very straight, relaxed, often with his hands clasped behind him. However, what I noticed most were his eyes. They were soft, deep, and quiet, and had a quality of intense stillness. I had the impression he could look into my soul and yet pass no judgement.

Bapak returned my greeting with a smile. He was very friendly and made me feel at ease. However, throughout the lunch and afterwards, I was very conscious of his presence. Whereas another person's strong presence may have diverted my attention, Bapak's presence had the reverse effect. It made me increasingly aware of myself and of everything I was doing. In this heightened state, I did everything with the utmost care, affected by his deep inner quietness. I was to find out later that my experience of self-awareness and the wish to do things well—to my utmost—was the common experience of many when near to Bapak.

He acted in a very pleasant and congenial way. He showed a great interest in where we lived and during the meal talked mostly about ordinary things. His voice was steady and he often laughed. He said nothing about his early spiritual life; however a book had recently been published telling his story, *Concerning Subud* by John Bennett.

Chapter Two

BAPAK WAS BORN near Semarang in Central Java, on June 22, 1901, a date which coincided with the birthday of the Prophet Muhammad on the Islamic calendar. The baby was named Sukarno, but with that name, he was always ill so it was changed to Muhammad Subuh, to correspond with the time of his birth, 5:00 A.M.—Subuh,* meaning dawn.

He was raised by his grandparents. At school he was taught in Javanese and Indonesian, and later in the Dutch language. When his grandfather died, Bapak took a job and studied book-keeping, taking over the care of his parents and younger brother and sister.

One night in Semarang in the summer of 1925, when he was twenty-four years of age, he received the latihan. He had gone out for a walk and at about 1.00 A.M. on his way home, he was startled by a light shining from above. He looked up to see a ball of radiant white light fall on his head. His body started shaking and his chest heaving. He hurried home and, lying on his bed, he surrendered to God. He then arose, but not from his own will, and performed his Islamic prayers. From then on he was woken almost every night and made to move: martial arts, dancing, singing new melodies, and so on.

In the years that followed, many friends interested in spiritual matters used to visit Bapak's house regularly to seek advice. He continued to receive and follow these movements of his inner self, which he later called the latihan kejiwaan and, although these people came in contact with the life force that he was receiving, Bapak said he felt that it was not yet the time to open people.

In 1932 he had a number of strong spiritual experiences, and as a result, he felt it necessary to give up work in order to devote himself totally to the latihan. The confirmation for doing this came around the time of his birthday in June with his experience of a spiritual Ascension. He then understood that it was his mission and his task to transmit to everyone who asked for it the latihan that he had received.

During World War II, he moved to Yogyakarta and by 1945 there were about three hundred people following the latihan. He gave the group the name *Susila Budhi Dharma*, or SUBUD for short.

. . .

---

* Subuh: The word Subuh has no direct connection with the word Subud (see Glossary).

Bapak Muhammad Subuh

BAPAK GAVE eight talks during his stay in New York, some attended by up to seven hundred members. I frequently sat in the front row a few metres from him and listened with intense interest. He sat in an armchair on the stage with his translator to his left. He was totally at ease and leaned slightly forward as he spoke into the microphone. His hands, when not making occasional expressive gestures, hung relaxed from the armrests of the chair. His words flowed easily without effort, rich in feeling, and as he spoke, I experienced a new and deeper inner peace.

I felt that it was not only what he said that was important—and he was explaining what was going on in my soul—but also that his being lifted up my inner state. When I left his talks, I often retired alone for a short time to integrate the feeling.

In his third talk on May 3, he spoke of the coming of the latihan and its significance for mankind:

Bapak gives thanks to Almighty God that he is, at last, able to arrive in New York and meet all of you. Your presence here shows that you are sympathetic toward our spiritual training, SUBUD, Susila Budhi Dharma. It is indeed like a symbol that at this present moment God requires from all of you that you shall no longer neglect your worship, lest you go so far away from Him that it will be too late to return.

It has always been like this in the history of the world and of mankind. Because of many difficulties which hamper the worship of God, and because of conditions of the present time which stir the hearts and minds of men, help from God becomes necessary. . . .

Bapak has not received this by learning from a teacher, nor from a man, but through the will of the Almighty God. Bapak has received this spiritual help, tranquilly and joyfully, as a state of being which is the will of the Creator and therefore not to be refused. Man cannot deny the Power and Beneficence of God, for it is contained in all that has been given to man; and perhaps it is also the will of God that what has been received by Bapak will be disseminated to all mankind, so that they also may find their own true path and know their own true lives. [5]

During his stay in New York, as well as talks to members, Bapak attended the latihans and when requested gave personal advice to individuals. This was to become the pattern of his visits to groups around the world. About the committee's activity, he simply advised us to organise it in accordance with the laws of the country.

Chapter Two

From the beginning, Bapak emphasised that the latihan is to be practised 'in life':

Bapak received this latihan while he was still in an original state, which means he was still working, still using his mind and his heart. This indicates that God wishes men to find a way to him without the necessity of leaving a normal mode of living in the world. It is not necessary for you who have received the latihan to retire from society, seclude yourself, or leave everything to which you are accustomed. You should continue working and using your mind. You are still required to earn a livelihood and provide for your family. But now that you have received Subud there will be within you, in addition to what is already present, a knowledge that God protects you, guides you, guards you and is ever-present in your life and in all you do. [6]

I had been opened less than a year and listened with rapt attention to every word as he continued to explain how the latihan would develop in us:

The coming of what all of you have received is really an infinite grace, for we are no longer simply to follow and conform to advice, but we are now to practise the reality of it, so that inevitably we will come to believe because of the experience of life and its vibrations within our own beings.

The presence of life within you in this way will bring you to realise and experience for yourselves the reality of what has been told by the Prophets in the days of old, that God is within you, and that you are always protected and He is always present, and that you should therefore worship Him. Remember your own house, the house of God within your own being.

In this way we can approach and find God through walking, through the movements of our hands, through seeing, through listening, through smelling as we should with our nose, through speaking and tasting in the way the mouth should speak and taste. So that in the fulfilment of our obligations in this world—a clerk in his office, an actor on the stage in his acting, a ballet dancer in his dancing—there is felt the greatness of God, and one should not forget Him.

In this way the truth is materialised within one's being, as, for example, a hand that is going to strike another person who should not be struck will be prevented from doing so, for the truth is already materialised in that hand. The same is true in seeing something that is not good, where the eyes of themselves will turn away from it, because the lawful truth is already materialised within the seeing. So also with your ears, which will no longer like to listen to people quarrelling. [7]

Although I felt that the significance of what he said was enormous—the hope of mankind, Bapak nevertheless spoke without trying to convince. He did not insist or try to impress. He spoke without force or the slightest emotionality. We soon learned that in his talks Bapak was receiving what he was saying—the words coming to him from beyond his thinking processes.

Bapak explained that Subud was not a teaching and that he was not a teacher. However, I came to understand many things about the spiritual life and the process of the Subud latihan through these clarifications. They helped me greatly when I had to face my own process of purification. He confirmed my experience:

You have faults and impurities and disordered feelings. These have come down to you from your ancestors. You must not imagine they have not handed on their faults, for they have.

Bapak's role was as a spiritual guide, giving explanations about the latihan to those already opened. "In Subud," he said, "we have experience first and explanations afterwards." For many years he continued in his talks to emphasise this necessity for experience:

Evidently, then, what Bapak obtained from Almighty God—what he calls the latihan kejiwaan of Subud—he obtained exclusively by the will of God, so that mankind might be able to become aware of and understand the essence of all the advice already given by the Messengers of God in days gone by ... Hence the latihan can be said to be of a practical nature.

It is not just something to hear about, something to be taught and advised, but something which at the same time can be witnessed and proved. So the latihan kejiwaan really provides proof of what has been taught to mankind from the distant past up to the present day.

The latihan you receive may indeed appear outwardly to have no meaning. In fact many people do not understand that all these things, such as the movements* you receive, are guidance and direction from God. Many people fail to understand; and why? Because this latihan truly cannot be understood with the mind. [8]

While Subud was expanding in the USA, it had meantime spread to many other countries. Bapak later described the coming of Subud to the West:

---

* Movements in the latihan: Spontaneous walking, gestures, making sounds, etc.

Chapter Two

At the time when Bapak received the latihan, he was told among other things that after another great war, the Second World War, he would have to travel around the world and make this latihan known to mankind. That was still in the year 1932. . . .

After the Second World War, when Bapak had moved to Yogyakarta, a foreigner Husein Rofé, came to Bapak seeking spiritual knowledge. . . . Bapak opened him. As Rofé's profession was writing for the Press, after some time he wrote an article [in Turkish] about receiving the latihan for a paper circulating in Turkey and Cyprus. Through this article Rofé was invited to open people in Cyprus who, when they moved to England soon afterwards, invited Bapak to England. . . .

Mr. Bennett happened to be holding a Gurdjieff seminar there. Because of this seminar, pupils of Gurdjieff from everywhere had come to Coombe Springs. These included people from South Africa, Ceylon, Holland, Germany, France, North America, Chile, and Peru. . . .

All this was quite by chance. Bapak had not reckoned on people from countries outside England being there. Bapak opened all these people, many hundreds. Bapak had to stay seven months. . . . The people returning to their various countries, after receiving the latihan, probably said it was very beneficial, . . . because Subud began to spread in other countries. [9]

When a Subud group was established, Bapak appointed "helpers"* to introduce others. He never suggested that we make propaganda about Subud and the latihan, in fact, quite otherwise. He advised the helpers:

The helper who talks to someone about Subud, to attract him to Subud, must never do it by trying to influence or pressure him in coming to Subud. The way to do it is, as it were, like telling a story. But, of course, a helper must be able to ask himself, when he tells the story about Subud, is he himself a good example of what he is telling? Because if he tells a wonderful story about Subud and he himself is a mess, then the person who is listening will not be very impressed by what he says. [10]

In the years that followed, Bapak's talks became a regular part of Subud life and were published and distributed to the membership. He finally gave some two thousand talks.

---

* Helpers: Those who according to Bapak had enough experience of the latihan kejiwaan of Subud to be able to pass on the contact to others.

Bapak's talks were attended by members only. Much of what he said was to meet our personal needs, and increasingly he provided direction for the activities of the Subud Brotherhood. He travelled around the world many times, giving talks to groups and at Subud Congresses. Most Subud members knew Bapak through their attendance at his talks. In this way almost the entire membership became familiar with his endearing personal qualities and characteristics.

When Bapak gave a talk, he was always punctual. He would arrive with members of his family and a translator. His family would sit in the front row, one of them first looking to see that he had everything he needed.

Bapak would take his time to adjust the microphone to the distance that was comfortable and to check with the technician and the interpreter to make sure that they were ready. He took longer about this than a speaker would normally do. It had the appearance of being purely practical, but the effect on the audience was to help them become ready in their feelings.

Even then, Bapak always waited before starting to speak. Later I understood he waited until a force from a higher level was strong in him. On one occasion later, he waited maybe fifteen minutes before starting, then suddenly said, "Ya!" meaning: "Yes, it has now come!" He also explained that when he speaks he never uses a prepared text. "The talk comes of its own accord." he said. "The way Bapak gives his talks is already arranged."

When everything was settled, Bapak would begin his talk with the kindly form of address: Saudara Saudara (Brothers and Sisters). Then followed a formal introduction, which often set a high tone, acknowledging the Greatness of God, before moving to the topic:

Brothers and Sisters. It is true that Bapak has already many times explained about the nature of the latihan kejiwaan. . . . We can state with complete clarity and conviction that the latihan is nothing else but a gift from God Almighty, and what we experience in the latihan is the guidance of the Power of God Almighty.

Now it is sure that there are nevertheless still many of you who ask yourselves: 'Is that really true?' Because all of us, including Bapak, are living in an age where we experience many things which tend towards the awakening of the thinking mind and we are subject to many influences which impinge on us and which have the tendency to awaken the nafsu.* So if we wish to answer this question, if we look for proof, we do not have to look far, we only need to look at the reality of the latihan itself. [11]

* *Nafsu*: the passions that animate feeling and thinking.

Chapter Two

Bapak spoke in Indonesian and would often talk for two or three hours, including the time for translation into English. He showed unlimited patience waiting for the translation to take place each time he paused.

In his talks he usually included something specific to the occasion or directed to the needs of someone in the audience. On one occasion Bapak was talking to a gathering which included visitors from a European country.

He referred to his last visit to that country and related how the members in charge of arrangements had gone to unnecessary extremes to guard his privacy. He said that he had felt isolated; he could see from his high window that members wanted to visit him, but those in charge did not let anyone in. "Bapak in fact wanted," he said, "to mix with the members on this occasion." His comment helped the members from that country overcome a strong national characteristic—to be over-organised at the expense of spontaneity.

Bapak did also appreciate his privacy and could help people see their errors in this regard without even saying anything. Once in Briarcliff when a person sneaked in to be near him, he quietly left the room.

BAPAK TRAVELLED extensively, generally with members of his family. Nowhere was his dedication to his mission more apparent. With each group he gave talks and attended latihans, sometimes travelling in the day and giving a talk the same evening. His activity for the welfare of the brotherhood went beyond ordinary human endurance. The whole time I never saw him upset or complaining if he was tired.

When he travelled he was always dressed in a well-tailored conventional style suit. The only thing that was not Western was that he would frequently wear a *petji*, an Indonesian Muslim hat of black velvet without a brim. He wore glasses all the time, except for reading.

Bapak was cared for extremely well wherever he went, not because he needed it or desired it but because the wish of people was so strong to please him. It was the event of the year for those he visited. He was mindful of the expenses of accommodation and travel and often talked of ways of mitigating these costs. He mostly ate Indonesian food, and the cooking was in the hands of the women who took care of him. For this reason, wherever he stayed, the accommodation was arranged so it was possible to cook for him, often in a Subud member's home, which he preferred.

Bapak Muhammad Subuh

Bapak was never a public figure. He did not try to be known. He did not try to influence people. The people who came to receive the latihan were guided to do so by their own feelings. When he dealt with people, there was no discrimination in his attitude. He often insisted he was just an ordinary man and never set himself apart. But to us he was extraordinary. His love of all people, his humanity, his spiritual receiving, his spiritual wisdom were extraordinary. All this he wanted to share.

There is no religious instruction in Subud. Bapak encouraged Subud members to continue with their religious practices but not to mix them with the latihan of Subud. He explained that the latihan is different from the prayers that come from the heart and mind. In the latihan we put aside our will and our normal prayers. In that half hour, we only receive and follow the power of God, which guides us directly and individually from beyond our desire to ask for favours.

Bapak further explained that purification, as one of the results of the latihan, progresses in accordance with our nature, needs, and capacity. He said that we would increasingly experience inner peace, even though this peace would be intermittently disturbed by the process of purification. As we grow, changes will be noticeable to ourselves and hopefully to those around us. He emphasised that we should never neglect our latihan. We had to practise it to maintain progress.

All these things I was able to confirm as time went on. I saw changes and was grateful and at times felt the heaviness of my process. I found that for us who have come into Subud as a first generation it is not always light or easy. But then, I say to myself, I don't wish to continue to be as I have always been, living my mistakes over and over. I realise that purification is a continuing process, without end in my lifetime.

I never ceased to wonder at Bapak's understanding of the spiritual nature of man and the spiritual history of mankind, insight which was as far as I know not available elsewhere. Yet he had never studied these things in a formal way. All this outpouring of wisdom was enveloped in an ineffable aura of love and compassion.

Bapak occasionally suggested that a member go to Cilandak* for more intense help. This might be to provide an environment in which they could go through an accelerated purification. Sometimes this led to physical healing, as with my close friend from Mexico who was diagnosed as having glioma,

---

* Cilandak: The suburb of Jakarta where Bapak established his home and an International Subud Centre.

a brain cancer, and had been told that without an operation she had only one month to live. Bapak invited her to stay in Cilandak and to do frequent latihans. After some weeks she was completely cured. The actress Eva Bartok was another case, much publicised in England in 1957, when by following the latihan she avoided a tumour operation and her unborn baby was saved.

Bapak, however, was not a healer and Subud didn't make claims that the latihan would heal. Healing may be the result of the latihan 'because the latihan is awakened by a life force which is not influenced by the heart and mind and so parts of the body previously weak may gain power again.' In other words, the healing is only something consequent to the latihan, not its intention. To those in Subud, healing may or may not happen.

Bapak lived very much within the culture of his country and his religion. This affected all who lived in or visited Cilandak, particularly in the days when his wife, Ibu,* was alive. Religious observances like Idul Fitre, the festival at the end of the Ramadan fast, and every event of significance in a person's life—birthdays, marriages, circumcisions, deaths, and even moving into a new house—would be acknowledged with a thanksgiving meal called a *selamatan*.**

BAPAK MADE no show of his spiritual receiving although some occasions were dramatic to those near him. My mother, Mayko, told me of her experience of an occurrence in Mexico City at a small gathering with Bapak in the house of a Subud member, Hosanna Baron. Clementina, Mayko's maid, was also there. Mayko said:

'What happened was unexpected and was felt by everyone in the room. It was a strong spiritual happening and those present reported a variety of personal experiences. It did not happen by Bapak's will. He was totally relaxed. Words poured out from him. Ibu went down on her knees and was crying in front of everyone, overwhelmed by the high force that had come. It was very powerful. One member reported seeing, as in a vision, Muhammad standing on one side of Bapak and, on the other, Jesus Christ.'

Later I asked Hosanna about the incident. She told me:

"It started with Bapak sending for members who had arranged gifts for his family. The Rickenbackers and the Owenses, who started the idea, were there.

---

* Ibu means mother in Indonesian and is a term of respect.
** Selamatan: A religious celebration with prayers and food.

The meeting started normally, but Bapak soon began to receive very strongly. I became aware that a strong and high force had come into the room as Bapak continued to talk. The force was overwhelming for most, causing people to weep and some to fall to the floor. This was in the large living room, which opens from the entry hall. The hall had a floor-to-ceiling mirror along one wall. In the midst of the happening, there was an explosive sound in the hall and the entire mirror fell to the floor in pieces the size of corn kernels."

One of the members told my husband, Erling, that he could see that something very strong was going on because people were weeping, falling to the ground, and so on. He said that someone was trying to translate but it was impossible to understand him because of his emotion.

A friend of ours, the wife of an economist working with the United Nations, was also present. She told Erling she saw Jesus beside Bapak. In her next latihan, Jesus again appeared to her, embraced her, and said, "Now I will always be with you." As a result, she said, "I was in an intense religious state for the following year and became extremely devout."

Clearly everyone present at this happening was differently affected by the high force. Such a dramatic manifestation was not typical of Bapak's activity but was consistent with my certainty of his extraordinary spirituality. He did not however divert anyone's worship of God by becoming an object of adoration himself.

Chapter Three
Bapak Explains Subud, USA

A NEW PURPOSE and direction in living began for me when I received the latihan of Subud. I now had an inner life that gave its own tone to what I was doing. I wanted to stay close to it. Once I had received the contact in September 1958, all that was required of me was the personal act of sincere surrender to God in the latihan.

No longer was I able to go along in a completely automatic way. For the first time I knew what it was to act from a source inside myself distinct from the ideas and values of my past. I started to be aware of my inner self, as well as my outer self. I had started to become the observer and the observed.

Sometimes I suddenly had a new insight. It was given and I then had to grow into it. The process felt totally natural, as did everything about the latihan. It was an instinctive harmonising force. For example, my perceptions of right behaviour started to come under question. Nowhere was this more apparent than with my family. As wife and mother, I began to see where I could be more flexible and patient.

The effect also became evident in areas of myself that I had no idea needed to be changed. As a person I was awakened to my own individuality and started to have a new confidence in my own judgements. This was a significant break from the rigidity of my upbringing.

At times the changes happening in other people due to the latihan seemed more obvious to me than my own. They became relaxed, were less intense about their opinions, more accepting, and often obviously more happy. This did not depend on strong latihan experiences. One who had obviously changed significantly in these ways complained that she didn't feel very much in her latihan.

I continued to attend the latihan diligently twice a week and made new friends. After latihan we would often go out for a meal or on Sunday to the home of someone for tea. There was a new kind of closeness. We talked about this as closeness of our inner feeling, but in fact we didn't know exactly what it was.

Chapter Three

What was clear was that opening ourselves to God in the latihan had the result of connected us with each other at a deep level.

Meantime my mother had had a strange experience. My brother was in England and I in New York, while Mayko was in Chile. As soon as my brother and I started to do the latihan in 1958, Mayko became mysteriously ill. She knew nothing of what we were doing. This could be put down to coincidence, if it were not for the nature of the illness. Her strange illness was that she became weak and would lose her balance. She could not keep her head up straight. She decided to go to her birthplace, Punta Arenas, to visit her mother and family. Nothing changed, her condition slowly worsened. She returned to Santiago and visited the family doctor, who put her in hospital for a complete checkup. When it was done, he said, "Mrs. Petric, there is absolutely nothing wrong with you!" This was typical of Subud illness connected with spiritual purification. I came to believe that this was as a result of her son and daughter's starting the latihan.

There was some outer evidence. My mother had been a heavy smoker for many years. It had happened accidentally when my father brought home a package of American cigarettes from the US company where he worked in northern Chile. Mayko tried one and she was hooked. She wanted to stop but couldn't. Silently she made a promise to God that, if she ever had the chance to stop, she would. During this strange illness, she could not smoke and she never touched a cigarette again. When she wrote to me about this, I realised that it had happened immediately after my brother and I had started the latihan, and that it was the beginning of a process of purification in her.

When my brother returned to Chile, he helped to arrange the visit of Bapak and Ibu to Santiago to open the first group in April 1959. Mayko was there but didn't know what was going on. She asked my brother, "What is happening?" He, in his masculine way, answered, "This is very good for you, just go into the room there!" She went in and the opening began. She responded immediately and from that moment, her latihan was always very strong.

. . .

Meantime, in late December 1958, John and Elizabeth Bennett arrived in New York from Coombe Springs to help with preparations for Bapak's visit. In February, we invited them to spend their weekends in our home at Briarcliff.

John Bennett was an impressive man, not only for his large stature, but also his enormous energy and his lively interest in everything. He had a strong presence and would give you his whole attention when he spoke. He was highly intelligent—a scientist, a philosopher, and a writer—and disarmingly sincere and charming. He was a linguist and had learnt enough Indonesian in a few weeks to understand Bapak's book *Susila Budhi Dharma*. Elizabeth was a helper and had a quiet confidence and friendliness, which I found very supportive. During her stay she became very fond of Cathy, who was two at the time.

In New York, John Bennett gave public talks and radio interviews and we began to open new people. By the time the Bennetts left for Mexico on March 9 —to prepare for Bapak's visit to Mexico City—we were six hundred active members in New York, and by the time Bapak left in June, we were a thousand.

John Bennett gave two talks in Mexico City, and about fifty men and women had been opened. On his return to New York, he related how on Easter Friday, whilst in latihan with a man in a state of deep distress, he had had a very strong experience of Jesus's suffering on the Cross and later of the Divine Christ. This experience had affected him deeply, he said. I was very impressed by this.

Later I was able to observe that one person in the latihan can experience something that another person needs to experience and cannot manage for him- or herself—such a state, however, can never be self-willed. When it happens, it is given.

Bapak gave five talks to members in the French Institute building and three to the helpers and committee in the Subud Hall. He started on May 3 with an explanation about the need for patience when the spiritual life has been neglected and the awareness of the soul covered up by the activity of heart and mind. It was implicit in this that the spiritual dimension of our existence cannot be reached just by thinking about it:

There are many of us, mature adults, adept in the working of the heart and mind, who wish for spiritual progress to take place quickly. Strong desires of the heart and mind cause us to be impatient. But remember that your own spiritual development began very recently—and that the mind and senses have been exercising and working since the time you were a child. So much time has been spent in the exercising of the brain and senses that spiritual growth has been left lagging far behind.

Chapter Three

Bapak presents the example of a newborn baby. Although it cannot distinguish definite forms or shapes or objects, cannot hear or interpret definite sounds, it can already receive something which does not come from its outside environment, but which comes from the soul. We can observe that sometimes the little child seems happy, sometimes sad; and we assume that this is a normal response. But in reality these reactions are not due to the environment, but to the strong contact which the child has with the soul. He has not yet become involved with the influences of the world. Therefore it is said that a baby is sinless and beloved of God. Gradually the little child learns to distinguish objects, to hear sounds, to move and to taste sweet and sour. Little by little it loses the close communion with the soul and becomes more involved with its environment. This process of learning about earthly matters continues until the child becomes an adult and then usually the things of the earth are far more significant than spiritual matters. Because of this highly developed involvement with earthly matters, the adult's concept of God and Heaven will not be far removed from that which has filled his heart and mind. . . . But God cannot be conceived by those who use senses and intellect to the exclusion of the spirit.

Bapak said that, as God knows us better than we know ourselves, all we need to do is to receive. He explained the process of the spiritual exercise which we were beginning to experience in these terms:

For all of you who have already received [the latihan] the way is opened for future spiritual development. . . . You need do nothing in the latihan but receive—you need no direction from your mind and heart. Freed from them you will feel more consciousness, more awareness of that which God's will has ordained for you. . . .

The latihan begins with physical movement. As the experiences become deeper and more significant, they will gradually penetrate the walls of the senses. When these have been purified, although it takes time, the walls of understanding are penetrated and eventually the walls of self-consciousness. By self-consciousness is meant a conscious awareness of inner participation from beginning to end [of life]. In this way you will become conscious of how "I live," where "I came from," how "I will be after death," and where "I will go." [12]

Bapak went on in later talks to describe the various forces* that form the inner content of man, some lower and some higher than the human level. He talked about the effect of the lower forces on our behaviour and how the latihan would purify us of our mistakes—which were our mismanagement of the lower forces.

---

* Pak Subuh's book *Susila Budhi Dharma* describes the forces or essences in all things and the effect of the quality of these forces on our human behaviour.

He emphasised that his talks were not a teaching but were information about what may be experienced by us in the course of the latihan. He said that the latihan of Subud is the practice and the reality of what has been advised by the Prophets Abraham, Moses, Jesus, and Muhammad in time past, who have received the revelation or grace from Almighty God. He briefly described the essence of each message—Abraham, the belief in the being of God; Moses, the distinction between right and wrong; Jesus, that there is life after death; and Muhammad, that all power is in the hands of God, both in the world and in the life after death. He referred to the symbolism of the death and resurrection of Jesus as it related to the latihan:

The three higher powers* can be received by man, that is to say, their working can be received within his being, only when he is able to bring his passions, his thinking and his feeling to a state of quietness or stillness.

The significance of this state, in which thoughts, feelings and passions are brought to a standstill, is that the man is dead. Those men who received grace in days of old, therefore, have repeatedly declared that in order to know and to realise the true, the real life, which it is both necessary and possible for man to know, he is required to die before he really does die; that is to say, he should experience death before he really dies. This is symbolised in the death and resurrection of Jesus Christ, which represents the return of life from death. [13]

On May 13 Bapak explained, "The vivification of the members of the body [by the latihan] is the development of the inner feeling** which results from, and proceeds parallel with, the growth of the soul." ... "When we die," he said, "when the thoughts and mind cease to function, the soul will then take over all the functions, so that we can continue a blissful life after death."

Bapak had introduced us to "testing" at an early stage of our latihan experience. He did this by example during his talks in New York in 1959. Testing was the name given to receiving answers to questions in the latihan state. Its function is to check the progress of the latihan in oneself or to gain insight into a problem.

---

* The three higher powers, rohani, rabbani, and rachmani that manifest in Saints, Prophets, and Messengers of God.

** "Inner feeling" is another term which is used by Bapak in a specific way in Subud. It refers to the feeling of the inner self experienced in the latihan state, when we are inwardly separated from our nafsu (passions)—judgements, our emotions, and our opinions.

Chapter Three

Bapak explained that testing was carried out by simply doing the latihan after asking a question:

In order to be able to receive and to feel a test, you are not required to do anything but to remain in the state of receiving your latihan; that is, not to think and imagine things, not to identify with anything, not to represent any picture for yourself, but only receive as in the latihan. Testing in its nature is similar to following the latihan. [14]

In "testing" the answer to the question is received in whatever form the person is able to receive it.

Bapak used the term "received" or "a receiving" in a specialised sense in Subud. It is a translation from the Indonesian root word *terima*, meaning acceptance. Something that is "received" or "a receiving" is something accepted by the person in the latihan, in a state of surrender to God. It may be physical experience, such as movements of the body—for example, gestures which are meaningful and can be interpreted. It may be direct knowing about one's condition or situation—like a refined intuition. It may be an understanding which has wide application.

Something we receive in the latihan is experienced as coming to our inner feeling from inside as a gift of God. To receive clearly, the activity of our thoughts and emotions has to be out of the way.

I was very impressed by my first experience of testing. It was after one of the 1959 New York talks. Bapak said that he would test so we could come to our own proof as to where the latihan comes from—a high or a low spiritual source. He put the questions and we received by simply following our latihan. He asked:

*"Where is Heaven?"** [Representing a high source].

Then: *"Where is Hell?"* [Representing a low source].

After we experienced that, he asked us:

"Where does the latihan come from?"

I did not believe such an experience to be possible. However, when I followed the test, "Where is Heaven?" I clearly felt a great peace, a condition beyond any disturbance. Then when we tested, "Where is Hell?" I felt unimaginable horror and anguish. It was so strong for some that Bapak had to stop the test.

---

* This was a question about a spiritual state, not intended to imply a physical place.

For the question, "Where does the latihan come from?" I received a similar feeling of deep peace. It was clear to me from my receiving that the latihan came from a high, good source—a heavenly place and not from a low satanic level. It was convincing, even though I, as a novice, may not have received it completely. However, what made most impression was the increased intensity of the latihan during the test. Bapak often used testing thereafter to help people have a deeper experience of the latihan.

Bapak said, "There are [need be] no secrets in Subud," meaning that through the latihan you can develop a new sensitivity. He also said that testing is a temporary short cut to this sensitivity, which the latihan ultimately brings as a natural facility.

During one of the meetings in May 1959, and much to my surprise, Bapak appointed some of us to become helpers. Ten women and ten men. I was included. He explained that it was necessary to have designated persons to talk to probationers and open new people. "Even though you are not yet real helpers," he said, "it is necessary to arrange this while Bapak is here."

It was to be a training period. The most important part of our program was to have a latihan for helpers once a week. This was in addition to our latihan in the group twice a week. Already it was becoming clear that, although the group latihan was initially restricted to twice a week, it was intended ultimately to permeate our lives and become ever-present. In our new role, a few months later, we tested questions from members and for ourselves. Testing at this stage was always conducted in a group, never by individual helpers. Although I felt fallible, I accepted it as a learning process and came to this work with the utmost respect and sincerity. Testing until we found a consensus of understanding among ten or more helpers resulted in our answers being well accepted by the membership.

It was common at that time to test our course of action. For example, when someone had a strong desire to do something, he or she could check their inner guidance on the matter. Emotional ideas would often dissolve during the testing in favour of a different approach. Difficulties with each other were also handled in this way. This brought resolution of problems and also widened our experience of the latihan.

Testing was practice for becoming familiar with inner guidance. Often the latihan worked in our lives without formal testing. A friend told me at this time how one day she felt herself starting to get angry with one of her children when, to her complete surprise, she found the anger checked and a quiet feeling took over. She said the effect on her child was astounding. The child immediately stopped crying and ran to her lovingly to say she was sorry.

Another effect of the latihan which I began to notice was remorse. It was nothing to do with my religion or my values or the opinion of others. If I transgressed my inner feeling with an attitude or behaviour that was inappropriate, I would feel remorse. It came with a certainty that could not be doubted. This I felt was the result of a 'sin against myself.' The standard by which I was judged was not written in any book or derived from any dogma, but came from my innermost self.

In June 1959, after leaving New York, Bapak visited Chicago, Denver, and Tucson on his way to the West Coast of the USA. On arrival in San Francisco, he decided there should be an organisation called Subud North America (SNA). In New York, Bapak had confirmed Erling's appointment as Chairman of Subud New York, with the added responsibility to arrange for its incorporation.* Now Bapak sent a message to Erling asking him to be Chairman of SNA and organise a SNA Congress having as one of its principal objectives the legal incorporation of SNA. Bapak then visited Vancouver and flew on to England for the First World Subud Congress held at Coombe Springs. It is reported that there were four hundred delegates from forty different countries. In two years Subud had spread around the world.

Meanwhile, before Bapak had left the USA, he had suggested that Sjafrudin Achmad, the Indonesian helper at Coombe Springs, should move to Los Angeles to be available to members in North America. Erling arranged Sjafrudin's visa, and he stayed with us in Briarcliff for several weeks before going on to Los Angeles.

Sjafrudin was a young Sumatran of slim build and light complexion with dark and friendly eyes. He was outgoing and smiled a lot. He told us that he had first met Bapak when he (Sjafrudin) was a student at the university in Yogyakarta. He was unassuming about himself, but I soon found him to be deeply spiritual.

---

* Subud New York was incorporated in the category of religious organisations. Although Bapak had said that 'Subud is not a religion,' he had also said that 'Subud is the essence of all true religions,' and there was no doubt that the primary activity of Subud was a religious activity—the worship of God.

Bapak Explains Subud, USA

One Sunday afternoon Sjafrudin gave a talk to the group at the New York Subud House. As I listened to him, I felt my spiritual state raised. I felt intensely my own existence, my worship of God, and my relationship to everyone and everything around me. I realised that he was receiving a high spiritual force which had also enveloped me. This was the first time I experienced how it was to be taken in this way to a higher spiritual state. Others at the meeting reported a similar experience.

Although Sjafrudin's manner was easygoing, I found him to be very sensitive with other people. One morning he was in the kitchen while I was baking. I began to feel depressed but kept the feeling to myself. He sensed that something was happening to me and said in his direct manner, "What is the matter? Are you all right?" I said I was feeling strange. He went on to explain how the latihan can bring about purification and we can find ourselves in a lower state when it happens. It was this sensitivity, kindness, and understanding that made him a popular helper.

Sjafrudin's presence also had the effect of reminding me if I got far away from my latihan. At one stage we took him on a car tour. During a long drive, the children became restless and momentarily I became annoyed with them. Immediately I experienced remorse. It was as if Sjafrudin's presence had acted like a mirror for myself.

During those weeks in New York, Erling and Sjafrudin would sit up late at night, usually staying quiet for long time until a subject presented itself. Erling told to me later some of the more interesting things that were discussed.

Sjafrudin had described the death of Bapak's son, Haryadi, in 1954. Haryadi, he said, had an experience of leaving this world and when he returned, he told Bapak that he did not wish to continue to live here. Bapak said that he needed him. A year later, Haryadi told Bapak that he had received an indication from God that he was free to choose between continuing his life on earth or passing over to the other side. He had decided to leave. Bapak agreed, but asked Haryadi to stay a few more days. During these days, Haryadi asked Sjafrudin to accompany him on visits to each of his friends. Sjafrudin was unaware of the discussions between Bapak and Haryadi, and it was only in retrospect that Sjafrudin realised that Haryadi's purpose in these visits was to say goodbye.

Chapter Three

One morning while the family was having breakfast, Haryadi asked Bapak, "Is it all right now?" Bapak said, "Yes." Haryadi went upstairs and they could hear him splashing in the bathroom. After a while there was silence. Bapak went upstairs and then called the family. Haryadi was seated against the wall, dead. Sjafrudin said that he felt as if the house was vibrating until after the burial service the following day.

On another occasion, Sjafrudin told how, in latihan, he had seen his Sumatran fiancée walking away from him and another young woman walking towards him. He realised that this meant that he would not marry his fiancée of those days. As he said this, it came into Erling's mind, *Bapak's daughter*, but he said nothing to Sjafrudin.

The first SNA Congress was held in Denver in August 1960. It lasted four days and was attended by about sixty members. Erling was elected chairman for the following year (and was to be re-elected in 1961 and 1962). When establishing the organisation, he proposed that SNA be purely a service organisation with no power to give directives, its main function being a communications and information centre. Later, publications were taken over as a Subud enterprise, owned and managed by Dan Cahill, a printer. In due course, Subud North America, which included members from the USA and Canada but not Mexico, was legalised in Colorado and, like Subud New York, it was incorporated under the law governing religious organisations.

From Denver we travelled for three months around the USA by car, visiting the Subud groups. This included Los Angeles, where Sjafrudin joined us for a visit to New Mexico and the Grand Canyon. Back in New York, Erling was asked by the committee to give a public talk on Subud. Several hundred people attended, and about sixty persons filled out forms expressing their interest in joining Subud.

In late 1961, Bapak wrote to Erling proposing that Erling and I, together with Sjafrudin, should visit the Subud groups in Mexico and South America. Planning for our trip proceeded and while writing to Bapak about some details, Erling felt he should mention his recent receiving about Sjafrudin's marrying. With Sjafrudin's enthusiastic approval, Erling added at the end of his letter, 'I feel that it is now time that Sjafrudin marries the young woman whom he is intended to marry.'

In his reply to Erling, Bapak said, "In regard to your comment about Sjafrudin, Bapak agrees with you." Erling telephoned Sjafrudin and read him Bapak's reply. Within a few weeks, Sjafrudin had left for Indonesia. Soon afterwards Sjafrudin and Bapak's daughter, Hardiyati, were married.

On January 20, 1962, Erling and I left for Mexico and South America. We visited groups in Mexico City, Lima, Santiago, Buenos Aires, Sao Paulo, and Rio de Janeiro, staying several days with each and two months in Chile. We attended latihans and, when requested, Erling gave talks in Spanish. By the time we returned home on April 15, Bapak had asked the SNA National Committee to arrange and host the Second Subud World Congress.

This Congress was to run from July 5 to July 26, 1963. Erling as Chairman of SNA supervised the arrangements and was Interim Chairman of the Congress. The venue was Briarcliff College, a finishing school for girls, which was vacant for the summer holidays. It was a stately college in English style, red brick buildings of mostly three floors and huge park-like grounds of trees and lawns. It had excellent facilities for the Congress meetings and ample comfortable accommodation for the three hundred delegates.

Bapak meanwhile left Jakarta on February 24, 1963, first going to Australia, New Zealand, Mexico, and South America, before coming to the USA for the Congress.

One day in June, as the time of the Congress approached, my brother telephoned from Florida and said Bapak wanted to know where he would be staying during the Congress. I told him that Bapak had a choice. He and his party could either stay in a very private and nice apartment in the college or in our house about five minutes drive from Briarcliff College. The answer came back, in our house.

Bapak arrived in New York on June 20. He came with Ibu, Usman (his translator), and Usman's wife, Aminah, and they were accommodated in the Manhattan apartment of Whitmore Ovington, a newspaper journalist. Soon afterwards, Bapak said to Erling that he would like to spend his birthday, June 22, at our house.

When the day came, Bapak arrived in the early afternoon with Ibu and the Usmans. We also invited to the birthday tea a few close Subud friends, including Livingston Dodson, Vice-Chairman of SNA, and Varindra Vittachi, both of whom were to become active in the organisation of Subud affairs.

Chapter Three

Erling gave Bapak a gold Rolex wrist watch, and my brother gave him a matching gold watch-band. Rolex was at that time one of the self-winding watches, and Bapak was later to use it to illustrate his advice to not neglect the latihan. "The latihan," he said, "is like a Rolex [self-winding] watch; if you don't keep it moving, it will stop."

After the visit we all drove back to Manhattan to the Subud House for Bapak's birthday talk to the New York group.

During the two weeks before the Congress, Bapak gave five talks and testing at Subud House on East Twenty-first Street, New York. I went to all of them, thankful for my good fortune. Bapak was to me the person who had been chosen to bring to mankind the most important gift of our times—a contact with the power of God.

On July 5 Bapak and his party moved to our house for the Congress. Fortunately we had a large house, for soon we had thirteen people in residence, among them Daniel Ruzo, an anthropologist from Peru, and his wife, Delia. Off the kitchen was a closed-in porch. Members who wanted to be near Bapak and his party could sit there. My mother, Mayko, often baked fruit pies and other delicacies to make these visitors feel welcome. The house was kept as quiet as possible out of respect for Bapak and his party, and yet it was alive with activity.

Mayko and her maid, Clementina, had arrived from Chile a month before and were staying with us. Clementina had changed considerably. My diary records the day of her opening:

Clementina has become more than my mother's maid; she is her devoted companion. She is also ready to do anything I need, which is a great help with so many people in the house. She is looking very pretty, blue eyes, perfect white teeth, beautiful olive skin and naturally curly black hair. Nobody could imagine that as a young teenager she was living in poverty in Santiago, too shy to come out of her room and getting under the bed whenever anyone came to visit. When she was occasionally given jobs, I heard, like washing clothes, she would hide her money, hoping to be able to save it, only to find that her own sisters had stolen it. Now, since working for Mayko, she has blossomed.

Ibu is so delightfully unpredictable and spontaneous. Clementina was helping with the cooking when Ibu called me to her room and asked, "Does Clementina want to be opened?" "I don't know," I said, "but I'll ask her." But Clementina said, "No!" and went on stirring the pot. I relayed this to Ibu.

"Oh!" said Ibu, "tell her to come." I called Clementina and we entered the bedroom. Ibu said, "Clementina, take off your shoes." To me she said to join in the latihan. Ibu proceeded to do the latihan with us both and Clementina was opened. . . . Only Ibu could do this.

The Second Subud World Congress at Briarcliff College started with a talk by Bapak on July 8. He pointed to the spiritual character of a Subud Congress:

A Subud Congress is a gathering of people who worship God, are obedient to God, have faith in God and surrender to God. . . . It is to be a Congress at which everything will be determined through the power of God which we receive in the quiet and stillness of our inner feeling. [15]

At Bapak's suggestion the procedure of making Congress decisions through testing was established. On the third day, the permanent Congress chairman was selected in this way and, later in the Congress, the members of a new international committee.

In his second talk, Bapak emphasised the separation of the activities of the committees from spiritual matters. This was to be a recurring theme of Subud. Regarding social work and suggestions that we help the sick with latihan, Bapak said that we have to be sincere, meaning that we must carry through thoroughly anything that we start. This means providing places to care for the sick. "In this respect," he said, "the way of Subud is not different from the way of religions—a struggle of man to worship Almighty God and to serve his fellow man. Social work is a sign of the link between one soul and another. . . . The organisation has to take on these tasks, but we have to begin with ourselves, the needs that are already amongst us, in our groups. To do this effectively we should set up enterprises to provide the funds."

Explaining the spiritual side further, Bapak said that in the group latihan we were being trained to experience the unity that God wills for man:

When you are in the latihan you will not feel that you are in a strange place. In the latihan you feel united with your own inner self and this means that in truth you are united with the human race. In the latihan you will sometimes feel sad if there if someone there who is suffering, or you will feel happy when those beside you are happy. It is clear from this that, in the latihan, it is willed that we should unite. It is only man's heart and mind that takes no pleasure in this closeness. [16]

Chapter Three

The Congress went on to establish an international executive committee for Subud. It was called Subud International Services (S.I.S.), and Erling was appointed head of a drafting committee to prepare its statutes.

Bapak illustrated the application of testing to the process of choosing the committee members. A helper was called to stand out in front of the assembly in the latihan state. Bapak then asked the helper to test the nominee's suitability for the position. Bapak asked the question: "Show [in a state of latihan] the capacity, ability, and quality of so-and-so (the nominee)?" We could all see the nominee's qualities and suitability by the physical responses of the helper—for example, either capable, confident movements or weak, tentative, and distressed gestures.

Bapak himself demonstrated testing by standing up, asking a question, and letting his latihan move him to show the answer. For example, to show how we are affected by the material force, he tested, 'How does a lady walk when [under the influence of] wearing expensive jewellery?' His coquettish walk showed her completely inflated by the jewellery and the audience laughed with delight.

Bapak also used testing with us to show us our progress in the latihan—what parts of us had come spiritually alive. Bapak would first witness our latihan and gauge our condition, then ask us to: "Stop, stand still, and receive" while he posed the questions. He varied the test questions to suit the experience of those present. I was always grateful if Bapak tested me. After a testing session, I felt I would never be quite the same again. It helped me to change or understand. I was also interested when it was somebody else. I learned much about human nature in general.

It was in the seventh talk that Bapak touched on a question close to my heart about the relationship of the spiritual to the material in Subud:

It may be that there are members who feel: "Why must the spiritual way be mixed up with money, with enterprises, with undertakings of various kinds? Will that not retard the way of the spirit?" Let Bapak explain it like this: The spiritual latihan of Subud has appeared at this time when the mind of man is highly developed. From this we can guess and feel that it is the will of God at the present time that while earning our living and attending to worldly matters, and also while close to, or involved in material things, we shall not forget our worship of God, because God is with us in all circumstances. [17]

About the latihan, Bapak said, some members are at first bothered by their minds in the latihan. He said: "It is not necessary for you to prevent thought, just let it be!—because gradually you will experience the separation between thinking and inner feeling, and then the thinking which is constantly at work will stop by itself."

One night after arriving back late from one of his talks, Bapak said he would like to have tea in the living-room. There he talked about his Ascension in 1932. He told it again in later years. This is taken from Bapak's autobiography:

I felt extremely sleepy and went to my room and lay down, surrendering to God. At once I felt myself lengthen, widen and expand into a sphere and then felt suddenly released and freed into a great space. Far away was a group of stars like diamonds in an earring. I asked myself what this was, and received the reply that what I saw was the universe that I had left. I assumed that I was dead and kept repeating, Allahu Akbar—God is Almighty. . . .

Then I travelled with great speed across a huge expanse until I could see mountains, seven of them like cones of light, stacked one above the other. Inside the first was a vast panorama with God's creatures clad in white, all praising Almighty God. I passed up from cone to cone until I reached the sixth where I felt completely powerless. I felt myself saying repeatedly, Allahu Akbar. . . .

Finally I entered the seventh cone. There I had no direction and no purpose other than to say Allah, Allah, Allah. But from there I could see anything and everything that was distant, including the world. Then I felt something, a key, penetrate the palm of my hand.* [18]

Bapak said he then found himself return with extraordinary speed to more normal surroundings and realised he was looking down on the lights of Semarang. In a moment he was above his house and then inside his room. There he saw himself lying with his hands folded.

'Carefully I approached and kissed the forehead,' he said, 'at that instant the one who was kissed and I who kissed awoke.'

Next morning his mother told him that she had awoken in the night and when she looked from her bed she saw the stars below and felt she was in the sky.

---

* Bapak usually spoke of himself in third person as Bapak, but this experience was related in the nominative singular I.

Chapter Three

ON SOME EVENINGS, Bapak would sit in the living room and watch television. David, aged seven, would come in, or Bapak would call him. Bapak would sit David by his side and rub his head. After a few days, David said to Erling, "Daddy, I have currents running in my arms and legs." Erling explained to him that this was life forces (of the latihan), doing a work of purification and bringing in a new life.

Meanwhile at the Subud Congress, Bapak mentioned something that connected this receiving of the latihan by David with a prediction made by a clairvoyant in Chile before we heard about Subud. Bapak said that the latihan should form a three-barred cross within the practitioner of the latihan. "It is a cross of light," he said, "with the main bar at the level of the shoulders, and two shorter cross-bars at the level above the bridge of the nose and at the level of the heart."

The prediction had occurred in August 1956 when Erling and I went to see Madam Laila, a Russian who was at that time front-page news in the government newspaper in Santiago for her success in foretelling world events. Erling was seeking some confirmation of his spiritual receiving. Madam Laila's way of reading was to take the right hand of the person in her left hand, go into a trance, and write on a pad. She would then come out of the trance and read what she had written. Erling sat across the table from her, with David, who was nine months old, on his knee. After she had read Erling's hand, she asked, "Will you let me read your little boy?" She went through her routine, came out of the trance, and began to read and comment. She said, "When he is seven years old, people will come from all over the world to the place where he is living. It will be in another country near a very large city, larger than Santiago. Amongst the people who come, will be some with crowns[*] on their heads. They will give David his inheritance. But the main thing that will interest him is a cross of gold." (She had drawn it in the trance—it had three cross bars, one long main bar and two short bars above and below.).

At the Congress, Bapak gave ten talks. I found one particular session dramatic and revealing. It was the morning that Bapak tested the condition of the spiritual body of a number of the men. As he tested he explained: "You only have one arm" or "You have arms but no legs" etc.[**] It was touching to see that those tested were grateful to Bapak for having disclosed to them their spiritual state.

---

[*] Crowns perhaps symbolised spiritual enlightenment.
[**] Meaning that they were not yet spiritually whole.

Bapak Explains Subud, USA

In addition to Bapak's talks, there were latihans every day and meetings on a variety of Subud activities. The mood was light and harmonious, and outside the summer weather was clear and warm. It had been a memorable visit.

Bapak asked Erling to accompany him on visits to Subud groups in the USA and Canada. They left for Washington, D.C. Later I joined the party in Detroit. We found a suite for Bapak on the fourth floor of an apartment-hotel overlooking a park. It was spacious and well-appointed, and we were able to rent another across the hall for ourselves. We left our front door open during the days so that Bapak and Ibu could come to our apartment whenever they felt like it.

One morning Bapak came to our apartment with a woman member who had come to ask questions. After Aminah had translated, he told the woman to start her latihan and asked me to join in. Then he joined in himself. Bapak then tested. He asked the questions and told me to receive the answers through my latihan for the woman. I was nervous but I was able to continue. The feeling was—as we say in Chile— *"Atragame tierra!"* (Earth swallow me!) but I always did what Bapak asked me to do.

My resolve always to do what Bapak said did not result from allowing him to become a father figure, taking responsibility for my decisions. It derived from my respect for the latihan. My own experience told me I could trust the guidance of the latihan, but my receiving was still clouded by my habits of thought and emotion. Bapak was closer to the latihan than I, and therefore his guidance was clearer and more comprehensive than mine.

That is not to say that I was not somewhat in awe of Bapak. I was, but not Bapak as a person, but rather as the carrier of a revelation. It was the revelation —the latihan—which created the awe and respect. From Bapak's side, it was his wish, often expressed, that everyone of us would come to the point where we could receive our own guidance in our own latihan.

After Detroit, Bapak continued his trip to Los Angeles where the local group had invited him. Erling and I returned home, Erling to catch up on some work and I to be with my children and my mother, who had stayed behind. Erling then flew out to meet Bapak in San Francisco. There he rented a large station-wagon and took him on a day-long outing to Yosemite National Park to visit a grove of giant sequoia, the world's largest trees. Bapak enjoyed it. He wanted to see and know the country. After a further trip to the Columbia River, Bapak asked Erling to go with him to Toronto and drive him to see Niagara Falls.

Chapter Three

Returning from this last drive, he announced that he had decided to postpone his trip to Europe and asked Erling if he and his party could return to our home in Briarcliff to rest for a while. The party arrived in October 1963.

One morning I was in the kitchen with Aminah, preparing food. Bapak was in the sitting room with Erling and members of the new S.I.S. Committee, one of whom was Reynold Osborne. Aminah went off to see if Bapak needed anything. When she returned she said to me. "You are coming to live in Indonesia, in Cilandak." I took it to be a joke—it was her nature to joke a lot. Such a preposterous idea could not be true. However she insisted that Bapak was serious and was at that moment talking to Erling about it.

Erling later related the conversation to me:

Reynold Osborne asked Bapak, "What is Erling going to do?"

Bapak replied: "Erling is coming to live in Indonesia!"

Reynold: "What about his family?"

Bapak: "They are coming too!"

Reynold: "What about his home and his business?"

Bapak: "He will sell them!"

When Erling told me, I found myself in a state of total disbelief. I knew where Indonesia was. But living there—that was inconceivable! The last thing I wanted to do was to move from the USA, take my children out of school, and sell my home. I started to feel very stressed. Even though I continued to do my latihan as usual, I felt the demand was beyond my capacity. Erling was far less surprised than I was. He said that he had known that one day he was going to move to the tropics.

The date for our departure was not fixed, but suddenly there were countless things to do. During the year that followed, we sold the business, the house, and most of our belongings. I was very concerned for David and Cathy and about the unknown life in Asia. I tried unsuccessfully to adjust to the idea of going to live in a country about which I knew absolutely nothing.

The words that I heard in the latihan soon after I was opened would often come back to me, *'Put your trust in God and not in man.'*

. . .

We left our house in Briarcliff and its comfortable way of life on December 8, 1964. We obtained two-year visas for Indonesia in San Francisco, then flew on to visit friends for a few days in the Philippines. Our scheduled arrival date in Jakarta was January 31, 1965.

During one night in our hotel in Manila, I was suddenly awakened and overwhelmed by a strong spiritual force. I found myself on my knees on the floor in a state of ecstatic prayer. This experience did much to reassure me that our move to Indonesia was right!

Chapter Four
Guests at a Difficult Time, Indonesia

IT WAS WELL AFTER midnight when we landed at Jakarta. The empty airport was poorly lit, and water lay in large pools everywhere from recent rains. The tropical air was heavy with strange smells. Unfamiliar sounds tinkled, croaked, and buzzed in the surrounding gloom. As I walked from the plane towards the terminal building, my heart jumped as I almost stepped on a huge squashed insect as large as my hand, wings and legs outspread. I had never seen anything like it. I pushed the image out of my mind. I looked anxiously ahead and grasped Cathy's hand tighter. "I don't want to believe it!" I said to myself.

The airport building was grim and deserted. Soldiers in combat uniforms looked at us curiously, holding their sub-machine guns at the ready as if unsure of us. Or was there some other threat? Fortunately, I saw the Usmans and someone else wave from beyond the immigration desk. It turned out to be a member of Bapak's secretariat, Brodjo. I waved back. I noticed an uncertain look from the government official as he thumbed through our passports. 'American?' he questioned Erling.

Brodjo's amiable smile and calm were reassuring. He seemed to know the customs officers, and soon our bags were chalked and his driver began to take them away. I decided to go to the women's room. I heard my footsteps echo on the cement floor of the empty hall. I found a very small cubicle with an Asian-type lavatory. Everything was wet and a tap dripped unchecked on the stained concrete. In the wall at floor level was a semi-circular opening to let the water out. As I looked at the drainage hole, I saw in the opening two big eyes watching me. Incredulous, I stared at the thing. Suddenly I realised that they were the eyes of a huge toad.

We drove in two cars through almost deserted city streets which ran beside dark canals. Our wheels spattered the occasional slow-moving bicycle rickshaw. Then long facades of old-fashioned two-storey buildings and shops finally gave way to bungalows and trees as we entered the new residential suburb of Kebayoran and passed through to a district market. Brodjo said it was called Blok A.

Chapter Four

Here vendors lined both sides of the road, still selling at small makeshift stalls by the light of flickering lamps. A few hundred metres more and we were out of the built-up area, our headlights cutting holes in the velvet blackness. It was the middle of the rainy season, and from there on, the narrow road was deserted, pot-holed, and muddy all the way to the district of Cilandak.

At 2:00 A.M. we turned past a huddled figure at a gate and drove into the Subud compound. Through the trees about a hundred metres away, I could see the white light of single lamp on the porch of a building. All else was utter darkness. As we drove up to the building, which turned out to be the two-storey guesthouse, I saw Bapak waiting for us. He had a huge flashlight in his hand. He welcomed us warmly. For a moment my tiredness was forgotten. Ibu and Rochanawati were there, Sjafrudin and Robert Winkler, all of whom we had met before in the States. Brodjo introduced the two other members of Bapak's secretariat, Sudarto and Prio Hartono.

Bapak explained that a small house was being enlarged for us near the north boundary of the compound. It was not yet finished, he said, so meanwhile he would put us in the Usmans' newly built house, which was unoccupied, as they still lived outside the compound.

I had just sat down on a rattan chair when a huge bug suddenly whirred loudly past my face towards the pressure lamp, almost hitting me. I realised to my dismay that the squashed insect I had seen at the airport had been indeed real.

Bapak, with much kindness, took us to the house. It was small, with two bedrooms, one with a master bed covered by a mosquito net, tucked in. The other room for the children, with two beds, was also fitted with mosquito nets. To my horror I saw an enormous spider on the inside of the netting of the master bed. I am terrified of spiders, but in the presence of Bapak, I said nothing. I just thought to myself, *I will deal with this later.*

As soon as everyone left, I said to Erling that we had to find that spider and get rid of it. We undid the bed and looked everywhere but couldn't find it. There was nothing I could do, so I finally went to bed and for a long time just lay there unable to go to sleep, feeling that it was lurking somewhere in the darkness. When I had to get up in the middle of the night to go to the lavatory, I felt certain that I would meet the spider. I grasped my flashlight tightly. In what was the smallest cubicle I had ever seen, sure enough, there it was sitting on the white wall half a metre from me, dark and hairy. *I'll never survive Indonesia.* I thought.

Guests at a Difficult Time, Indonesia

With daylight things were better, and I started the marathon task of adjustment to a new way of life. Over the following months, I was to learn the language and customs and set up a home in the most primitive conditions, without electricity or running water.

The first thing was to find servants—without whom an expatriate family could not live in Indonesia—a maid, a houseboy, and a cook. The houseboy came from central Java. He was neat and clean in appearance, perfectly behaved, gentle, polite, and respectful towards us as his employers. His name was Sariman. I had had good servants in Chile, but I had never met one with such model qualities.

Everyone was kind and helpful, and I was introduced to shopping in the small market close by. The rains had turned the ground into mud, especially between the bamboo stalls. The only thing to do was to wear rubber thongs, aptly called flip-flops, which flipped red mud up the back of my legs and dress. I quickly learned to bargain for everything, as was the custom. Fresh food was inexpensive for us, but I argued my way down to the lowest price in order not to cause inflation for others. Small boys would carry my purchases—including all kinds of tropical fruits—in woven baskets for a few *rupiah*.

It took me some time to get used to the night. There were strange smells and unknown noises in the dark. At night the jambu tree in particular exudes a strong aroma, and if I woke up, this new smell made me feel disoriented. The appearance and the noises of the *djaga malam*, the night-watchman, were eerie. Wearing a sarong in the normal way as a skirt and another draped over his head and shoulders against the night air, he looked like a hunchback. There was always a goat with him.

The land, which had been purchased in 1960, was about two hectares, with its boundary at the back of the guesthouse; beyond that were paddy fields. A house for Bapak was under construction, set back about ten metres from the road. It was at the concrete frame stage when we arrived. This was a good time to build if you had foreign currency. The Indonesian *rupiah* was losing exchange value, and building costs were low in Western terms. This meant that a substantial house could be built at a very low cost using American dollars.

There was a large latihan hall within the compound. It was a simple timber-framed building with a tile roof and concrete floor. I believe it was a second-hand army building. The front was partitioned off, used partly as an office for

Chapter Four

the secretariat and partly as a recreation area. The back of the building was also partitioned and was divided into two apartments for Sudarto and Prio, both married with several children. Many things in the compound were improvised. Water was pumped by hand from shallow wells and carried to the houses by the maids. In times of heavy rain, surface water from higher ground, laden with red soil, would flood across the compound, turning the roads and pathways into muddy rivers.

Bapak and Ibu lived on the upper floor in the east wing of the guesthouse, which overlooked the paddy fields. Rochanawati also stayed there, in a room adjacent to Bapak and Ibu's larger room. Hardiyati, Bapak's youngest daughter, lived with Sjafrudin, her husband, and their baby in the west wing. There was a small dining room and a kitchen on the same floor. Verandahs along both sides gave some sitting space. Bapak had a small desk with a typewriter in his room.

The Ramadhan* fast had started when we arrived. I soon learned that Indonesia is a predominantly Islamic country where the Ramadhan fast is universally respected—if not strictly adhered to—by the community. It is one of the compulsory tenets, or five pillars, of the religion and is the major religious observance of the year. It is a thirty-day fast, abstaining from food, water, and smoking between the dawn and sunset prayers.

I did not take part in the fast, but I did join everyone else for the Idul Fitre celebration on Bapak's verandah. Idul Fitre is the customary celebration and public holiday at the end of Ramadhan. Everybody asks forgiveness of each other and, as a symbol of a clean start, puts on new clothes. Indonesians travel to their family homes to pay respects to their parents and elders. There is normally a big *selamatan*.

The women in Bapak's family persuaded me to put on Javanese clothes for the occasion. I complied more from a sense of politeness than from a wish to conform to custom. As I sat in the tight pleated batik sarong and buttoned lace blouse with long sleeves, I struggled to relate to the scene of a totally foreign culture that was unfolding before me. When it came to asking forgiveness, Bapak's family came one by one to Bapak and knelt before him, touching his knee with their folded hands and uttering the traditional words, *Minta ma'af lahir dan batin.* (I ask forgiveness for my outer and inner mistakes.) I only understood in part what was happening around me, and the emotions were beyond my comprehension. I felt rather overwhelmed by it all.

---

* Indonesian spelling of the Arabic month Ramadan.

Guests at a Difficult Time, Indonesia

Bapak gave few talks to gatherings of members. During the six months following the Ramadhan, he gave only three talks to the women and one at Idul Fitre. This may have been because of the increasingly tense political situation, which discouraged meetings, and the fact that for safety reasons Jakarta members could not travel on the roads at night.

Although there were few formal talks, Bapak would sit out and chat every evening with those who lived in the compound. Often he would appear on our verandah for a talk with Erling, and Usman would translate. Also we would visit Bapak, climbing to the top floor of the guesthouse and sitting on the small porch at the top of the stairs. Talk would range over many topics, occasionally spiritual or personal matters, but most often about practical matters concerning life in the compound.

Ibu appeared in the role of the family mother. At that time she did not have a retinue of women friends, as she did later. Indonesian women generally stayed indoors in the evening and did not take part in the sitting out with Bapak. Rochanawati spent a lot of time in her room. She was always pleasant and self-effacing.

Amongst those living in Cilandak were some who, by disposition, were drawn deeply into the spiritual life. They preferred to dwell in the spiritual dimension of experience rather than in the normal life of the world around them. Those who were genuinely close to their latihan in this way were often able to be of help to other people. Rochanawati was such a person. I had met her in New York in 1959 and realised that she was an extremely sensitive person who felt the emanations of another's inner state. She suffered very much as a result.

What was remarkable was her capacity constantly to surrender her condition to God. She was not openly active in giving advice, but when a situation was congenial to her inner feeling, she was willing to offer valuable help. She would often call me to her room and talk to me. Her spiritual insight and intuition of a world that we seldom see was extremely clear and focussed. Bapak remarked of her, 'Rochanawati is [spiritually] older than her mother.'

The unusual circumstances of living in such a small community brought its own problems, particularly under the pressure of events in the country. I noticed that for some days an American lady who had been one of the witnesses at my opening in New York had stopped speaking to me. Since I had not done anything to offend her, I said nothing. Eventually she came to me.

Chapter Four

She complained, "I have been told that you have suggested to Rochanawati that I should leave Indonesia." I said that I had done nothing of the sort. She was convinced but suggested we go and explain this to Rochanawati. When we arrived at Rochanawati's room, my friend had hardly started to explain when Rochanawati said, "Stop! I never listen to gossip!" That was the end of it.

I found adjusting to life in Indonesia in 1965 very difficult—the hot and humid climate, the rudimentary conditions, and the limitations of a new language. It was also difficult at times to get personal relationships right. Respect for another person's feelings come first in any discussion between Indonesians. If you disagreed with someone, you were expected to handle the matter with a given protocol of care and subtlety. I found that Indonesian people achieved what they wanted, or communicated what they needed, with greater circumspection than was normal for us in the USA. As they were accustomed to this approach, they were also inclined to be more sensitive to violations of their code, and it was easy for a newly-arrived foreigner unwittingly to upset someone. This was an East-West cultural problem. If something was unresolved, I might, at best, sense that something was wrong, but the Indonesian would not come out and say so.

This problem came up for Erling over cutting the trees. Mas Usman was Bapak's interpreter and treasurer, taking care of the financial management of the property, its building program and security. He had an arrangement with a local villager, called "the gardener," to live in a hut on the compound. This man would cut quite large branches off the trees to feed his goats to the point where the trees started to look grossly deformed. Erling became concerned as the gardener started to saw a large branch from a tree in front of the guesthouse, and, in a few newly acquired words of Indonesian, he told the goat owner to stop.

Later when Aminah was very touchy about something else, she said to Erling, "I'll spare your trees if you will spare my feelings." With this the problem came out and the matter was settled.

Arising from the tree incident, Erling said to Sjafrudin that he believed there should be a small committee to take care of community matters, as no-one in the compound was taking responsibility. Soon afterwards Bapak came to our house and asked Erling about the committee idea. "Who do you think should be members?" Bapak asked. Erling suggested that it might comprise about six people, Indonesian and foreign (not including himself), whom he named, representing each of the current activities in the compound: financial management, construction, the secretariat, architecture, matters affecting foreign guests, and family matters. A few days later, Bapak announced the formation of the committee. All its members were Indonesian. Some order was established, and years later foreign residents were appointed to this committee.

There were many things I had to learn to accept as part of the normal life in Indonesia. The Subud compound at Cilandak was a construction site, with several houses partly completed. Many aspects of the building work used raw materials prepared on the site; river stones for foundations were brought and broken, timber hand-sawn and plaster mixed from lime and brick crushed by hand.

Soon after I arrived, I found the workers on our new house sawing wood in a most primitive way. A large log was placed on a trestle and two Indonesians, one above and one below, laboured all day with a huge double-ended pit-saw, cutting it into planks. It brought me to tears to see these two peasants, dressed only in sarongs, pushing back and forth for hours in the tropical sun.

I also had my share of minor household dramas that characterised the restricted life of Cilandak in those times, where small things loomed large. Many Indonesians keep caged birds, either hanging on the porches of their houses or mounted on tall bamboo poles. They attribute symbolic significance to certain species and value others for their distinctive calls, such as doves, which sang uniquely up the octave. One day there appeared a cage with a grey owl inside, hanging from a big tree in front of the guesthouse. The cage was so small that the poor bird barely fitted. I could not stand its miserable situation and had to look away. I was learning to think of myself as a guest in the compound and felt helpless to interfere. An hour later the owl and cage were on the ground outside my house. I could not believe my luck—how could this misery follow me to my own house?

I soon discovered that Rochanawati, who was very fond of Cathy, had arranged with a servant to buy a bird as a present for Cathy. I immediately freed the owl from his prison and put it on a branch of the tree. I tied a long line to its foot so it had some movement but could not escape. That seemed the best compromise. It sat there looking down on us for a few weeks, accepting bits of meat, then one day mysteriously disappeared. Some said it had been stolen for resale.

Chapter Four

Throughout my settling-in, I was learning Indonesian. I took lessons every day from Pak Ishak, a Subud member and school teacher with a good command of English, who lived nearby. Initially I concentrated on the vocabulary I needed for talking to the servants. Later, I enjoyed the ability to express the shades of feeling* I was picking up in all my relationships with the Indonesians. Their manner was soft, courteous, and discreet. Bahasa Indonesia, an adaptation of the Malay language, was also—as is Spanish—spoken with a more lively emphasis than English. Much later I was to take an interest in Indonesian popular music and find that its easy rhythm owed much to early Portuguese influences.

Bapak, realising our need for transport while we were awaiting our household goods and station-wagon from the USA, lent us an Opel station-wagon. Erling used it to drive the children to and from school. It was in this car that I had my first experience of Indonesian traffic outside the city. Bapak invited us to go with him for the day to his small farm at Cipanas in the mountains, about two hours drive from Jakarta. Our driver was told to follow Adji, Bapak's teenage grandson, driving another car.

The dual carriageway was busy with loaded trucks of all sizes, buses packed with people, cars, and mini-buses, all travelling as fast as they could manage. As well there was local village traffic of three-wheel taxis, motor scooters, bullock carts, rickshaws, bicycles, and pedestrians loaded down with market produce. Drivers tried to pass everyone else by weaving in and out of the stream of oncoming traffic at high speed, with horns blaring. Adji joined this stream with all the bravado of youth. To be on the road at all was dangerous—wrecks on the side of the road testified to this—but to let yourself be driven by somebody else was an act of faith or obedience. Our driver terrified me by driving faster than anyone else to try to keep Adji in sight. The strategy seemed to be a kind of brinkmanship—to stay in the centre of the road as long as possible, only giving way to the approaching vehicle at the last second if it did not!

An hour later much to my relief, we had to slow down as we came to a winding road up the mountain through the tea estates. As we climbed into the cool air, I looked back and caught my breath. The view far below was magnificent, a vast rice plain of green and yellow paddy-fields stretching out

---

* The word *feeling* is used, as far as possible, to describe a judgement of value—for example here, agreeable or disagreeable. Feeling defined in this way is not emotion (which is involuntary) and not intuition (hunch). This definition of feeling is important in understanding Indonesians, who, I found, more commonly made judgements by feeling than by thinking.

Guests at a Difficult Time, Indonesia

to a distant horizon softened by a pale blue haze. Suddenly I found myself in a beautiful and exotic land as yet unknown to me. What had seemed to be spreading settlements of orange-tiled white-washed houses turned out to be a narrow band of ribbon development. There were villages too, but from this altitude, they appeared as clusters of trees and coconut palms. My feelings lightened and I started to appreciate the bright colours of the tea picker's clothing and the smiling and waving of children as we passed.

At the farm everyone relaxed. Ibu disappeared to her room and her maids set about preparing lunch. I felt the tension of Jakarta drop away and breathed in the fresh mountain air like an unbelievable luxury.

In Cilandak the car would sometimes, without warning, disappear from our front yard. It happened one day just when the children were to go to school, so I went to see Bapak. He was sitting on his terrace, and as I arrived, Ibu came out the door of her bedroom. I explained as politely as I could that the car was missing, implying that Adji was responsible. Ibu became angry. That I might be finding fault with her grandson was not—definitely not—acceptable. I said no more. As I left Bapak gave me a look that said, "With Ibu, my dear, on the subject of her grandson ... you are on your own!" From then on, however, the car stopped disappearing from our front yard.

Erling told me that one evening Bapak had made the following suggestion: "Erling, you are bringing in US dollars to pay your expenses. Usman tells me that some of your money is in savings banks earning only four per cent per annum. Why don't you bring in ten thousand US dollars and convert them to Indonesian rupiah? You can lend the money to Usman at one per cent per month, which will be enough for you to live on."

"But, Bapak," Erling said, "the present rate of loss of the rupiah versus the US dollar is four hundred per cent per year. Whatever I convert will be worth only a quarter in US dollars by the end of the year." Erling said he thought Usman didn't fully understand the practicalities of inflation. There was much discussion and the matter was dropped. Erling later discovered that in Jakarta at that time personal loans were extended at rates of interest of anything up to five per cent per week. Of course many such loans were never repaid.

Outside the Subud compound, the political mood was becoming increasingly hostile towards the USA. The normally peaceful Indonesian people had been stirred up by Sukarno and the PKI Communist party into a

Chapter Four

state of hatred against the Americans and the English. In Jakarta there were huge posters showing Uncle Sam being kicked and saying 'Americans Go Home!' Because of the danger to its nationals, the US Government instructed all Americans to leave Indonesia.

One day Bapak sent us a message that he was going to Bali and wanted Erling and me and the children to go with him. This suggestion was almost too much for me. I felt I was doing all I could cope with in adjusting to Indonesia and managing a home for the family without then having to go to Bali. But of course we agreed. The party consisted of Bapak, Usman, Erling, myself, our children, David and Cathy, and Landon Gray and his wife.

When the plane landed at the Den Pasar, Bali, there were two open-back trucks full of anti-American demonstrators outside the airport. They were shouting at us in chorus, "Kill the Americans!" There were large bloody-looking banners daubed with dripping red paint. It was very threatening, and the police ushered us to safety around the back of the plane. When we drove away, these trucks went ahead and stopped us in order to demonstrate some more. I heard afterwards that we had been mistaken for US Embassy officials who had been expected on that flight.

We lodged in the city in a typical old single-storey Indonesian hotel. Our room had only one window, and there was no possible cross ventilation. At the back was a bathroom, which had an abominable smell. The mattress was lumpy, damp, and stinking.

Next day, Erling went off with Landon Gray to look for better accommodation. I waited at the house where Bapak was staying, and I sat chatting with Usman at one end of the ornamental Balinese terrace. Bapak was in an armchair at the other end. He called me and said, "The chief of police here in Den Pasar wants to be opened. Actually he is not ready but Bapak will open him . . ." Here he paused and, pointing his finger at me for emphasis, said, "for you!" I was baffled as to what Bapak meant, but I never asked him questions. I thought and thought, *Why would Bapak open the chief of police for me? What could I possibly have to do with him?*

Erling now came back with the news that he had found a nice place, so we and the Grays moved in. It had individual huts and was picturesque, with sloping thatch roofs. It was clean and right on the beach. Bapak moved there too.

Guests at a Difficult Time, Indonesia

At dawn of the day we were due to leave, Bapak said that, instead of going directly to Jakarta, he would go to Surabaya in East Java, Semarang, and Yogyakarta and that he wanted Erling to go with him. He said that the Grays and I should return to Jakarta as planned. Bapak, Usman, and Erling left soon afterwards.

When later I went with Landon to pay the hotel bill, we were told in an abrupt manner that the seats reserved for us on the plane had been taken by government officials. We decided we had better move to a hotel nearer the airport. On arrival at this other hotel, I realised that Erling had taken all our passports. The desk staff became very unpleasant and sent me to the police station. I went alone, leaving the children with the Grays. The police questioned me for more than an hour and then released me. All the time I was there, I could hear soldiers drilling outside the window. As they marched they shouted slogans about killing the Americans.

I returned to the hotel, where all five of us had been given a single room without a window. It was hot, muggy, and smelly. I could not sleep and spent the night on a chair outside the door. Early the next morning, we tried to get on a plane, but we could not get any seats. I began to be very uneasy. Suddenly I remembered the chief of police. Of course I should call him. He had become very friendly—like one of us—when he was opened by Bapak. I called him and explained our situation. He immediately sent one of his personal assistants with a jeep. I cannot recall how many times that man took us back and forth to the airport, day after day, waiting with us each time to see if we could get on a plane, and bringing us back to the hotel. By now the children had diarrhoea, and the airport toilets were indescribably bad. He never left us for a moment, finally waving goodbye as our plane lifted off. Bapak's opening of the chief of police had indeed been for me.

In Jakarta the public became increasingly aggressive towards the USA, but we went on settling in. Once we went to the house of an American family, who were leaving in a hurry and selling everything, and bought good household equipment at reasonable prices. These people were fleeing for their lives, and it brought home to me the risk of our staying. Here I was learning how, with the help of the latihan, I could stay centred and keep moving—undeterred—in the direction I had decided upon.

Chapter Four

But far more important than the equipment, I found and employed Morsini, who had been their cook. Trained by them, she was a jewel in the kitchen and beautiful, graceful, and polite.

When the building of our house was finished and I was ready to move, Bapak sent for me. "You are moving today?" he asked. "Yes, Bapak," I said. "Then you must have a selamatan tonight and invite everybody in the compound. Bapak will come too."

I agreed but as I walked back home my mind was racing, *How am I going to manage to move, and have a big party on the same day?* I thought it was impossible. However I had not yet experienced Indonesian hospitality in a case like this. As soon as Morsini heard, she mobilised help; she made saté and others in the compound brought all kinds of delicious dishes. Sariman arranged the moving. Everything was perfect and ready on time. Bapak gave a long talk in Indonesian to the forty or so guests. Mrs Subardjo, wife of the former Foreign Minister of Indonesia, told me that he said many things that she had never heard before. She didn't elaborate except to say that he said that one day my heart and Bapak's heart would become one.

Though our new house was small, we had all that was necessary for the simple life of the compound. I now established a routine with the children and the servants. However, I would still cry sometimes, for no apparent reason. One day I was crying when Hosanna Baron, who had come from Mexico to see Bapak, came into my tiny room. She said to me, "I don't blame you for crying. I would too, if I had to listen to 'that' every day." "That" was the sound of Indonesian soldiers marching back and forth half a block away, chanting hate of the Americans and preparing to kill. Spontaneously she took from her neck a gold chain bearing the Miraculous Medal and put it on me. The Miraculous Medal carries the promise of the Virgin that all who wear it will be protected by her. It was made according to the instructions of the Virgin during a visitation to Catherine Laboure, a Catholic nun who lived in Paris in the nineteenth century.

The situation became more and more tense. Rochanawati did latihan with us women every night and sent us home repeating the name of God. One morning she said to me that she could see around her in the compound a kind of beauty which we as yet could not see. I asked her, "How many years does one have to be in Subud before one is able to see this?" She answered, "It is not a matter of years; it depends on where you are when you start."

Guests at a Difficult Time, Indonesia

One night when Bapak was away from Jakarta for a few days, I woke up at around 2:00 A.M. feeling disturbed and itchy. I asked Erling to put the lights on. He did so and went into the living-room. I heard footsteps outside a little window next to me but paid no attention because there were always noises in the compound at night. Then I heard a strange guttural sound. I put on my robe and went to the living-room. What I saw paralysed me with fear. At the same time, something in me said, "Be very careful!" so I uttered no sound.

Erling was against the wall with his hands up. A swarthy Indonesian with a moustache that hung inches below his chin stood with a machete poised above Erling's head. The Indonesian wore a shirt open to the waist and a sarong. There were two others with him dressed in military fatigues, one with a rifle and bayonet held against Erling's stomach, the other with a pistol.

The leader, the one with the long moustache, ordered the uniformed man with the pistol to go outside and close the shutters of our bedroom while he ushered us into our bedroom. Fortunately that night I had felt I should close the door to the children's room.

Erling and I sat on opposite sides of the bed. The leader wanted money. I showed him my purse, and he insisted that I open it. For a moment I was so close to him that anyone viewing from outside would have thought that we were the best of friends. For a split second as he looked into my purse, amazingly I felt as if he were my brother and I thought, *This is a strange situation!* My mouth was dry from fear. He was not satisfied. He insisted there was more. As it transpired, someone had tipped them off that we had in our house money from the sale of an electric refrigerator. We had hidden three million *rupiah* (the equivalent of eight hundred American dollars) in a briefcase in a concealed drawer built into the back of the bedhead. We gave it all to the bandits. Then the leader produced a rope to tie us up. As he did, I said to him in Indonesian, *"Tidak usah, tidak usah!"* (It's not necessary, it's not necessary!). As I experienced that strange mixture of emotions—fear and closeness—he accepted this and instead used the rope to tie up all Erling's clothes and belongings into a bundle.

As they prepared to leave, Erling said, "Tunggu" (wait) and slowly opened again the briefcase that contained the money. He took out our passports, insurance policies, and traveller's cheques, then his wallet with credit cards and four one hundred American dollar bills. The leader inspected each item as Erling threw them on the bed. The bandits took only the large bundle of *rupiah* because they did not understand the value of the other items.

Chapter Four

The guerilla leader then threatened us, saying that if we told anybody about what had happened, they would come back and—pointing to the window—"Kill you all, through there."

I thought afterwards, *what strange things we do under stress*. When it all started, I looked at my watch and then again when they left. They were with us for thirty minutes, from 2:10 A.M. to 2:40 A.M. We waited quietly for another thirty minutes, then woke our houseboy, who was sleeping on the floor in the kitchen. He had, fortunately, slept through the whole incident. We sent him to call Robert Winkler, who lived behind the latihan hall about a hundred metres away. He was aghast! How could this have happened in Bapak's house?

The next day, when the word got around, those who lived in the compound came to express their sadness and support. The sincerity was very moving. Mas Sudarto from Bapak's secretariat clung to Erling and wept copiously on his shoulder. The only exceptions were our nearest neighbours, who were responsible for security in the compound. Husband and wife criticised us, saying that we should take a good look at ourselves. Something must be very wrong with Erling and me, they said, "to deserve such a bad experience." However, the following day, they had bolts fitted to their windows and doors and hired a special guard for their house!

After the robbery I was very frightened for my family and myself. When Mariamah Wichmann, a single lady who had come from Coombe Springs to live in Cilandak, heard about it, she came to sleep in my house. She slept on a sofa in the living-room for three or four days, the very place where the robbers had threatened us. Hers was a wonderful gesture.

A few days later, the gang of robbers returned to our nearest neighbours' house. They tied up the watchman, broke in and stole everything outside and inside, sewing machines, radios, children's bicycles, and much more. There were a dozen of them, and they brought a truck to load up. Bapak was notified. He came down immediately and had the Indonesian men in the compound armed. Later they were appointed by the commander of the military district as members of the civil defence to form a night guard.

Those days were extremely difficult. We had latihans every night, and Rochanawati used to give us advice on how to lead our lives. She suggested that the only way to face the situation, especially at night, was to say inwardly 'God, God,' incessantly. I followed her advice and was able to sleep.

In the middle of all this, Hardiyati said to me that I should take very good care of my family because the bandits stole children. This added to my distress almost beyond endurance. What could I do? All children played in the grounds of the compound. It was impossible for them to be kept indoors in such small premises and in that heat.

I was, of course, not alone in my anxiety. The political tension of the country filled everybody with fear and doubt. The struggle for domination of the Indonesian people by the Communist party, the PKI, backed by China, was a struggle for the hearts and minds of a hundred million people, the biggest Islamic nation in the world. President Sukarno was playing a dangerous game playing off the East against the West, thinking that he could control the PKI and factions within the army. China was providing arms.

On Bapak's advice, most of the foreign guests had left. Then one day in July, Robert Winkler came to our house. He said Bapak had called him to suggest that, because the situation had become so dangerous, he should move into the German Embassy quarters in the city. He told us that he had asked Bapak, "What about Erling and his family?" Bapak had answered, "If he were to ask me, I would say, he should leave as soon as possible."

Erling went immediately to see Bapak who said, "Yes, it is better for you to leave for a while. When the situation is normal again you should return." Erling said, "Well I have sold everything in the USA so I think I will go to Australia." "Yes," said Bapak, "but New Zealand is better for you." Erling found out later that the reason why Bapak did not call us and speak to us personally was that he had invited us to come and we were his guests. According to Javanese custom, Bapak could not propose that we leave.

Nobody was more pleased than I. We packed and left our household effects with the Indonesian families. On July 8, 1965, we flew out of Jakarta to the safety, normality, and cooler climate of Sydney, just five months after our arrival in Indonesia. A few days later, I was starting a new phase of my life in New Zealand.

On September 30, 1965, the political turmoil in Indonesia reached its climax. Six generals were murdered in a failed coup d'etat. The tension was broken, but half a million people were killed in one of the worst slaughters of modern times.

Chapter Five
Intermission in New Zealand

IT WAS A GREAT RELIEF to arrive in New Zealand after the tense political situation and difficult living conditions in Indonesia. We were met by Subud members at the airport and within a few days found a comfortable furnished house to rent in Takapuna, north of Auckland. The beach was a hundred metres away and a school for David and Cathy within walking distance.

I found the local people friendly and relaxed and the amenities of the area very good. But at first I was not sure if I could adjust to New Zealand—so much so that I remember wondering, *Where on earth am I?* There was little that I could relate to in this new country. I was more at home with the activity of cities than with rural life, which New Zealand suggested. Of course it was only a matter of time before I made friends and became familiar with my surroundings. Then I found that Auckland had much to offer. Meantime, I set about making a new home.

For Erling, there were many features of New Zealand that he immediately responded to. He enjoys being near the ocean and likes open views and beautiful scenery, abundantly present in our area. The light of the southern latitude brought out the colours of land and ocean, and the clear atmosphere accentuated the broad sweeps of sky.

We began to attend the Subud group latihan in rented premises near the city centre. The group totalled about seventy, among them Tom and Vivian Pope, whom Bapak had also advised to come here from Indonesia.

In Indonesia almost everything I did was related to Subud and to activities within the Cilandak community. Here in New Zealand, my Subud life was limited to attendance at latihan. I learnt that Auckland had one of three Subud groups in New Zealand, the others being in Wellington and Christchurch. A national organisation to service the country-wide activities was just forming—the first National Congress of Subud took place in the capital city, Wellington, in October 1965. Erling attended while I stayed at home with the children.

Chapter Five

I had no inkling that one day I would do active helper's work at a national level in New Zealand. At the congress Erling and Tom Pope showed a film and slides of Cilandak. Lamaan (later Raymond) van Sommers, who had designed the guesthouse in Cilandak in 1960, was elected the first National Chairman of Subud New Zealand. He was to become a very close friend of our family.

As had become the custom, Bapak sent a message to this first gathering. He reminded us of the qualities of Susila Budhi Dharma as a basis for conducting a congress:

What is necessary for Bapak to advise you is that you should not forget the qualities of Subud in discussing the business of congress, meaning you should behave with patience and calm, willing to give and take, showing mutual respect and considerateness to one another. You should in fact always remember God the Almighty and not think only of your own interest. [19]

After the intense activity of the early spread of Subud in the USA and the drama of life in Indonesia, Subud in New Zealand was, to me, quiet. However, for local members the process of the latihan seemed to be just as dramatic as elsewhere. I remember Erling telling me of one man in the group who was going through an accelerated purification. His behaviour, which stemmed from an undiagnosed mental illness, kept several men helpers occupied as they gradually learned the appropriate degree of care.

The person who had brought the latihan to New Zealand was Christopher Baynes, whose family was closely associated with the Swiss psychiatrist, C.G. Jung. Christopher had been a member of John Bennett's Gurdjieff Institute in Coombe Springs and was amongst the first to receive the latihan in England in 1957. He and his wife, Lorna, had immigrated to New Zealand with their young family and were living on a farm in Hawkes Bay. Erling had corresponded with Christopher from 1960 to 1963 and went to visit him while attending the Congress in Wellington.

If things had remained as they were, I would have become more active in the Subud group, but destiny had something else in store. In January 1966 I had the following dream:

A cleaning lady came to the door of my house and gave me a container with very special coffee. The aroma was exquisite. I realised that to serve such a coffee I would need to have a very clean cup. I began to wash and dry the cups, but as I dried each one, I found a small mark on the outer side near the bottom of the cup.

Intermission in New Zealand

When I tried to remove it, a small chip fell out and the cup was useless. I began to worry, thinking there are a limited number of cups, soon they would all be gone and Erling would be disappointed.

Because of the strong impact of the dream, I wrote to Sudarto in Bapak's secretariat, who had a reputation for interpreting symbolism. He replied that the dream was telling me that we should have more children. I told Erling and he reminded me that while we were in Cilandak, Bapak had also said that he hoped we would have more children.

In February I became pregnant with our third child.

That month Rochanawati died. We received the news by telegram from Robert Winkler in Cilandak and told David and Cathy, who accepted it without comment. About a week later, Cathy asked, "Is it possible that M'bayu has died?" I realised then that Cathy only knew Rochanawati by the name *M'bayu*, which means elder sister in Javanese.

"Of course," I said, "don't you remember that I told you last week that Rochanawati had died?" Cathy sobbed and ran to her bedroom, shutting the door. I heard her crying, then she suddenly stopped. An hour later she came out.

Afterwards I learned that Rochanawati had appeared to Cathy in her room early that morning. "M'bayu said she had come to say goodbye," Cathy said, "I could smell that the batik she was wearing was a new one. After she left I wondered why she had come to say goodbye. When I ran back to my room crying, she came again. She told me not to cry as she was very happy where she was. I told M'bayu that I wasn't crying for her but for me, because I wouldn't be able to see her again. Then she talked a long time to me until I felt better."

As my pregnancy progressed, I could feel the latihan continuously. I became very sensitive. About the fifth month, the baby started to kick vigorously. Also at that time my gynaecologist picked up two heart beats from the child. He couldn't find any evidence of twins and seemed puzzled and a little concerned.

When I was about six months pregnant, I had another clear dream:

I dreamed that I was pregnant. I stood in the centre of the kitchen. It was exactly as in real life. Suddenly in front of me and about two paces away stood the Virgin Mary. With her was a young girl. Mary was dressed very simply in a three-quarter length white dress with a light blue sash. She talked to me for a long time non-stop in a strange language that I had never heard before.

Chapter Five

I stood there listening but not understanding. I was just as I was at the time, six months pregnant. She then stopped talking and came close to me. She put her hand on my tummy and said in English, "And don't worry about the baby. The reason why it moves so much inside is because it is going to be a ruler."

. . . I woke up.

The baby was born on November 10, 1966. It was a girl and everything went well. We had asked Bapak for a name.* It was customary in those days for Bapak to give the first letter of a name for a new baby by mail and the parents then supplied a list of suitable names from which he could choose. This time he sent a cable with the name already chosen, it read: "The right name is Sandra." I was filled with joy when I saw it.

During these days, Erling saw an advertisement for an attractive farm on Waiheke Island in the Gulf of Huaraki, about twenty kilometres by ferry from downtown Auckland. The farm adjoined the all-weather deep-water ferry port at Matiatia Bay and was offered in two parts, one each side of the port road. Erling decided to form a company, Church Bay Farm Ltd, and with Louis Patten, an American Subud member, to buy the southern part of five hundred hectares. It consisted of low rolling hills of grassland interrupted by ravines and stands of native trees, including huge flowering pohutukawas along the rocky shoreline. It was stocked with sheep and cattle. There were three houses, one of which was spacious and almost new.

On December 17, 1966, we moved from Takapuna to the farm. Sandra was one month old. It was early summer and everything was at its best. The house was on top of a high hill, with a vast all-round view of the ocean and the islands of the Gulf. Fresh breezes, charged with ozone, blew up from the cliffs and across the unmown grass of the headland. The sunlight sparkled on the blue-green water, clear all the way to an horizon without haze. A distant band of cloud, which gives New Zealand the name of "The Land of the Long White Cloud," slowly passed in ordered formation. At night, our home being far away from street lamps and houses, the clear sky was awesome with its canopy of stars, so bright that on a moonless night there was enough light from them to distinguish the land against the dark ocean. From my bedroom window, I could see the distant points of light of Auckland city far across the Gulf.

---

* Giving of names in Subud: see Chapter Eight.

Intermission in New Zealand

To carry out a long-term program of development of the farm, Erling employed a manager and sought regular advice from farm experts. As a result the property improved over the next two years. David and Cathy went to school on the island. We bought ponies for them, and Cathy developed a passionate love for horses. Every afternoon after school, she could be seen galloping her pony, Taffy, across the hills, her hair flying.

I took turns with Erling going to Auckland for latihan. In this way each of us went once a week. As the ferry ran only during daylight hours, we would stay overnight with the Longcrofts, who lived in Howick, a southern suburb. Charles Longcroft had been chairman of Subud Coombe Springs group. His wife, Harlinah, later moved to Cilandak, where she lived for many years, becoming an official historian of the Subud movement.

One morning we were with David and Sandra in the family room, and I asked David to fetch Sandra's bib from her room. He was then nine years old. He returned with a puzzled look. "When I came into Sandra's room," he said, "I saw a bare pine board laid across her crib. On the board there was a book bound in black leather, with gold lettering: 'The X-Holy Bible.' I turned to get the bib off the shelf and when I turned back both the board and the book were gone."

Before we moved to the farm, Subud New Zealand held its Second National Congress in Christchurch. Erling showed a film of the Briarcliff Congress. The active membership of Subud in New Zealand was then a little more than a hundred, out of a total of five hundred who had been opened. Fifty attended the congress. The coming Subud World Congress in Japan was discussed and the possibility of a visit by Bapak to New Zealand sometime afterwards was enthusiastically endorsed.

In July 1967 Erling received a letter from Bapak, asking him to join Bapak in Cilandak and go to the Third Subud World Congress in Tokyo. Erling took David with him. In Cilandak, Erling found that Sjafrudin had just died. He was only thirty-five years old and left his wife and a family of four children.

Erling told me when he got back that during the Congress, Bapak had asked him about our returning to live in Cilandak. Erling said that he had agreed to come as soon as possible. Erling then arranged with Louis Patten, who was also attending the Tokyo Congress, to move with his family from California to the farm as we moved back to Cilandak.

Chapter Five

At the end of January 1968, Erling travelled to Cilandak to see to the completion of our house. While he was there, he was asked to Bapak's office to discuss a potential forestry project. He later told me that when he arrived at the office, he found Bapak with Usman, Mas Dono, Prio Hartono, and Sjarif Horthy. Erling's account, I believe, throws light on the way in which Bapak accepted the advice from those around him on business and other worldly matters.

Bapak spoke, with Usman translating: "We are very fortunate that some of our Subud brothers who are section heads in the Forestry Department have been able to obtain for us an exclusive concession to harvest ten thousand hectares of Meranti hardwood in southern Sumatra. Bapak proposes that you and Sjarif supply the capital, whilst Usman, Prio Hartono, and Mas Dono will do the work."

Erling said he immediately felt a sinking sensation, which from long experience he had learned was a warning of an unfavourable outcome. He asked, "Who among the brothers here has experience in the lumber business?" There was silence and Erling continued, "I also have no experience in the lumber business. My observation is that when a person enters a business outside his field of expertise, he loses a lot of money, paying for his inexperience. Maybe he loses it all."

"But," Bapak replied, "You are a businessman, you know how to organise these things successfully." There was some discussion between Bapak and Usman. Then Usman said, "Bapak says you are thinking too much. Just go ahead and do it."

Erling answered, "Bapak, I am not thinking, I am feeling, and my feeling about this proposal is not good. I have been warned off bad proposals all my life in the same way." Bapak responded, "Bapak does not insist." Erling said he would discuss the matter with Sjarif and return to Bapak with a suggestion the next day. The following morning Erling proposed that he and Sjarif prepare a feasibility study and that the Indonesians appointed by Bapak would take a look at the concession area. Bapak agreed to this approach.

The sequel was that later that year, when we returned to Cilandak, Mas Dono came to Erling and said, "We're all very happy that you didn't agree to the Sumatra lumber project. Prio and I went to the concession and found that it is a swamp with no roads. The trees are infested with beetles, which would make the timber worthless."

Intermission in New Zealand

At that time, Husein Rofé, who brought the latihan to the West in 1957, was also visiting Cilandak and when Bapak took a post-Ramadhan trip to East Java in February 1968, Husein and Erling went along, sharing a taxi. While Bapak went to his mother's house in Semarang, Erling and Husein stayed with Pak Slamet at a member's mountain house. Pak Slamet, who was among the first persons to receive the latihan from Bapak, was an artist with a highly developed capacity for portraying a person's spiritual future in symbolic imagery. The four men sat up late talking. At 2:00 A.M. Pak Slamet said, "Erling's daughter (Sandra) has just come into the room and is standing near the table. She says, 'I am the old mother.'" No one commented and the matter was left unresolved.

In early May 1968, Mayko came to New Zealand to see her grand-daughter, Sandra, for the first time. Mayko had been in Lima, Peru, for Bapak's visit a month earlier and had followed him to Cali, Bogota, Colombia, and Mexico City. She told me of her many spiritual experiences during this trip.

With Mayko was Clementina. When Clementina saw Sandra it was love at first sight. She picked her up and from there on, I was never to change her or feed her again. Clementina simply took over the care of Sandra. When Mayko left, Clementina stayed with us.

Clementina told us how in Chile she had had a dream in which she saw a little girl near her and a voice said, "You must go and take care of this child." This was about the time that Sandra was born. When she saw Sandra, she immediately recognised her as the little girl in her dream.*

Meantime it was confirmed that Bapak would come to New Zealand that same May at the end of his world trip. We offered the Auckland Subud committee the use of our house for Bapak's stay. Rachman Mitchell, who was visiting New Zealand and had never been on Waiheke Island, said that he felt this would be unfair to the members. The group was in Auckland, an hour and a half away by ferry.

Harlinah Longcroft, who knew our house, suggested to Rachman that they both visit us on Waiheke Island. It was a bright sunny day with a few broken white clouds. I collected them from the wharf and drove them back up the steep hill,

---

* Bapak's explanation about dreams at the Tokyo Congress in 1967 was that, whereas most dreams are a projection of a person's own unresolved concerns, there are "sometimes, too, dreams which are an indication of what is going to happen." Clementina's dream appears to come into the latter category.

Chapter Five

parking the jeep next to the house. Rachman got out and stood there a long time, looking at the vast view of sky, ocean, and islands. He seemed stunned. Then he turned to me and said, "Of course Bapak should stay here!"

Bapak arrived at our house in the mid-May 1968. I was waiting at the door with Sandra. As Bapak got out of the car, Sandra took one look at him and threw herself into his arms. It was an acceptance she had never shown for anyone else. I was amazed.

The next morning Bapak pointed to Sandra and said in English, "Very strong." Erling jokingly made a gesture of strength, flexing his arm muscle. Bapak smiled and said, "No . . . in the latihan." Sandra loved being with Bapak and showed him her affection by bringing books and placing them all around him. Bapak laughed and let her be.

Sandra began to disappear in the afternoons. We discovered that she was knocking on Bapak's door. He would let her in and, as we found out later from Bapak, she was doing the latihan with him—which she initiated spontaneously and Bapak accepted. She was then aged eighteen months.

The party consisted of Bapak, Ibu, Usman (translating), and Aminah (cooking). They all fitted in comfortably and stayed for ten days. About half the New Zealand membership came for Bapak's stay and were helped to find accommodation on the island. We rented the Oneroa municipal hall for Bapak's talks and latihans. Bapak's five talks included clarifications about not mixing Subud with other spiritual methods, how the growth of Subud depends on the helpers, and the difference between belief and spiritual experience.

For us in the house, the days were taken up looking after the guests. We fed everybody who was actively helping. Although it was winter, the weather was mild and there were many sunny days. On the weekends members would sit in the garden to be near Bapak and Ibu. Some of the women who liked being with Ibu sat on the terrace, waiting until she called one or another of them.

I have a picture of Bapak printed indelibly on my mind. It was early in the morning of the day of his departure. He was sitting in the living-room with his back to the wide view of sea and sky. He was in a long-sleeved shirt, no tie, and very relaxed. Aminah and I were in the kitchen preparing breakfast. Usman was at the table having coffee.

Intermission in New Zealand

We all stopped what we were doing as Bapak began to talk. *This is amazing,* I thought, *Bapak is talking about the Secret of Fatima.** I remembered at once what Erling had told me about this. Usman remained at the table, Aminah came from the kitchen and stood near the counter, and I stood against the door to the living-room. Together we listened. Usman translated for us but only intermittently. I sensed he felt it would be inappropriate to interrupt.

Bapak talked for some time about the Miracle of Fatima and of wide expectations of help for mankind from God.** Among reports by people who had received indications, he said, was the expectation that "Salvation would come with a man from the East and that his name was Muhammad."

The time came for Bapak to depart. Because many members wanted to go with him to the airport, we all left on the larger morning ferry. We sat together on benches, accentuating the feeling of closeness that had grown between us all during that wonderful visit.

In Auckland the group took the party to Subud House and gave them lunch, while waiting for the plane. It was at this time that Bapak suggested that Mayko should live in Cilandak. It was Thursday and Mayko was fasting. (Monday and Thursday fasting was a Javanese custom undertaken to help make correct decisions in life's activities.) The Subud House comprised a hall for latihan and a house. Mayko wanted to be out of the way, so she went into the latihan hall. She saw it was empty and sat away from the door on a solitary chair. She started to put up her long hair, which had come undone, into a bun when suddenly to her surprise Bapak and Usman came in. Bapak asked Usman to bring a chair and table and together they sat in the corner of the hall diagonally opposite to Mayko. Mayko said she felt Bapak's presence was overwhelming. She felt she could not stay but could not leave either. She started silently to cry.

---

* The third message from the Virgin Mary of Fatima given to Sister Lucia in 1917 was a secret which was to have been disclosed to the world by the Roman Catholic Church in 1960 but has not been released.

Erling told me that while he was travelling in Europe in 1953, he was introduced to a personal friend of Pope Pius XII, Bernard Fay. M. Fay had just returned from spending three months with the Pope at Castel Gandolfo. After a long intimate conversation, M. Fay said that Pope Pius XII had told him he brought Sister Lucia of Fatima to Rome and instructed her under obedience to reveal the third message of Fatima to him. Sister Lucia did so.

Then M. Fay went on to say, "And we know that we are about to see the Second Coming. We know that it will come from outside the Church. We know that it will come from the East."

** Bapak related some of these stories on July 24, 1967, at the Tokyo Congress and then later, in December 1979 in Cilandak, he said that the Second Coming was not a man, contrary to people's expectations.

73

Chapter Five

After some time Bapak went to the house for his lunch. He then came to the kitchen where I was standing at a table, buttering bread. He said, "Can your mother come to Cilandak immediately?" "I don't know, Bapak," I said, "but I'll ask her." I went into the hall where Mayko was still sitting on the chair. I knelt on the floor and related Bapak's message to her. She was taken aback but answered quietly and simply, "If it is the Will of God, I will." When Bapak had this answer, he called Erling and asked him to arrange for Mayko to travel with Bapak to Jakarta. She was to join Bapak in Melbourne, then follow along with him to Perth, Singapore, and Jakarta. Mayko said later that when she returned home after this decision, she was filled with spiritual bliss. A few days later, we put her on a plane. Bapak's decision to arrange for Mayko to go with him to Indonesia immediately after his New Zealand visit came as a surprise to all of us, but it was typical of the special kindness he always showed my mother.

I do not pretend to understand Mayko's destiny. She was not a very educated person, but she had instinctive wisdom. She had a strong presence, partly I believe an innate quality and partly derived from long and hard experience. She was well liked by those who knew her. She was deeply religious and a devoted Catholic. Being called Mayko, mother, instead of by her own name, Anastasia Marusic, suited her. By living in the mother role, her personal self could be in the background as she preferred. She nevertheless had a strong will. She had to have. She had had a difficult childhood, a rough marriage with a lot of suffering. That her life had a large measure of fate is illustrated by her story of meeting my father. She told me that at the age of seventeen she was walking on the street with her sister in Punta Arenas, when a man went by. She felt, *This is the man that I will marry.* Sometime later the man, Guido Petric, came to ask for her hand in marriage, and it was agreed.

Mayko told me that she had several strong experiences with Bapak, but she did not feel that it was right to talk about them, as a rule. I respected her reticence. One of the few incidents she did describe impressed me greatly and I believe that it may be unique in the history of Bapak.

Mayko joined Bapak in Melbourne to go to Cilandak. There she was given the responsibility to take care of Bapak's clothes. It was a job she liked very much, and it suited her to be out of sight. The party was staying in the Subud House, which had been a large private home. She told me that very late one night, when she knew everyone would be asleep, she went into the living-room to put Bapak's clothes to dry near the dying fire. She arranged them and sat nearby on a chair.

Intermission in New Zealand

"The room was dark," she said, "except for a slight glow from the embers. Suddenly the door opened and Bapak came in. He walked across to an upright piano not far from where I was sitting. He put his arms on the piano and bent his head on to his arms and cried in total disconsolation. As suddenly as he had started, he stopped and quietly left."

For many years this incident remained a complete mystery to me. Then one day, in a state of latihan, I experienced spontaneous crying on behalf of another person who could not cry for herself. It was from the depths of my inner feeling, without the sentiment of the heart or the intention of the mind. From this I could understand why Bapak had cried for Mayko, who had many inner woundings beyond her capacity to heal.

Bapak's trip continued to Perth, Singapore, and Jakarta. From Cilandak I received a letter from Mayko, thanking me for buying her a first-class ticket. I hadn't; it seems she was taken care of by someone on the plane. She said that when flying in the same cabin with Bapak, she was constantly enveloped in a heavenly feeling. As soon as the plane started its descent into Jakarta airport, she felt that this was the end of her bliss. She said, "I knew that my purification process would begin." Her intuition was right.

After Bapak's visit we settled our affairs in New Zealand as quickly as possible in order to return to Indonesia. I still had some misgivings, but David was very excited with the idea. When I asked him why he was so enthusiastic about Indonesia, he replied, "Can you think of a better place?" We went via the United States and it was three and a half months before our visas for Indonesia were ready and we took the polar route to Jakarta, arriving on November 2, 1968. Mayko and the Usmans were at the airport to meet us.

∼

Chapter Six
Life Near Bapak, Indonesia

CILANDAK HAD CHANGED considerably since I was there three years before. It was now an established community of fifteen or so families, and a steady stream of overseas visitors came and went through the guesthouse. Whereas Bapak had originally invited certain people to come and help, now he was agreeing to the requests of many people who wished to visit for their own needs. There were additional buildings and improved guest amenities—a dining room and kitchen. The property was now named Wisma Subud, meaning The House of Subud, to distinguish the compound from the district of Cilandak, and it was registered in the name of Yayasan Dana Subud, the Subud Foundation. Within Subud it was called the International Subud Spiritual Centre. However, in one important sense it hadn't changed; the compound still had the feeling of being Bapak's home.

Bapak was giving more talks and testing—to explain and explore the potential of the latihan. Indonesians were coming in larger numbers to Wisma Subud for latihan, and Bapak was encouraging the Indonesian membership to see itself as part of world Subud.

Bapak's house had been completed. Affectionately known as the Big House, it was an elegant white concrete framed two-storey building with high ceilings and a curved vaulted roof. The layout was Western, as was much of the architecture of Jakarta. On the ground floor, there was a large living and dining room, used mostly to receive guests and for entertaining, and Bapak's office. The second floor contained bedrooms and rooms for members of the family, many of whom, children and grand-children, stayed in the house at various times. There was a garden on the terrace, with an aviary. Here one could sometimes see from a distance Bapak and Ibu sitting out together. This openness was a measure of Bapak's accessibility, but he was protected by the respect that his presence commanded. We never imposed ourselves on him or his family life.

Chapter Six

The land sloped away from the road so that the back of the Big House was three storeys. On this lower side were garages and the wide stone staircase that was our entrance to the house and Bapak's office from the compound.

Another one and a half hectares of land had now been purchased at the rear of the property, and the building program had extended the housing for permanent residents and visitors. The guesthouse, where Bapak had lived in 1965, now had a third floor. The extra land was fenced and a brick perimeter wall built for security, according to local practice. Trees, many of them tropical fruit species—mango, rambutan, jack-fruit, durian, guava, and others—had been preserved, lawns kept neat, and bright tropical plants cultivated. Roads were improved and stormwater drains built of river stone to mitigate the wet season flooding.

I was quite impressed by our new home. It was of concrete in a contemporary style, painted white, and had two floors. It was spacious, with large areas of window and wide verandahs all around. I realised that we were very lucky to have it.

It was here on the first night after we moved in, that Bapak's sensitivity was most dramatically illustrated. Sandra, who was two years old at the time, was in a small bed in the room with us. When we put off the lights, Sandra started to scream. She was extremely agitated, something we had never experienced before. I didn't know what to do; nothing would appease her.

Suddenly Bapak entered our bedroom. He went over to Sandra's bed and rubbed her head with his hand for a few minutes. She immediately stopped; she was completely soothed. He suggested that she should have a dim light near her and arranged for a lamp to be sent from his house. Sandra never cried at night again.

Gradually Erling furnished the house. We retrieved the beds and other furniture that had been kept for us from our previous stay. I soon found that the new house had one major disadvantage. It had an uninsulated flat concrete roof, which made the upstairs like an oven at afternoon siesta time. The electricity supply in the compound was still insufficient for air-conditioning. We gave Mayko a bedroom with her own bathroom downstairs, where it was cooler. The rest of us slept upstairs, except for Clementina, who had her own room—a brick and tile sleepout—in the garden. Sandra was so attached to Clementina that after a time we provided an extra bed so that she could sleep in Clementina's room, whenever she wished.

Life Near Bapak, Indonesia

It was customary to have furniture made to measure, and one day my mother saw a huge teak table arrive for our dining room. She was dismayed and said, "It looks as if Erling is preparing to live here for years!" I realised that the idea of settling permanently in Indonesia was threatening to her. She had left Chile a few months earlier with a return ticket and now found herself in a foreign place that she knew nothing about. She was isolated by language and age, and it was not in her nature to live so far away from her own country. Although she was there on Bapak's advice—and she believed whole-heartedly in the latihan and in Bapak—she felt the time would come when this commitment should be gracefully relinquished.

Clementina I believe had no real idea where she was. Every so often she would come to me to say that she wanted to go back to Chile to her family. I would always agree and would offer to get her a ticket. Each time she would return and say, "Mrs Week, I can't go because I just can't leave Sandra." Clementina was a wonderful help to me. She took meticulous care of Sandra. This was particularly important with regard to hygiene. She saw to it that Sandra was kept from eating anything which could carry the many tropical diseases and internal parasites which were prevalent.

We arrived on November 2, 1968 and on November 10 celebrated Sandra's second birthday, inviting the many children of all nationalities living in the compound. The following day David was thirteen.

Meanwhile I heard that the Ramadhan fast was approaching. Although I considered it an Islamic observance, I felt by now that I shouldn't completely ignore it. I thought, *I will fast on the weekends only.* Soon afterwards Ibu called me and said, "You will do the Ramadhan fast, yes?" I explained what I intended. She was silent for a while and then explained that the Ramadhan was important for us all, whether we were Christian or Muslim. "The Ramadhan fast," she said, "is an opportunity given by God to make a sacrifice and the sacrifice is important because it works as a purification for our mistakes." I decided to follow her advice.

David became friendly with many of the Subud members, both Indonesians and foreign guests, and heard about the Ramadhan fast. He told his father that he wanted to do it, strictly. I was appalled. As a mother I was worried at the thought of David going without food and water from 3:00 A.M. to 6:00 P.M. every day for a whole month. Erling felt it would be a good experience for David. In the end it was agreed that we would all do the Ramadhan fast that year.

Chapter Six

Our house was attached across an open hallway and staircase to another building of the same size consisting of two apartments. Tom and Vivian Pope lived downstairs and Eva Bartok (now Ilaina) with her mother upstairs. Ilaina and I became great friends. Her daughter Deanna and my Cathy were about the same age and became instant companions. They went together in our car to the International School in Kebayoran, Jakarta.

My life now in Indonesia was completely different from my earlier experience. Not only had the living standard in Cilandak improved, but also outside in Jakarta the situation was peaceful and friendly. Conditions for the people of Indonesia were continually improving. A visitor may have noticed that many simple Western foods, such as butter and honey, were still rare and powdered milk a luxury, and that the cost of imported goods was generally prohibitive, but as residents we quickly adjusted to local products. I changed to, and enjoyed, an Indonesian diet. We had the advantage of foreign currency incomes and so could afford to choose the best of what was available. I had our clothes made by local dressmakers, often using traditional batiks for dresses and shirts.

By mid-1969 when the population of Cilandak was about thirty families, there was a selamatan almost weekly and Bapak attended them all. As was the custom, everyone was invited. We dressed in our best clothes and sat—often on mats or cushions on the floor—quietly sharing food and tea, or listening to Bapak if he felt like giving a talk. The life of the Subud community revolved around Bapak's activities. His talks, latihans, selamatans or travelling were everybody's first priority.

Bapak spent much of his time in his office, writing. Letters arrived in many languages and were first translated into Indonesian by the secretariat. He then prepared his replies on a typewriter or in longhand, in classical script, which the secretariat re-translated and typed. Archives show that over the years Bapak wrote approximately fifty-five thousand pages of replies to correspondence in his own hand.

After working in the morning, Bapak would go to the secretariat and stay talking for some time, occasionally testing an answer to a question. At night he would sit up with the men members on the verandah of one the houses or outside the secretariat in the warm night air, talking until midnight or later. When he finally went back to his house, it was often to work until 2:00 A.M.

Life Near Bapak, Indonesia

Bapak was accessible to Subud members but left it to the helpers and the secretariat to speak to non-Subud people, such as those newly interested in Subud. Occasionally he would meet a government official, such as when Subud was required to register with the Department of Religion.

In Cilandak, Bapak frequently gave a talk on Sunday mornings. Often the decision was made on the day. A messenger would arrive at my door to announce that in a couple of hours time Bapak would give a talk, either to all members in the large latihan hall or to the women helpers in his house. Somehow the message would get out to members in Jakarta, and a hundred people or more people would attend. Sunday, even in that Islamic environment, felt like the holy day of the week and was set aside by residents and members for latihans or a talk by Bapak.

His talks were the most important event for me. The women helpers had a latihan with Ibu in the Big House on the first Sunday of every month, and afterwards Bapak would talk to us. Over the months he covered many issues and tested many things, some arising from recurring questions in members' letters, which we as helpers might later encounter.

Typical of these was his advice to use testing to resolve a disagreement between members:

The latihan which you receive and follow awakens the inner feeling that is clean and pure and free from the influence of the nafsu (passions)—the influence of the nafsu [that] always causes you to behave improperly, for example, inclining you to push yourself forward and to claim that you are in the right; having the inclination to boast and to humiliate others. In short, because of the influence of the nafsu, one forgets harmony and brotherhood with one another.

The feelings of affection for one another, and of valuing and respecting one another, are there because the influence of the nafsu over the heart and mind, is (as if) forgotten. The latihan, in reality, is like a protection for you from the influence of the nafsu.

If you remember this and are protected by the latihan, then you will have respect for one another, you will help one another, and be harmonious with one another. For this reason Bapak hopes that you will try and solve anything that causes disharmony amongst you by testing together, and that you will obey the answer you receive from the testing. [20]

He then went on to test the reality of this with us.

I always felt he was sharing his work rather than teaching us something. Usually I found that Bapak's explanations put the question in a more comprehensive context. Once, however, although I was very impressed by what he said, I found it conflicted with my Catholic beliefs. He said that nobody can know God:

"If a man came to Bapak and said: 'Bapak, I have seen God,' then Bapak would say, 'And what was He like?' If the man answered, 'Oh, the most beautiful, the highest and the most good,' then Bapak would answer, 'And was He also bad and terrible and evil?' And the man would say, 'Oh, no, Bapak!' Then Bapak would have to answer, 'In that case, you have not seen God. Because the most beautiful, the most good, and the most benevolent, that is God. And the most terrible and most cruel, that is God too.'"

I decided that, because I had difficulty accepting this, the best I could do was to suspend judgement and think no more about it. Some years later I came to understand its truth.

Bapak also gave talks to the men helpers. These were held in the latihan hall every second Friday night during 1969 and sometimes lasted all night. During one such session, Bapak said to Erling (with Usman translating), "Erling, tell us an experience."

Erling told of an experience that he had in the latihan shortly after we arrived in Cilandak the year before:

"I was standing on a hill looking up at the sky and in the sky was the earth, twice the size of the moon. I realised everyone in the world was [like me] outside looking at the sky, seeing this impossible thing. Then a very bright source of light appeared above the earth and a number of rays of light shone down, hitting the earth in different points on the different continents."

Bapak asked, "How many rays of light were there?"

Erling answered, "I realised after the experience that this was important and I tried to remember how it appeared. I decided that there were more than twelve and fewer than fifty."

Bapak said, "More than thirty and fewer than forty."

Erling continued relating his latihan experience:

"I then found myself walking into a big park in which there was a research building . . . I went up on to the verandah and saw Subud people walking around. I realised it was a Subud building—actually it was Subud itself. I looked into the window of the first room at the end of the building. In it there was a Javanese dancer and nothing else. (I understood this was the first phase of Subud.)

"Then I looked through another window into the second room which was at an angle to the first. In this second room there was a computer about the size of a steamer trunk. I thought, 'I'll be able to know when this is happening by looking at the manufacturer's plate on the computer.'

"I entered the room and looked for a plate and found one. The brass plate had a date on it which said: 1987 . . . then it changed to 1988, 1989, 1990, 1991. Then it stopped."

Bapak turned to Usman and asked, "How long is it from now (1969) until then?" Usman answered and Bapak said, "Yes, about twenty years from now. This is an example of an experience which will actually happen and afterwards [later] nobody on earth will be able to say that God does not exist. At that time there will be between thirty and forty *rohani** souls come into the world."

Erling told me that Bapak had also asked him, whether he understood anything more about the computer. On his way home, Erling said, he realised that all the rohani souls were connected into the computer and that the understanding of all of them was programmed into it. If asked a question, each could call up the answer from the common computer.

ONE SUNDAY morning I awoke depressed and wanting to leave Indonesia. I decided that I would! I was very determined; I would not let even my marriage and children stop me. That morning someone came with a message to say that Bapak would give a talk to the women in the old latihan hall. I decided I would sit in the back row against the wall. This way Bapak would not see me. I was afraid that if he did, he would read what was in my heart.

Bapak talked, and halfway through he decided we needed a break. He invited everyone to go out to the verandah for makanan ketjil (a snack). As I walked out, he saw me. When the session was resumed, I again sat in the back

---

* *Rohani*: the perfect human level, characterised by complete surrender to God's Will.

Chapter Six

row against the wall. He started his talk like this, "Many people come here from far, far away just to be near Bapak. Look at Irma (my name then), she has come all the way from Chile, just to be near Bapak!" I immediately knew he had seen everything in me. How could I possibly leave after such a statement? By his action Bapak healed my distress and helped me to get through what proved to be only a temporary condition.

As time went on, my thoughts of leaving faded. I became accustomed to the way of life. As I became more fluent in the language, I enjoyed a closer relationship with my Indonesian Subud sisters. I began to visit those in the compound and also near neighbours, like Ismana, Bapak's daughter-in-law. I also joined the American Club, which helped. It was a pleasant easy-going place where I could relax, swim, and play tennis.

And there were many moments that touched the exotic. One evening Mayko, Clementina, Sandra, and I went to Blok M, a residential area of Jakarta, for evening Mass at the Catholic church. It was just dusk. The harshness of the equatorial sunlight was forgotten and the dazzling gold of a tropical sunset was beginning to fade. The colour of the sky was changing the trees from green to luminous blues and purple. The busy motor traffic had given way to the quieter hum of rickshaws and the bells of bicycles. It was as if the heat of human activity had cooled with the cooling of the day. People now sat out on their porches and vendors stopped their peddling to squat and rest on the road side. Our driver parked the car and we walked through the coloured stalls of the flower market towards the church. The scent of tuberoses filled the still evening air. As we climbed slowly up the graded steps to the church, I was deeply touched to hear through the open doors the sound of the congregation singing those very hymns that I had sung so many times in Spanish, in my childhood in Chile. Now they were sung in Indonesian with all the sweet timbre of Indonesian voices. It was a moment of wonder and enchantment.

The daily routine within our closed community also brought its minor tests and had its funny moments. One day I took Sandra to the dentist. The elderly dentist looked at her and said, "There is nothing wrong; I have nothing to do." "But," I objected, "what about this, and that other one over there?" pointing out to him the obvious holes. His reply was, "Oh! Well, you can't blame me if my eyes are not so good anymore."

Life Near Bapak, Indonesia

The close proximity of neighbours in Wisma Subud could be a problem. Because it was so hot in our bedroom, I kept all the windows and doors open day and night. It was the habit of local people to get up early, so often before I was ready to get up I was awakened by the neighbour's maid starting to pound the husks off rice at dawn. Our neighbours on the other side, from the USA, bought a parrot for one of their children. Its cage was put in a large jack-fruit tree that grew between our houses. This bird made the most terrible squawking, so that there was no way that I could rest at siesta. The girl was so attached to it that I had to threaten to douse the bird with water before it was moved. A similar strategy ended the dawn rice pounding!

But I only found complete relief from noise two years later when the electricity supply was sufficient to have an air-conditioner and I could finally close up the bedroom.

Next to the guesthouse lived an Indonesian family, the Sudarsonos. The father was an artist and the three older children were talented musicians. Rukmini, the daughter, also was a Javanese classical dancer. In the evening the family had a small enterprise selling Indonesian-style fruit drinks to foreign guests on their terrace and the three, Atok, Rukmini, and Adi, aged twenty-two, twenty, and nineteen, would entertain by playing their guitars and singing. Erling would sometimes sit there with a visitor and would tell me how much he enjoyed the melodious *krontjong* (popular Indonesian music).

One day as I was coming from a *selamatan* in Bapak's house I was approached by Mrs Sudarsono who asked me if I would teach her children some Spanish songs. I happily agreed. It was, as I thought, fun to do. They played by ear and learned quickly. We had sessions two or three times a week, and they soon became very accomplished. Later they entertained outside the compound and even performed on Indonesian National Television.

At Tuti's (Bapak's grand-daughter's) birthday party in the Big House, the Sudarsono trio and I surprised and delighted Tuti by singing her the Mexican birthday song, 'Las Mananita.' I had no idea how popular this would become and that it would be taken up by the whole compound.

From then on we were asked to sing at other birthdays and celebrations. Bapak, who came to all the parties, obviously enjoyed the music. Sometimes, I didn't intend to sing, but Bapak would call me anyway. All this led to the

Chapter Six

French, the Germans, and other national groups preparing songs and dressing in their traditional costumes for Bapak's sixty-eighth birthday selamatan. It was an all-night affair and the most memorable of all those I attended in Cilandak.

By now I was content to live in Indonesia. I often went to the Big House in the evening, and Sandra was taken there by Clementina at Bapak's invitation so she could play with his grand-children. On these visits I would meet Ismana. She told me she was going to Australia with her husband, Haryono, Bapak's son. They were invited to visit the Subud groups in Melbourne and Sydney. "Would you like to come with me?" she asked me teasingly. Then one day she repeated the question seriously. I said that I would have to talk to Erling. She went in to another room for a few minutes then came back and said, "I have asked Bapak and he says, Yes! You should come with me to Australia."

I was rather shocked. How could she do this until I had consulted Erling? I told her that she would have to tell Erling herself!. She simply said to him, "Bapak says Istimah should come with me and Haryono to Australia." Erling laughed. He knew Ismana had arranged it so he couldn't say no. "If Bapak has decided," he said, "of course she can go."

We went to Melbourne and Sydney for altogether two weeks during September and October 1969. Everyone was very hospitable, with dinners at the Subud House and invitations to members' homes. Extra latihans were scheduled and many people came to see Haryono and Ismana with personal questions. Ismana was an experienced helper and answered the women's questions with great insight and understanding. She was loving and had the capacity to deal with members' problems in a light and unattached way. It was a delight to be with her, and also I learnt a great deal. She explained that the latihan brings problems to the surface. Before receiving the latihan, we live our lives continuously acting and reacting according to our nature and its shortcomings. As the years go by, this automatic way of being becomes more fixed so that our souls are imprisoned in the forces of our behaviour. When the latihan starts, the power of God working from inside us breaks down or weakens this hold on us.

Haryono was quite at ease with foreigners. As a director of Indonesia's national gold mine, he had worked for many years with overseas consultants. To his role of Subud helper, he brought a quiet and light touch to problem solving. Later on in Sydney he had to deal with a serious split in the local group.

Life Near Bapak, Indonesia

By carefully listening to both sides and bringing them face to face, he was able to gradually diffuse the tension. We ended up going out together for a day-long picnic. Although there was not a complete reconciliation, Haryono's even-handedness helped to reduce the enmity between the sides.

In early December, the Councillors of the Asian Zone gathered in Cilandak. Councillors are the national representatives of each country, a man and a woman for the spiritual side and a third person for the organisational side. The councillors of all countries together made up the members of the Subud World Congress. Subud worldwide was further divided into seven zones with the same councillors as zonal delegates. This was the first Asian Zone Conference and was held during Ramadhan.

Bapak opened the meetings and commented on the delegates' reports. Problems in the reports were often particular to a country's culture and religious background. Shyam Bose, the Councillor for India, said there were difficulties in India because members and helpers were still involved in other methods and spiritual practices. Bapak explained what is different about the way of the latihan:

What people have heard, experienced and believed is so ingrained in them that what is in the nature of a tradition has become an instinct which they do not wish to put aside. However, it is necessary [for those in Subud] that all these things be put aside, but not in a way that will disturb people.

It is true that this latihan kejiwaan is not in conflict with the various religions—quite the opposite. It will unveil the realities of religion which cannot yet be understood, even by those who profess a religion.

As an example Bapak will speak about India. In India many people believe in karma and reincarnation and in mystical training such as the practice of samadi (a state reached through meditation). It is just the same here in Indonesia and elsewhere. These things are a way or a religious discipline from an era of long ago. In former times the range of man's thinking had not yet reached the extent that it has now. Thus today many people have become learned, but only outwardly believe in their religion; inwardly they do not believe in it because they have no evidence or proof. With the coming of the latihan kejiwaan of Subud, that which was previously secret in religion will be revealed and people will no longer wish to keep all this secret. . . .

Chapter Six

The nature of religious secrets is such that they cannot be revealed by man, but only by the power of God. God will certainly not do this through the inner self of man [acting] on his own. No! In reality it is "the man who receives" who is able to uncover the secrets which are still locked up in religions. In this way man will have more devotion to the content of religion and will know truly whether he may take this step or may not take that step.

Bapak went on to say that Christians, Muslims, Buddhists, and others will each become aware of the truth of their religions, revealed to them through the power of God in the latihan. He continued:

This is what Bapak means when he says that the closed veils have been opened already, so that man can become someone who does not just blindly follow but will really know the closeness of God. If a man knows that he is brought close to God, he will not dare to continue to sin. He will become a man who is honest, a man who truly loves his fellow human beings. He will become a man who has the true human qualities, a man with the character of Susila Budhi Dharma. [21]

At about this time, Bapak described the coming of the latihan in terms that left a lasting impression on me. He said that every time the world was in trouble God had sent a Messenger. He mentioned Abraham, Moses, Jesus, and Muhammad. "But," he said, "this time He has come Himself. Therefore, this is our last chance, because what more can come than God Himself?"

After the Idul Fitre celebration, Bapak and his family went on a nine-day car journey around Java. It was the customary visit to elders at the end of Ramadhan, but on this occasion, it was extended to include the main Subud groups. He went first to Semarang to meet his mother, sister, and other relatives at the house where he had first experienced the latihan. He then continued to East and Central Java, including Temanggung—Ibu's birthplace—finally Purworedjo, to the house of the Regent, and Bandung in the West. He gave talks to the Subud groups at every stop, which, according to Erling (who went along), were well attended by new as well as long-time members.

Back in Jakarta, Ibu's sixty-third birthday selamatan on February 17 was a big occasion. It was celebrated with music and a supper, members playing and singing her favourite songs. Bapak gave a talk, sang a song for her, and played the gambang—all things which delighted Ibu.

Ibu liked to go to the family house in the hills at Cipanas. She was often not in good health and would say, "But Ibu feels very well here." Bapak began making the trip more often. He talked about enlarging the house to make it more comfortable for Ibu to stay overnight. Towards the end of February, he and Ibu, with some family and Subud members, travelled up on a Friday morning for a selamatan to mark the beginning of the construction of a two-storey extension to the house. It was a very happy affair, and it seemed to me that Bapak was making a special effort to please Ibu.

By May 1970, we could already see preparations for the 1971 Subud World Congress. Guesthouse cottages were being built. A new water borehole had been drilled to a deep aquifer in readiness for the increased Congress population. Then on Bapak's birthday, a selamatan was held to mark the start of construction of a large new latihan hall. It was to seat twelve hundred people and to be built as a clear space with no interior columns. The design was simple and contemporary, a partial white dome in concrete, floating atop a symmetrical cross floor plan. To mark the start of construction in accordance with Javanese custom, a bullock's head was buried on the site. It was a colourful spectacle, marked by much delight from the children watching these ancient rituals. After the ceremony, the guests were fed with traditional food cooked in Ibu's kitchen and served under the trees.

Bapak also ceremoniously turned on new electricity generators from Australia, which had enough capacity for day-time running of air-conditioning, a great step forward, as the old equipment had become heavily overloaded.

This was Bapak's sixty-ninth birthday, and in the evening, some four hundred people came to pay their respects. The festivities were quieter than on previous birthdays as the household was preparing for Bapak's departure overseas.

Meantime, unexpected events were already shaping one of the most momentous experiences of my Subud life—Bapak's coming world journey.

Chapter Seven
Bapak's World Tour, 1970

BY THE END OF 1969, Bapak had completed three around-the-world journeys and had given more than five hundred recorded talks to Subud groups. Bapak travelled, he said, "to fulfil his responsibility to pass on the latihan to everybody who asks for it—to pass on the contact with the Power of God Almighty, and then to give instruction and explanation of what this is."

There is in Indonesia an active tradition of Javanese mystical movements. According to Michaël Rogge's* study of the literature of anthropologists in recent decades, there is no record of a spiritual exercise similar to the latihan kejiwaan of Subud. He also observes that although some of the *kepercayaan* (beliefs) have memberships within Indonesia larger than Subud, only Subud has become known worldwide and attracted significant foreign membership. In this respect Bapak's world journeys have been unique for Indonesia.

Early in June 1970, Bapak invited Erling and David to join him on a fourth world tour, which was to take in thirty Subud groups in twenty countries over a period of three and a half months. Just a month earlier, Bapak had suggested that Erling help PT International Design Consultants (IDC), the Subud Architects and Engineers enterprise in Cilandak, with their application to the government for foreign investment status. The negotiation had reached a critical stage, so Erling had to decline Bapak's invitation in favour of this responsibility.

I was disappointed that David, now aged fourteen, would miss this opportunity and decided to talk to Bapak about it. I went to Bapak's house, but he was with a guest. I left a message with Tuti, suggesting that perhaps I could go with David to the first group visit on the tour, and return from there. Tuti brought back the answer from Bapak: he agreed, but then I should go on the whole trip. I was staggered. I had never considered that possibility—leaving the family behind was unthinkable. Immediately I tried again to see Bapak, but again he was occupied. After two more attempts, I gave up. I thought to myself, *This is getting beyond me! . . . I leave it up to God now!*

---
* Michaël Rogge: Discussion paper, "Subud at Cross-Roads," Amsterdam, 1991

Chapter Seven

That evening Sandra, then four, had been invited to a birthday party for Isti, Ismana's daughter by her first marriage (Ismana was the wife of Bapak's son Haryono). Their house was a few minutes walk from the Subud compound. I took Sandra and as I entered the living room, I saw to my surprise Bapak sitting on a sofa just inside. I went on with Sandra to another room where the children were gathered.

As I stood there with the children, Bapak beckoned me to sit on a stool near him. He said that I was coming on the trip as part of the party. Then, moving his right hand in a circle, representing travelling around the world, he said, "From Jakarta . . . to Jakarta!"

"But, Bapak," I protested, "I cannot leave my husband and three children!" "Not three, two! David comes too. . . . And," he added, "you travel first class, with Bapak."

"But, Bapak . . . poor Erling . . . it's so expensive!" I was going from shock to shock. Bapak simply smiled and pointed up, saying, "Erling will get his money from God."

When I arrived home, I told Erling all Bapak had said. He looked a bit surprised, but with his usual generosity at once agreed that we would do as Bapak had suggested.

We had fewer than two weeks to get ready. Since we were travelling first class, it was possible to get seats on all thirty-five flights with Bapak at such short notice. Visas were obtained for our Chilean and USA passports, except for entry to South Africa, which had no diplomatic representation in Indonesia at the time. (When the time came to fly to South Africa, this lack of visas created a problem.)

Subud was at this time maturing in the world. Activities of all kinds flowered from the new associations of people following the latihan. Groups acquired premises for latihan, and members started working together in business enterprises, social welfare projects, and cultural activities. As Subud expanded, the organisational and helper services for local, national, and international cooperation were developed under Bapak's guidance.

In the midst of all this, increasing numbers of members worldwide were confronted with questions in their personal lives arising from the process of the latihan. Also committees and helpers came up against problems they couldn't solve. All this brought a stream of letters to Bapak, which reached more than one hundred a week.

Bapak's World Tour, 1970

When Bapak travelled, invitations from Subud organisations would arrive for him to visit particular groups and attend National Subud Congresses. Bapak's travels were an opportunity to instruct and explain about the latihan and the spiritual life face to face, taking into account the circumstances of his audiences. Every visit to groups was an occasion for clarifying goals. It was also a chance to solve hitherto intractable problems. For example, I saw a situation in which a difficulty between members had divided a group and had remained unresolved for months when dealt with by correspondence. Bapak not only solved the problem during his short visit, but his solution also served as an example to the whole brotherhood when tape recordings were distributed and his talks appeared in Subud publications.

As we travelled from city to city, I noticed the transformation of every group to a higher and lighter spiritual state during Bapak's visit. I could sense this change in the meetings. It wasn't possible for me to know the background of the groups that we visited—whether they were newly opened, or had particular problems of organisation, or whether there was disharmony between members and helpers, and so on—but I could pick up a lot from the direction of Bapak's talks as he focussed on the needs of the situation. For example in India, Bapak emphasised the need for a national organisation and regular national meetings, which made it clear that the membership had not yet built a relationship between the scattered groups of that large country. Every group and therefore every talk was different.

Bapak would often illustrate his talks by testing—in his words, "to give proof." On one occasion when he was talking about hard work, he tested with an Australian member the attitude of the various nationalities to work. After testing the Australian, the English, and the German attitudes, Bapak asked the member to show (by testing), "How does a Japanese work?" The Australian immediately began to elaborately mime working on a production line. The spontaneous transformation of the usually laid-back Australian to high-speed activity was so utterly convincing that it brought a burst of delighted laughter from the audience. Bapak frequently used contrasts like this to illustrate a point and was a master at producing a laugh when the time was right.

Every group made supreme efforts to be hospitable and please Bapak. Bapak in turn was loving, patient, and attentive, but most of all, his spirituality created in everyone a feeling of peace, joy, and harmony. By the end of a visit, everyone was uplifted, satisfied, and grateful. If I seem overly positive, it is because I was part of an experience which was totally positive. Bapak's activity was enveloped by the in-flowing of the grace of God. During the tour I recorded my impressions in a diary and in letters. Here are some excerpts that recall those days:

June 28, 1970

COLOMBO. We left Jakarta at ten o'clock on Wednesday morning. It was June 24, two days after Bapak's birthday. We were farewelled with the feeling of love and devotion which everyone has for Bapak, first at his house where he sat relaxed waiting for Ibu and chatting with his family, and again at the airport where a hundred or more brothers and sisters crowded into the departure lounge. I noticed the familiar faces of Subud members among the immigration officials, police, and military who facilitated our departure. For a while the airport was totally taken over by Subud. Bapak's mother, Eyang Kursinah, now in her nineties, was there, standing perfectly straight and serene, and with her my mother, Mayko, waving from the observation deck.

The party for the tour includes Bapak and Ibu, Usman (as translator), Tuti, Ismana, Mastuti, Lydia Duncan, David, and me. Everyone is dressing in European style except Ibu, who is wearing traditional Indonesian *kain* (sarong), *kebaya* (lace blouse) and a silk *selendang* (shawl). Bapak is wearing a light gaberdine suit and his black *petji* (Indonesian hat).

At Singapore airport we waited five hours for our connecting flight. Members from the small Subud groups in Singapore and Jahore Baru sat with us. They were of the many races and religions which make up the population of the island—Chinese, Malays, Indians, and Europeans from Buddhist, Hindu, Moslem, and Christian beliefs. They made every effort to see to Bapak's comfort, bringing him an armchair and cool drinks. He obviously enjoyed the conversation, much of it in Malay. He is looking strong and well. Bapak, like many Indonesian men, smokes *kretek* (clove) cigarettes, more as a social activity than as a need. There were very few ladies, but Ibu kept Lydia and me busy with her concerns about arrangements for the coming journey. The smell of Ibu's Blue Grass perfume pervaded our little group.

At Colombo we were met by a crowd of about a hundred members, the ladies looking graceful in their saris. A traditional garland of respect for a special person was placed on Bapak. The welcome had a family feeling like a long-awaited return. We were accommodated comfortably together in the large colonial-period house of Dr. Abeyawudera, a psychiatrist. He and his wife are very sincere and pleasant people.

The first night Bapak gave a talk and testing, which went on until after midnight. He joked about the large number of helpers, more than a third of the membership. It is usual in groups to have not more than one helper to ten members. He emphasised that helpers should not feel themselves different or above members. Inevitably some status gets attached to the job. We all sat on the floor Asian style and, because I was sitting close to Bapak, I was able to hear and understand almost every word of the Indonesian before it was translated. This promises well for the journey.

The second night Bapak did more testing with separate groups of men and women. There was much amusement at the tests that showed up our common human weaknesses. It had its serious side too—as a member wistfully said, "The testing showed that our group is not as satisfactory as many of us may have fondly believed, but perhaps it is a good thing to know the truth about ourselves."

Bapak's evening talk to the helpers and committee members was strong, pushing them to grow, not to be satisfied with just the pleasant feelings of the latihan. He said they should have their own Subud House and that as many as possible should go to the World Congress next year in Cilandak.

I am struck by the affection of the Ceylonese people. They show this endearing quality in many eloquent ways: flowers, music, the preparation of food, and a continuous giving-out of feelings of love and joy towards us all. They played music and we joined in the singing. In the party there is a very light feeling. We laugh a lot and tease each other in an Indonesian way. Ibu was happy to be here and was outgoing with the members. It was a beautiful and unique experience to see how Bapak works on a trip. I feel privileged to be able to travel with him and his family. I thank God for this wonderful experience.

July 4

POONA, INDIA. We arrived in Bombay from Colombo on Monday, June 29 and stayed overnight in a majestic, old-style colonial hotel. Next morning the party was driven in several cars up to Poona, in the hills, a long journey of about five hours. It was all quite different from Indonesia, dry land farming with oxen. I saw a lot of poverty, people living in shelters made of sacks and rags.

Here at Sangam, near Poona, I found that there are sixty members in residence and that they are taking the opportunity of Bapak's visit to hold the Subud India Third National Congress. Delegates have come from all the major Subud groups—Bombay, Delhi, Madras, Poona, and Calcutta.

Chapter Seven

The chairman reported that the brotherhood has an active membership of one hundred and twenty and that Subud is now registered in India as a Public Society and Charitable Public Trust.

As good hosts, the group has never mentioned the work and sacrifice that has gone into preparing for Bapak's visit, but behind the venue, the accommodation, the transport, the delicious food, the programming, the speeches, the entertainment, the flowers and garlands, not to mention the financing, I see everywhere the evidence of effort.

Bapak has attended most of the day-time Congress sessions, giving guidance on various issues as they arise. He has given talks and conducted latihans in the evenings. Maitreya Ramaswamy, the chairman of Subud India, in his gentle way described the spiritual effect of Bapak's visit as "gradually pervading everyone and everything until it made all activity a worship of God."

Shyam Bose is in charge of the arrangements. He is a long-time member of Subud and often comes to Cilandak. Although Bapak says the latihan is enough and does not need self-help practices, Shyam still insists on fasting. It is as if he cannot do enough to show (to himself) his devotion to God. David is very fond of him, and although they are two generations apart in age, they are often together.

Bapak gave five talks here, each focussing on a particular problem in India. Two were for the guidance of helpers—one about applicants to Subud and their needs and one for committees about an efficient national organisation. In all, he left a vision of an expanding Subud, with its own houses, enterprises, and charitable and educational activities. In his opening talk, he explained how in Subud it is the spiritual that leads the organisation:

Brothers and Sisters: The spiritual way cannot be organised because this is completely God's work, but since we have a brotherhood which consists of members, of all of you, this should be organised—if only to administer, manage, and run the worldly side of the brotherhood.

However, in your organisation you should never forget the most important thing of the brotherhood—the latihan kejiwaan, the worship—because it is through that worship that you may receive the guidance of Almighty God. This worship actually forms the right and sound base for you to be able, as an individual, to organise [your collective activities] in a right and proper way.

Bapak's World Tour, 1970

God has created man on earth so that he can organise his life in the best possible way, so that a world of peace and understanding and harmony can be created, where man as one human family can work and worship the one Almighty God. [22]

Long after the business of each day was over and late into the night, small groups could be seen sitting quietly together, sharing that indefinable spiritual feeling that latihan brings, immune to the demands of time or sleep.

July 5

LONDON. Yesterday we flew from Poona back to Bombay, then changed planes for London, getting in at 10:00 A.M. The plane stopped at Beirut, Geneva, and Paris on the way. In Geneva, I persuaded Ibu to get off the plane and breathe the wonderful crisp air. I made sure that she was well bundled up. She became invigorated and wanted to walk up and down the terminal. This is part of the delight of Ibu. She starts out saying she can't make the effort, but with a little encouragement, she agrees. At one moment she is the big mother and the next she becomes as a child, enjoying the simplest of things.

July 12

LEICESTER. David spends most of his time at Bapak's house even at the risk of missing a meal. When I went to the university today to take him to Bapak's house, I found him in his room playing his guitar and improvising. He bought the guitar in London for thirty pounds and loves it. There was an elderly lady with him. She said, "I am staying in a room two doors away and have been feeling nervous and depressed. Suddenly I heard this beautiful guitar playing, and I started to feel so quiet and peaceful. I just had to come to see who was playing."

The UK Congress is being held here during Bapak's visit. His first talk was an introduction to Subud, including a review of the history of the coming of the latihan to the West. He also talked about the question of his succession. Apparently there is something in the Subud UK Articles of Association stating that Bapak is the spiritual leader of Subud, which raised the question of who is to succeed him when he dies. Bapak said he cannot and may not answer, for only God can give an answer, if He so wills. "Unless God wills otherwise," he said, "the most there can be is, not a deputy, but a continuation through the latihan kejiwaan, which via yourselves is spread over the whole world."

Chapter Seven

Last night we all went to Bapak's fourth talk. We are becoming more sensitive to the forces around us, as we do more latihan. Ibu and Usman have encouraged me to spend my time at Bapak's house. In his talk Bapak explained about testing the effect of the nafsu [passions]:

This testing (which we have done together) is to enable your jiwa* [soul] to get to know the state of your physical body, which is constantly influenced by nafsu. For it is your jiwa [soul] that needs this latihan in order that the inner self, i.e., the jiwa [soul] may become the guide or director of your self as a whole, so that when eventually you die, your consciousness of life, your awareness of life, will be no different from your awareness of your state at the time of your earthly life. [23]

Between the talks I have been with some friends who are here for the UK Congress. Hosanna Baron and her husband, Laksir, said she will follow Bapak through Europe. I met Chris (Dominic) Rieu. So nice to talk to him again. He had earlier come to Cilandak to talk to Bapak about his proposal to write a book about Subud *(A Life Within a Life)* and we had become good friends.

That night I joined Bapak and the party to go to the helpers' meeting. Bapak again emphasised the importance of acting from the *jiwa* [soul] in our daily life, and also in the organisation of Subud affairs. "Don't let the organisation take over," he said.

As Bapak was preparing to do testing, I left the room for a glass of water. On the way I met Laksir. He was very upset because Hosanna had not been able to get into the helpers' meeting. I went out and saw Hosanna standing there. She was dressed in a very outlandish costume, a long coat reaching to her ankles and a large spectacular curly hairdo. A doorman nearby had refused to let her in as she did not have a helper's card. He asked me, "Do you know this lady? ... and is she a helper?" When I assured him that she was, he let Hosanna come in.

The situation was amusing. This stern man was guarding the door with all seriousness when he was confronted with this incredibly charismatic Mexican lady dressed in beautiful, but (for England) unconventional clothes.

I wonder if my original impulse to go out was a subconscious response to Hosanna's situation? Will there be a time when I will recognise such intuitions consciously?

---

* *Jiwa*: The spiritual content of the self (often translated as soul).

Bapak's World Tour, 1970

July 17

OSLO. This is a very clean and bright city with amazing clear air; even the people seem to shine. When we arrived we were driven directly to the Subud House. Here the group welcomed us in their multi-coloured national dress, singing a popular Indonesian song: *Naik, Naik, ke punjak gunung . . . etc.* (Climbing to the mountain top). The house is gorgeous, an old-style two storey brick home—high ceilings with an attic. It is located on the tree-lined street of the foreign embassies. The group have bought it and renovated it into a beautiful, cosy, and comfortable place.

Subud Scandinavia held their Annual Congress during Bapak's visit. On the evening of the first day, Bapak spoke about how our developed mind has come to lead us astray. On the third night, there were latihans and on the fourth day the final talk, in which Bapak talked about avoiding mistakes:

Bapak hopes that you will be sincere and diligent in your latihan. . . . You should be cautious, aware and careful in your attitude and behaviour so that you will not do anything wrong which would hamper the process of purification within you. How long the process of purification will take one cannot tell. . . .

You should be able, by yourself and for yourself, to correct yourself and help each other to cooperate to establish this harmony in the group. If later the group here becomes strong, then Bapak is sure that you will then be an example to society and people will be attracted to Subud. [24]

July 20

HAMBURG. We arrived on Friday July 18 and were taken to the Subud House. There were two hundred people or more for the visit, singing for Bapak as he arrived. They threw rose petals on him as he went and, since we were walking behind him, some fell on us too. I could hardly keep back my tears.

Bapak's talk was serious but full of encouragement and guidance. "Mankind has fallen," he said, "into the valley of forgetfulness, but now the Power of God is in us." He told the story of how in 1932 he had had a number of spiritual experiences including two which concerned receiving of books:

Bapak was in a state of latihan when Bapak received something very strange—if we think about it with our ordinary mind. Bapak received a book. It was the shape of a world atlas. Bapak was sitting, following the zikir (Islamic recitation). The book fell on Bapak's lap. Bapak was rather astonished at something falling on him, because, although Bapak was in his room, he felt at that moment as if he was in a wide open place.

Chapter Seven

Bapak opened the book. On the first page, where there is usually an introduction, there was a picture. It was of a man, a Sajid—an Arab, wearing a turban and a robe. As Bapak tried to read the caption, which was in Arabic, it changed to Latin characters and Bapak read: 'Prophet Muhammad, Messenger of God.' As Bapak read, he was amazed to see the figure in the picture nod in confirmation and slightly smile.

Bapak then turned to the next page. Here the picture was of many people. They were Bapak's countrymen. As Bapak looked, they moved. Some laughed, some cried, some asked forgiveness from God for their sins. Bapak turned the page and again there were more people. Some had white skin, some yellow, some black, some like Bapak. They too were making sounds—crying, laughing, asking forgiveness from God, singing. Bapak continued to turn five or six pages like that. Bapak then closed the book, thinking he would show it to his friends the next day. However, as he was holding it, it disappeared and Bapak felt like it had entered into his chest. Bapak felt uncomfortable and wondered what was happening. But there came an answer: "Don't be concerned. If you had the book, it might get lost. Now it is one with you, it can't be lost and it can't be far from you. As long as you live, it will be with you."

. . . Months passed, then one evening as Bapak was again sitting doing zikir, another book fell into his lap. This book was not so large as the first book, but it was thick like a dictionary. Bapak opened it and looked through the pages. All the pages were blank. Bapak was disappointed to receive a book without anything in it and wondered what was the use of it. Writing then appeared on the blank page: "There is meant to be nothing written here, because it is to be written when you ask a question."

Bapak then went on to ask all sorts of questions. "How will it be later?" and so. The book then disappeared just as the first book had done—Bapak was holding it and it disappeared inside him.

Among the things that Bapak was told in the book was that there would be a great world war. Then, after the war, it was God's will that Bapak would travel around the world to show the way for mankind to receive and experience the truth of what Bapak had received. . . . [25] *

He went on to say, "This was a very strange experience and Bapak hopes that you too will not just simply believe it. Hear it only. Don't believe something unless you are convinced by your own experience, by your own senses, and by your own understanding. Don't believe it until you can receive it for yourself."

---
* Provisional translation.

Bapak's World Tour, 1970

After the talk, at about 1:00 A.M., I went down to the living room where there were about a hundred people, singing as only Germans can sing! The hospitality and enthusiasm to please knows no bounds. The food was abundant and lavish. David again played his guitar. He plays with a lightness and a quality that touches people.

Tonight, Bapak gave his last talk. He talked about God "as a symbol to describe a certain power [that we sense]."

So far, travelling with Bapak has been one of the most wonderful experiences of my life. I feel as if the angels are following him and that we in the party are getting the benefit of it.

July 24

WOLFSBURG. We drove here from Hamburg this morning, and for the rest of the day, I was feeling rather exhausted. Ismana is unwell for the first time.

When I came down the stairs to attend Bapak's talk on the third evening, something strange happened to me. I felt as if there were a force enveloping me that made me unable to walk straight. I have never had such an experience. I went to the talk anyway and sat near Ibu. Suddenly Ibu looked at me and I saw that she realised I was feeling unwell. The situation got worse, so I excused myself and went to another room. There I cried copiously and from the depth of my being. A Subud brother looked in, and I asked him to take me home. Next morning, while I was still in bed, Tuti came and gave me a *radjah* (a Javanese runic cure) from Bapak. She said, "Now you know how Mayko feels sometimes." All I knew was that this condition made me extremely sensitive and unable to cope with the presence of other people.

This morning I felt better and took care of Ibu. Bapak played the *gambang* (a Javanese xylophone with wooden keys) for a long time. Hermine Rutz from the Wolfsburg group was with me, and we did latihan to the sound of the *gambang*. Bapak sang and told mythical stories and explained their meanings.

July 26

ROME. The schedule is now to stay just two days in each place and every night there is a talk, latihan, or testing. Normally, I think I would find such a program exhausting—not so much physically, but from the flood of feelings and thoughts coming from the many people I meet day after day. Instead I find I have all the energy I need. Moreover, I feel fresh and light.

Chapter Seven

The secret is of course that the latihan is flowing strongly in me most of the time so that I am not identifying with my emotions and thoughts. I experience myself as encapsulated in my own presence. When there are moments of exhaustion, which there are from time to time, they go away after a short time. Although I owe much of this state to being with Bapak, the experience is the direct result of the working of the latihan. I now understand better Bapak's explanation of how the latihan directs the forces of our daily activity: "... after separation, the forces may go on to flow spontaneously in their rightful directions." This leaves the inner feeling clear, clean, and quiet. Tiredness, it seems, comes from forces residing in the wrong place.

It may be said that this is no more than the natural condition for a human being, but I find it is both wonderful and extraordinary when I compare it with the more common everyday condition of being disturbed by concerns and thoughts.

I realise I am living in a way totally devoted to my spiritual life. It will be interesting to see how I cope when it is all over and how much permanent benefit remains. I am hopeful—I remember Bapak's words to the Indian Congress in Poona:

And the contact which Bapak has communicated to you will continue to work by itself and will always be present with you. Therefore do not fear that once Bapak goes away it will cease to work. Once it is present, it will continue to work; it will always remain present in the self of man or, to be more precise, within the self of each of you. [26]

July 30

MARSEILLES. Bapak seemed surprised to find that the majority of the forty or so men and women here for his visit are from elsewhere. On the second afternoon, Bapak came down to the garden where many members were sitting around, including the Spanish group, of about eight. Bapak talked and asked me to translate, first into Spanish and then into English. His talk was about testing and its importance and was a preparation for the testing session that he had scheduled with the members that night. Finally he gave a demonstration. It was just as well that he did, because many of the people there had no idea what testing was about.

Bapak's World Tour, 1970

August 2

PARIS. Bapak and Ibu are staying in the apartment of a Subud sister, an eye doctor, Patricia Auffret. She and Ibu are very fond of one another. Ibu wanted me to sleep in Tuti's bed in Ibu's room. This is very Indonesian—wanting to keep all the family together, so to speak—but as Ibu sleeps with all the lights on and gets up many times during the night, I decided I wouldn't. I was rather exhausted, and getting a good night's sleep seemed essential. I moved into a small hotel nearby.

Here again the members arranged to have their Subud National Congress during Bapak's visit. There are about one hundred French members and almost as many foreign visitors, making it a very international gathering.

The trip is hectic. There is something happening every night. Bapak never has any nights off, and no matter at what time we arrive, he starts the program that same night. Last night we had consecutive latihans. Paris has treated us very well. We had sunny days inwardly and outwardly.

August 9

HOLLAND. Bapak and Ibu stayed in the Tjalsma's house in The Hague and the latihans, talks, and testing were held in a church across town. There were about two hundred people here, eighty of them from abroad. Moving from group to group every two or three days, I notice the process of change in the feelings during each visit. The first day it is heavy. Then Bapak's talk invariably lifts up the feelings, and from there on, everything becomes light.

Here his first talk was entirely about the spiritual life. He explained the difference between Subud and other movements and how it is impossible to find God through the mind. In his second talk, he spoke a lot about marriage as a sacred institution. He said the character of children results from the inner quality of the parents. Because of this, he said, children of parents doing the latihan have a chance to be different, with less burden from inherited faults and weaknesses.

In the evening Bapak conducted testing and appointed two women as National Helpers. They have a history of not liking each another. Bapak said they were to work together. "So that North Korea and South Korea make peace!" he said.

Chapter Seven

When we arrived the reaction of some of the organising members toward Lydia, David, and myself was, 'What are you people doing with the party?" This made me feel uncomfortable, but as the days went by we were accepted as a part of the whole unit. For our departure, use of a private conference room was provided at the airport. There were about two hundred members present to farewell Bapak. The members sang old Dutch plainsong. Bapak sang a prayer. As they shook hands to say goodbye, some of the men and women started to sob, loud and clear. Bapak just smiled. It was very touching to see how emotional they were.

August 14

TORONTO. It took seventeen hours to fly here from Amsterdam. We slept only two and a half hours, then we were up again. Ibu is really tired.

Subud Canada held its Third National Congress to coincide with Bapak's visit. In his talks Bapak explained that the new national helpers and the group helpers are expected to take some of the responsibility for answering members' questions and so relieve Bapak of the increasing amount of correspondence that he is receiving.

August 17

SKYMONT, USA. Today we flew to Washington D.C. and came here by car. Skymont Camp is a Subud-owned ex-boys' camp in the Blue Ridge Mountains area of Virginia. It has large grounds and many of the Subud members are accommodated in tents. Bapak's house is simple and not very comfortable. Lydia, David, and I are in a small cottage behind Bapak's house. It is dirty and smells stale. It has two bedrooms, and we live there with Prio Hartono (previously a member of Bapak's secretariat in Cilandak), his wife, and two children, as well as two other ladies. The bathtub is broken. In the day-time, if people want to go to the bathroom, they have to go through our bedroom! It is very inconvenient.

This is the Subud USA National Congress and hundreds of members are expected to attend. Today is the twenty-fifth anniversary of Indonesian Independence, and in the evening, we had a selamatan to celebrate the occasion. The Indonesian ambassador to the USA sent a representative, and Bapak gave a short talk. This was interesting, as it highlighted the difficulty that Indonesians who are not in Subud have in distinguishing Subud from their many *kebatinan* or inner mystical disciplines in their country. He said:

Many people still think that the latihan kejiwaan of Subud is an inner way. Whereas, in the light of what has happened, and what all the members including Bapak himself have experienced, the latihan kejiwaan of Subud is not just an inner training, but is both inner and outer, of soul and of body.

A sign proving the real nature of the latihan is that you do not receive it passively but that you behave and move and act and function in just the same way as is usual for people living in this world. Therefore this latihan kejiwaan of Subud is in truth the latihan of life, not of death. Hence it is not right that you who have received the latihan kejiwaan should give up working. You must work, for this latihan is the latihan of life. [27]

August 19

SKYMONT. Bapak talked this morning to the full assembly of members about the spiritual side of Subud in the USA. He emphasised that the spiritual was more important than matters of administration, money, and so on. "The committee," he said, "only look after what is already done, what has already happened. But it is the helpers who have to put things together, so that [things] can come to maturity properly. . . ." He continued:

Bapak is happy to hear of an increase in membership, but is not really satisfied if the additional members cannot really understand what is Subud. Even to know the Scriptures of the great religions does not give a grasp of what the latihan is. For this reason it is no use for us to imitate the things that are already past. That would be as if God had existed in the past and now exists no longer, and as if God were only in the hereafter. It is not only the dead who meet God. God is the God of life— of all that He has created. [28]

Bapak then asked Prio Hartono—who had been sent here to North America by Bapak—to report on his activities. Prio said that when he arrived in the USA in October 1969, he felt there was confusion in the meetings and a lack of achievement. Since then, little by little, Subud North America had been restructured into six regions as Bapak wished and these were now operating effectively. He told how ten members had got together to start an enterprise and had purchased Skymont Camp.

August 22

SKYMONT. Ibu is enjoying having many of her lady friends together here. Today, being sunny, she went for a stroll with a small retinue. She was resting on my arm when suddenly she stopped and, pointing to me, said to the others: "You know . . . I like her because she is very Javanese."

Chapter Seven

August 25

SKYMONT. Bapak's presence here has given the gathering its spiritual direction. The latihans were the crucibles of transformation. They were held in tents and were extremely strong, with lots of sound and movement. Tuti said that Bapak is happy because there are so many Subud people. He gave seven talks and general testing sessions in the first three days.

In his talk on the morning of the third day, he spoke about his mission:

Bapak's mission is not only to bring two or three nations together but people of many races and nationalities, speaking different languages, embracing different faiths, having different customs and ways of life. This is really a heavy task and duty to fulfil. But since what Bapak is doing is the command of God, God will guide Bapak in anything that he will do in this world for this mission. * [29]

In contrast to the strong spiritual experience of being here together, the practical side has been a bit chaotic. Rain made everything muddy, and some of the people in tents have moved out to motels in the nearby town. The catering has its problems, and even the water is sometimes off. I'm sure many people worked very hard to make it a success, but the facilities were not adequate for such a large number. David seems to have enjoyed himself. There were social events every night. I've hardly seen him the whole week. In fact I didn't even try to find him, among so many people and trees! We leave for New York tomorrow, a stopover for Eire.

August 28

DUBLIN. We could not land in Ireland because of the fog, so we were diverted to Glasgow and had to wait for several hours before proceeding to Dublin. After the intense activity of Skymont and the long overnight flight, we arrived exhausted. We were taken to the house of a Subud woman. It was a large house, and she had meticulously arranged everything for our comfort. But when Bapak announced there was to be latihan and talk that night, we all gasped.

On the second night after the latihan, I sat with Ibu and the other ladies in the front row waiting for Bapak to begin his talk. Without formality Bapak suddenly called the woman who owned the house. He showed very clear displeasure because she had left the room during the testing the night before. Why had she done so? he asked her. She said something to the effect that she did not believe in testing. Bapak was stern with her. The woman apologised.

---

* This is a provisional translation of Bapak's talk.

Ibu, who had been very tired, suddenly straightened up, aware that something unusual was going on. After the incident the woman continued making every effort to see that Bapak and the party had everything they needed. I thought this was a wonderful gesture on her part. She was able to act as if nothing had happened.

August 29

MANCHESTER, UK. We have been here for a two-day visit. Bapak is greatly loved in England, and as usual people from other parts of Europe are visiting for the occasion. Tonight Bapak's testing changed. The helpers were asked to sit in the front, and Bapak tested their spiritual condition. Following the testing Bapak gave a short talk in which he explained:

In the accounts given by the Messengers of God, it has been said that when each man dies and enters the world of the grave, the life after death, every part of his body is questioned. His heart and mind are locked up, so that they are not the troublemakers—no longer able to justify things that are wrong. So, one by one the parts of your body will answer and tell what they have experienced while on earth. . . . By the Mercy of Almighty God, this has already been made clear to you [through the latihan], while you are still living in this world. [30]

September 1

LONDON. There was women's latihan and testing. The questions were directed to finding God's guidance about right attitudes towards our husbands, in the face of good fortune or unhappiness, and towards one another. I sat in the front and found the tests very helpful.

Tonight was a selamatan and Bapak's farewell talk in England. He explained about the uniqueness of the latihan of Subud:

In truth, brothers and sisters, the coming and growth of the latihan of Susila Budhi Dharma, Subud, is different from anything else. Only now, by the will of God and His grace, is mankind receiving such a thing.

Why is this? Bapak himself does not know the reason, but according to his receiving, everything runs parallel to and in line with the needs of mankind. Because of his outer needs, man has set his heart and mind to work, with the result that the longer the world goes on, the more progress is made and the wider human skills extend. God proceeds according to human strength and development, so the latihan is now necessary because the human intellect has now developed to the point at which man seems no longer to believe in anything that is holy.

Chapter Seven

Bapak used the word "separate" to explain a key experience of the latihan:

The latihan is a training which is all embracing. In the latihan we are trained to trust, surrender and worship the One God; trained to separate ourselves from our own lower forces; trained to form our own individuality; and much more. [31]

Bapak was farewelled for about an hour in a private room at London airport before we flew to Barcelona. There was a very close feeling between us, and friends cried as we left.

September 4

BARCELONIA. This is Bapak's first visit to Spain. There was a big welcome at the hotel and more than two hundred people came for the talks, although I believe about a third of these were foreign visitors. We had three days here. Bapak asked me to translate his talks into Spanish, from Usman's translation of Indonesian into English.

On the second morning, Bapak arranged latihans, first for the ladies. This went on for a long time and was followed by testing. After the women, Bapak called the men for their latihan. It was not usual for a woman to be in a men's latihan, but I was there to translate for the testing. The men's latihan was very strong—active, noisy, and intense. Some of the men perspired profusely. In addition the room had no ventilation and a low ceiling. It became increasingly hot, and I started to feel faint. I began to remember the strange feeling I had had when I nearly passed out in Wolfsburg. I became a bit panicky and prayed, 'Not here, God. Please, not here!'

At that moment I noticed Bapak look at me briefly. He had with him on the table a small round box of Valda gums (small Indonesian lozenges). He motioned to Usman to pass the box to me. I thought, *Bapak! . . . A Valda for what I am feeling?* It seemed outrageous to me. I said nothing and took the Valda. Unbelievable! In two minutes I felt completely well. I was able to go on translating with no problem at all. I knew for certain that Bapak had by his action done something to help my condition that had nothing to do with the lozenge.

September 8

LISBON. We have been here since September 5. Portugal has quite a different feeling from Spain—more serious. The members have been very loving, filling the car with flowers on our arrival, and making Bapak very comfortable in a house high up in the hills overlooking the countryside and the Atlantic Ocean.

Bapak held latihan and talks. There was an emphasis on strengthening the organisation and forming a national committee. The new chair-person is a woman. The members did a lot of singing, their way of expressing their gratitude for Bapak's visit.

Throughout the stay here, I have tried unsuccessfully to get South African visas for David and myself. When I told this to Bapak, he suggested I should get on the plane anyway and maybe Mr. Baerveldt in South Africa will be able to arrange our visas on our arrival. If this could not be done, he said, then I should fly on to Australia and meet him in Perth. I wasn't confident about this idea, but things were taken out of my hands. A young man, who is now following Bapak, and is in a kind of crisis (which makes him headstrong) was holding my passports and tickets. He decided, because of what Bapak had said, to get David and me on to the plane to South Africa—at all costs! I feel uncertain about this . . .

An hour out of Lisbon, the plane turned back and I spent the night sitting up with Bapak and Ibu in the airport lounge. This time together was incredibly light and intimate in feeling. No one felt tired, burdened, or anxious in any way.

September 17

PERTH. Just as I had anticipated, when we arrived in Johannesburg, there was trouble. The immigration officials at the airport were very angry that we had no visas, and Mr Baerveldt could do nothing to help. After midnight and tired from the long flight, David and I were put in a security room at the airport. Bapak and Ibu were very concerned. The following morning we applied for visas, but this was refused. That day we took the next plane out to Australia.

September 21

MELBOURNE. Bapak stayed one night in Perth. He gave a talk and did testing. After the testing he had the women who live in Cilandak do latihan in front of the members. I took part with Ismana, Tuti, and Mastuti. This was the first time we had done this on the trip. It was to demonstrate that the more you do the latihan, the more clearly and confidently you can follow the receiving.

We have now been here five days. The Australian National Congress has been arranged to coincide with Bapak's visit and members have come from all over the country. In Bapak's first talk, he explained about the influences of the forces which make up our experience, including the higher qualities that are possible for man:

Chapter Seven

There are four qualities of a holy man which have been shown by the Messengers of God in the past [Abraham, Moses, Jesus, and Muhammad]. The quality of sidik is the quality of wisdom, not cleverness or intelligence. The quality of amanat is the quality of one whose words give peace to the heart of man and whose behaviour is good. The quality of tablech is the quality of one who can make harmony among those who quarrel or disagree, the quality of one who can create understanding among men and who can make an honest man out of a thief. The quality of fatunah is the combination and realisation of the qualities of sidik, amanat, and tablech.

Helpers should be able to show these qualities, at least to some extent. [32]

October 6

KUALA LUMPUR. I slept the two nights here in the same room of the hotel with Ibu. Bapak was next door in a connecting room. It was very much an intimate family feeling. I took care of them both, serving them breakfast in the early morning. Today is my birthday. I followed the Javanese rite and asked Bapak's forgiveness and then thanked him for taking me on the trip. I do love Bapak and Ibu very much.

October 8

SINGAPORE. On the flight here, Ibu asked me to sit beside her and told me the following story:

One day during the trip, I was alone with Bapak and I longed for cooked apples. Then I thought to myself, *If someone came to my room and brought me some cooked apples, I would consider her part of Bapak's family.* At that moment, there was a knock at the door and you came in with a dish and said, "Ibu, I've brought you some cooked apples."

I felt to just accept her love and not try to understand what she meant.

Bapak gave a talk to the group about the four *nafsu* (passions), which affect man's life and our need to subordinate them and make them our servants. These passions come from the material, vegetable, animal, and human life forces. The effects include anger and conflict (material force), greed and selfishness (vegetable force), desire and ambition (animal force), and patience and acceptance (human force).

. . .

October 9

JAKARTA. We flew in at 8:00 P.M. As I walked with Ibu towards the airport terminal, I could see crowds of people waiting to welcome Bapak. Once inside the building, I felt a surge of thankfulness to God as family and friends gathered around us with their love and joy.

FOR DAYS I continued in the lightness of spirit of the journey. I had no inkling of the momentous events that were so soon to unfold. In a few months, I would be traumatised by events in Subud that sorely tested my faith.

Part Two

Chapter Eight
An Unexpected Gift

A WEEK AFTER returning from the world journey, came the new moon that signalled the beginning of the Muslim month of Ramadhan. I decided I would follow the fast, as I had done in previous years. The heightened spiritual state that I had enjoyed on my travels remained with me for some time and with it the sense of closeness to Bapak and Ibu.

The fast was becoming a regular practice for a number of Subud members of all religions, and this year there were some fifty overseas visitors who had come to Wisma Subud especially for the occasion.

Bapak did not insist that Subud members follow the Ramadhan fast. It was a matter of free choice. He simply said that there were great benefits for non-Muslims as there were for Muslims. Ramadhan is to the Muslims what Lent is to the Christians. Bapak explained the reason for the fast and that, like other religious practices, there are different levels to the experience:

This fast is said in Islam to be man's highest and most noble form of prehatin (self-denial), enabling him to be given the Qadar (revelation from God). The fast forbids eating, drinking, and smoking, but there is more to it than that.

There are five rukun (pillars) in the structure of Islam and four levels to that structure. The five pillars are the creed, ritual prayer, fast, alms-giving, and the pilgrimage to Mecca. The four levels are shari'at, tarikat, hakekat, and marifat.

The shari'at [of the creed] is fulfilled by declaring one's belief in the existence of God. It is expressed in the words "I bear witness that there is no God but Allah and that Muhammad is His Messenger." That is enough. For the tarikat ... what is needed is to recite the creed and to understand the inner significance of the worship. [Sufi practices are tarikat.]

Hakekat means reality. When you climb a tree, your climbing has become a reality for you. That is hakekat. ... The existence of the Power of God is real; the existence of God with His Power and His Messengers is real.

Chapter Eight

Hakekat is not unfamiliar to you [in Subud], of course, this arising of what Bapak always calls the vibration of life, felt at the moment you have ceased to think of anything except that you are standing before God and worship Him with trustful acceptance and sincere submission.

As to the marifat, Bapak does not need to say more, because after the hakekat one progresses automatically, for such is God's Will. After the flower, the seed is sure to set. After the seed has set, the fruit surely follows. That is the Will of Allah.

The fast, being a time when the inner self awakens, is therefore a time when you have to be quiet. If you can do what is required [according to the hakekat], you will know and have the fruits of the fast. So feelings such as the desire for food and so on will disappear, and thoughts that were straying all over the place will vanish. What may be called the best feelings will arise. If you have experienced all this, every good quality will appear, so that you will be really honest in what you feel. This will be expressed by your being able to know your faults and why you are as you are. Before that ability arises, you are as if shut off from your honesty, shut off from your sincerity.

It is said that, after twenty days of fasting, the twenty-first night is the time when the Lailatul Qadar, the Revelation of God, manifests in man's inner feeling. Where previously he had no affection for his fellow man, he now loves them. . . . A willingness to give to those in real want, the poor and the needy, will develop in him automatically. It comes of itself. This is the hakekat. [33]

This was my third Ramadhan fast. In the previous years, people in the compound had stayed awake the whole night, going to bed after the dawn prayer, but this year Bapak suggested we stay up only on the traditional Nights of Power, the five alternate nights from the twenty-first to the twenty-ninth. On the other nights, we would have some sleep until about 2:00 A.M., then after sahur, the last meal before the start of the day's fasting at 3:00 A.M., go back to bed again. The day-long fast from dawn until sunset was, at that latitude, usually from about 4:00 A.M. to 6:00 P.M.

For Subud people there was, as Bapak said, more to a successful Ramadhan fast than simply not eating and drinking. The restraint had to be carried through to attitudes, desires and bad habits of thought, such as finding fault with others. The intention was to find the deeper spiritual reality of the fasting and so come to an experience of one's true humanity.

An Unexpected Gift

The fast weakened my desire for activity and quietened my thinking. It slowed down my responses. I came to see how the life forces in the food we eat are a source of our passions. By taking care I could direct the lower life forces away from turning into anger, desire, impatience, and so on. As Bapak said, the fast was a gift of God. "The Ramadhan fast gives you the opportunity to experience and understand more about the spiritual life in one month than you would normally learn in the other eleven," he said.

Each year I found the experience was different. It started with noticing the lack of food and drink, then it changed to awareness of right attitudes and handling the feelings. It was a learning experience, and it was interesting to see that the body and the feelings remembered, each year's fast becoming an extension of the previous one.

As the days passed, my feelings became more clear and light. My heart and mind quietened and there arose natural feelings of charity, love, and compassion towards others. These were not qualities which I could claim as my own, but are potential in the inner heart of everyone. They were attributes of being a true human being. The giving of alms in this state was free of self-interest. I felt grateful and could understand why Ibu had said that the Ramadhan fast was an opportunity to love God.

The breaking of the fast each day, called *buka* in Indonesian, was, by custom, a time to sit quietly and eat something small and light. Erling and I would often sit alone, showered and relaxed, on the upstairs balcony as the sun began to set in a turquoise-coloured sky. Morsini would bring some juice and freshly cut mango. From the village mosque across the paddy fields would come the drum beat announcing the end of the fast, followed by the sonorous call to prayer, Allahu Akbar, Allahu Akbar (God is Great) from the loudspeaker of the minaret. It would echo again and again from distant mosques, filling the air with the praise of God. It was a magical moment.

After dinner we would serve a little tea and cake. This year there were a number of our friends among the overseas visitors, and many evenings we had guests coming to the house to chat quietly and enjoy the peaceful feeling that the fast produced.

On four occasions, Bapak gave talks to men and to women separately. On the twenty-ninth night of the fast, he gave a talk to all of us, which lasted until 3:00 A.M. He explained that the deeper reality of the pilgrimage to Mecca

Chapter Eight

(the hadj) is to experience the centre of life. "It is symbolised," Bapak said, "when you pray Allahu Akbar (God is Great). This centre of one's life is none other than the inner self of the worshipper." Bapak also explained that when one comes home from the *hadj* it is customary to change one's name. The word for name in Javanese means that which has been enthroned within. Ideally you have this experience of the inner self on the pilgrimage, so it is appropriate for you to have a new name.

You will notice in my narrative that people's first names sometimes change. This is not uncommon in Subud. Although the practice is part of Indonesian-Islamic culture, in Subud it is a matter of choice, based on a person's feeling for the need to change. Bapak gave new names when asked and occasionally suggested a change. He once gave this explanation:

There is no compulsion or obligation in Subud to change your name. It is up to you whether or not you wish to do so. However, a name does, in fact, have a strong influence on the self of man, because when a person is called by his name, he will certainly respond from his whole being, so that his entire self, when called by name, feels as if it is being awoken from sleep, or stirred out of passivity.

If a person or child is wrongly named, then when his inner feeling is awakened and rises, it becomes adjusted to a name which does not correspond to his inner self. As a result, his outer behaviour and his inner feeling are not in harmony. [34]

I was named Irma, after my father's sister. I never liked this name, but even though many Subud people went to Bapak to ask for a new name, I never felt inclined to do so. I nevertheless accepted what Bapak said, that a name does have a strong influence on the self of man and that the right name can change a person's character in a favourable way to correspond with his or her true inner nature.

Then, shortly after the world trip, I started to feel that I should have a new name. I was reluctant to ask Bapak for fear of getting an exotic multi-syllable Javanese or Islamic name, so I just waited. During the following week, Hardiyati, Bapak's daughter, unexpectedly said to me, "It feels as if you need a new name!"

When the once-a-month Sunday women helpers' latihan in the Big House came around again, I attended as usual. Bapak was expected to give his regular talk. This was December 20, 1970.

An Unexpected Gift

There were about twenty women, including Bapak's daughters and granddaughters. At the finish of the latihan, Ibu asked me to help turn her chair, which was in front and apart from the other women, so it faced Bapak at an angle. She then chatted with me about this and that. I began to feel that I should move away and sit next to the wall on the mats with the other women, but Ibu insisted that I sit next to her. When the family came, who customarily sat on the floor next to Ibu, my discomfort increased. I did not want to take their place and tried to get up again, but Ibu held my dress and made me stay. Ismana sat next to me and next to her Tuti and Muti.

Bapak gave a talk and then said, "Would you like me to test how the satanic forces can affect the inner feeling?" I heard the women against the wall saying, "Yes, Bapak!" I kept very quiet. Then Bapak said, "Who will come forward?" To my surprise I started to stand up—with a little last push by Ismana and the words, "Yes! go, go!" I was impelled; something in me just knew that I had to do it.

Bapak looked at me and said, "You?" I answered, "Yes, Bapak." "Are you sure?" he repeated. "Yes, Bapak," I answered. Bapak then proceeded, *"Show! How does it feel when the inner feeling is invaded by the satanic forces?"* Immediately I was filled with an indescribable agony. I felt everything in me was being torn to pieces. A great cry came out from the depth of my being.

I heard Bapak say, "Stop!" But I couldn't, so he repeated, "Stop! Stop!" Only then was I able to open my eyes, still crying. Then Bapak said, "Yes, that is how it is!" As I sat down, I saw many tearful faces.

Bapak continued his talk, which I don't remember, except that he said, "Not everyone here will receive a *rohani** soul. Maybe only five. Ibu will. Irma will." I was surprised because I imagined that Ibu was already at that level.

In the evening Bapak sent for me. Muti, one of his grand-daughters, was with him. She had a piece of paper and, as she gave it to me, Bapak said, "Here is your new name." I opened it and saw Istimah.

I was spontaneously filled with happiness. I loved it. And I had never heard the name before. I asked Bapak its meaning. He said, "Always obedient to the commandments of God." Then he added, "This name is both Javanese and Islamic. Javanese for your gracefulness and Islamic for your worship of God."

---
* Bapak explained that: "When the *rohani* power comes to influence the self of man, he will be conscious of and know that there is the power of God and he will be constantly aware of and know that there is a continuation of life which is more blissful than life on this earth."

Chapter Eight

I stood with Bapak and Muti on the porch for a little while. I was thrilled. Bapak was very kind and seemed to appreciate my reaction. He said how important it is to have one's right name; every time it is mentioned, it carries its meaning.

Next morning soon after dawn, Ibu sent for me. She said that I should announce my new name to all the residents in the traditional Indonesian manner. The way to do it was to have my maid cook a large amount of white rice and mix half of it with spices and tumeric to make it a golden beige. Then, showing me meticulously with graceful gestures, she said, "Put portions of each coloured rice into small baskets, making a pattern, and send to each household with a card saying: My new name is Istimah."

Thereafter, when I was addressed by this name, I immediately felt joyful and wholesome. From the moment I got the name Istimah, I felt I was a different person. It was as if the world trip with Bapak had worked like a pilgrimage, bringing me to my inner self and so to the need for a new name.

Chapter Nine
'Ibu Is Within You'

ONE TUESDAY MORNING at the end of January 1971, I was with others doing latihan in the hall in Cilandak with Ibu when she suddenly became ill. Bapak was called, and in a few minutes, he was by her side. Ibu had to be carried back to the Big House. Although she rallied a little during the following days, her condition after that deteriorated. The doctors treated her for her diabetes, but she never recovered.

A week or so after she fell ill, Bapak told all the women to stop visiting because it was becoming too crowded. He instituted a roster and asked me to be on it twice a day for four hours each time. There was not much one could do for Ibu; she just needed quiet attention and to be gently fed with liquids. At a certain moment, I realised that she would not live.

On Friday, January 12, Ibu suddenly got worse and Bapak asked me to telephone Singapore where Tuti had gone for dental treatment. While I was trying to get through, Maryam Kibble came to me and said, "It's too late!"

I went back to Ibu's room and found Dr. Rachman Mitchell giving her resuscitation. The family was there, also my mother and a few of the women helpers. Dr. Mitchell continued until Bapak said, "That is enough."

Ibu was then taken to the large second-floor living room for the wake. We stayed there through the night. Sometimes Bapak would say a few words. One of Ibu's granddaughters became very attached to me during those quiet hours. Maybe she needed the comfort of someone who was a mother, as her own mother had died.

The following day, Ibu's face was made up by a French lady member who was an expert in cosmetics. She was deeply attached to Ibu and wept all the while she was doing the make-up. The funeral was held the same day, according to Islamic custom, and Ibu was buried beside her daughter Rochanawati in the family tomb in Karet Cemetery in Jakarta.

Chapter Nine

During the days and weeks that followed, a series of special commemoratory selamatans were held in the evenings. I particularly recall the sixth night of the vigil. It was Ibu's birthday, the seventeenth of February 1971. Had she lived, Ibu would have been sixty-four. Instead of the usual joyful celebration, suddenly here I was attending a solemn ritual, the forty-night recitation of the Koran.

I remember it as if it were happening in the present:

Carefully, I make my way up the wide graded stone staircase at the back of Bapak's house. I leave my shoes inside the porch and enter the large living room. All furniture has been removed and the floor is covered, wall to wall, with carpets and overlapping mats of finely woven raffia. The glass chandeliers throw a pale broken light on the teak panels and a familiar portrait of Bapak.

I have arrived early so that I can choose where to sit, just inside the door to the right. There I have easy access in and out of the room, if I want ... Sitting on the floor, I like to support my back—here it is against the full-length mirrors. My long skirt of batik covers my legs.

The room fills slowly. The first to arrive also sit against the walls and those who come later form a second, inner row, cross-legged. They are all men in the centre. Most of the women have chosen to be in a group near the dining room to my left. This is the usual arrangement of seating for selamatans—so often held in this room—but the mood is quite different.

It all happened so quickly, so unexpectedly, Ibu's death. The vigil is quiet. The quietness is not sleepy, it's very wakeful. I feel deeply still inside. Everything but surrender has left my feelings. Ibu is in God's hands.

Bapak also sits on the mats. Near him are Haryono, his son, and other members of his family. His grand-daughters, Tuti and Muti, occasionally get up and go to other parts of the house. Such is their composure that their movement is hardly noticed.

The Koran verses (Al Qur'an sûrahs) are being chanted in the traditional Islamic mode. It is in Arabic and the recitation continues until after midnight. Some nights it has gone on until 2:00 A.M. The readers are all Subud members, mostly Indonesian and skilled at this kind of intoning. One is English, a scholar in Arabic. They are taking turns to read, and as is the custom, the reader cups his right hand against his ear as he reads. He seems to monitor and at the same time amplify his voice. The sound is not loud, but rich and resonant, like sung poetry. I feel both aware of myself and, at the same time, very close to everyone in the room.

'Ibu Is Within You'

This is as it should be for Ibu. Respectful to God—following the religious custom—and being in a state of latihan.

Two electric fans on tall stands add their regular whirring noise as they sweep from side to side, blowing air around the room above our heads. It's incredibly hot and humid. It's still the rainy season, but tonight there's been no rain. Trays of sweetened cold jasmine tea are brought in and the glasses passed hand to hand around the room. Also there are small plain cakes.

The chanting of the Koran drifts into the background as my thoughts return to Ibu. I remember the impact of Bapak's words on the day she died as we gathered upstairs around her coffin:

"Now, here is Ibu. What remains is only her body.
Her passions have left. Her soul has left."

And then, to all of us standing there:

"Yes, Ibu has left.
Where is Ibu? Ibu is within you."

Now, I can hardly believe I am taking part in this unfamiliar observance. As a Catholic, I have never known this Islamic experience. I am so grateful to be here. I think of myself as I was when I lived in Chile; I could never have imagined that I would one day be immersed in such an Asian atmosphere and be witnessing this significant event.

I look across at Bapak, and I think of him and Ibu together. I remember Ibu's lovely story: "One day after Ibu had met Bapak," she told me, "Ibu was walking with a friend on the street behind Bapak, but not close. Ibu looked at Bapak's back and as she looked, she pondered: 'I wonder if he is the man that I will marry.' Bapak turned around, looked at her, and said, 'Yes, it is I!'"

This room has so many memories of Ibu and Bapak together. Here we have had such wonderful birthday selamatans. Besides those held for Bapak, none were more special than those for Ibu, particularly the one in 1969. It was an evening party. All day the Subud ladies from Cilandak and from far as away as Jakarta were cooking and making preparations. Food of a dozen kinds, savoury and sweet, and fruit and drinks were set out on the long dining room table. The centre-piece was a *nasi tumpung*, the large decorated yellow rice mountain traditional for such occasions. To accommodate the overflow of guests, extra chairs were brought in and placed on the wide cool verandah in front of the house.

Chapter Nine

Ibu looked regal in a beautiful dark *kain* (pleated sarong) and lace *kebaya* (blouse). She sat with Bapak, each in a velvet upholstered armchair at the end of the long room. He wore the classical Javanese dress of sarong and buttoned jacket. They looked splendid, the embodiment of their exotic culture.

Everything was laden with tradition. Bapak and Ibu's family, children and grandchildren, dressed in Javanese costume, came in single line and paid their respects by kneeling and bowing their heads to their folded hands as they touched Ibu's knee.

Ibu loved music, so members played her favourite songs on the piano and many sang. But the highlight of the evening was the playing by Idris Sardi, one of Indonesia's most famous romantic violinists at that time. He played Ibu's favourite song, "Ramona," with characteristic intensity. We shared Ibu's pleasure as she listened enthralled with her eyes half closed.

I was sitting very close to Ibu and said to myself, "I hope I will remember this for the rest of my life."

Bapak and Ibu, how well they looked together! Surely it was destiny that he should have a spiritual companion with a high soul and an exceptional capacity to help others. Ibu also added the feminine dimension to Bapak's activities. Bapak related to everyone, but Ibu enabled women to come closer to him through her accessibility.

Ibu was indeed the most feminine of women. She loved perfume, clothes, beautiful things, romantic music. She was graceful and well-groomed. She had beautiful smooth olive skin and brown eyes. She often smiled and at times laughed with delight. She had fine black hair, long and straight. She often wore it loose at home or combed up with perfumed oil and rolled into a bun on the nape of her neck in classical Indonesian style. When she went out, it was adorned with combs and gold pins. Her hands were expressive, delicately shaped, and very flexible. She could bend them back easily if she wanted to imitate a Javanese dancer.

Ibu dressed in traditional Javanese costume, her *kebaya* lace blouse a light colour, and her batik *kain* an elegant classical design, hand-painted in browns, dark blues, and beige.

One of her customs when she went out was to carry a handkerchief in her purse drenched in cologne. For the years that I knew her, her favourite scent was Blue Grass. Sometimes she added a little Joy near her hair. On the world trip,

'Ibu Is Within You'

I would make up her face. It was like a ritual—cream, then powder, then her eyebrows and her eyelashes. Finally lips, with liner and some lipstick. Another lady would help with her hair.

Getting Ibu ready to go somewhere on time during a trip was an all-absorbing drama for those who helped. I loved to share in it. Everything had to be arranged meticulously, and Ibu had to participate with care in every detail.

Like most intensely feminine women, Ibu could be capricious or contrary because of a mood. Once in Barcelona as Bapak and Usman were leaving the hotel to be taken on a tour by members, Bapak said to me that I should come along. I thanked him and very quickly got ready to go. We were waiting in front of the elevator when suddenly Ibu appeared at her door. She had already decided not to go, and now she said, "I want Istimah to stay with me!"

Bapak said: "Look, you already have Lydia; you don't need Istimah. Besides, she should see the country of her origin." But Ibu kept insisting until Bapak, with a look at me and a gesture, gave up.

"Ibu, why don't you come too?" I asked.

To everyone's surprise, she said "OK," making it sound like Ooo Keeey! ... Then she enjoyed the outing, laughing and seeming to be quite enchanted by the scenery.

Ibu was not as a rule adverse to going out. She liked to take walks, moving slowly with a Subud lady, resting her hand on the lady's arm. In Cilandak, on a nice day, she might go along the road that ringed the compound, taking about half an hour for the short circuit. Sometimes she was accompanied when walking by a number of ladies, as when going from her house to the latihan hall on Sunday mornings. It was a colourful procession with one lady holding a parasol protecting Ibu from the blazing sun.

One of Ibu's idiosyncrasies in everyday life was a painstaking attention to detail. She even seemed irrational about this at times, as when checking and re-checking her luggage on a trip. Later I could appreciate her behaviour in this respect—it was her way of managing the forces of her environment. When I was doing frequent latihans, I found myself more sensitive to such forces and, as a result, more careful in handling them. How often we have to pay, by things going wrong, because of our carelessness, our lack of respect for simple routine tasks.

Chapter Nine

Ibu was conservative, not a champion of the emancipation of women as we know it. But in reality she encouraged emancipation from the inside. Strengthening a woman's inner femininity often did more for that woman's independence than any outer action. I think this is often better understood by women in the East than in the West.

Much of her advice on women's behaviour derived from her sensitivity and insight. However, her advice could sometimes be too subtle for the understanding of visitors from Western cultures. For example, she could experience the negative effect on a women's femininity of wearing trousers, and advised against it. This is something that American women, accustomed to jeans, may assume comes only from the Indonesian culture, within which, they think, women are not yet emancipated. In reality, this advice is pro-femininity, not anti-feminist.

Something more open to question has been Ibu's objection to mixed race marriages. She once told friends of mine, visiting from Chile, that "marriages between East and West, do not work." Upon which, I said to Ibu, "What about so and so?" —an Indonesian man married to a European woman. Ibu answered, "And have you any idea how many times he comes to see me, crying in despair?"

Ibu was very respectful of her own traditions and through her example, while in Cilandak, I followed many of the customs of Indonesian society and of the Islamic religion. The most important was the Ramadhan fast. In 1968, before the start, Ibu made one of her beautiful and gentle gestures. She sent to every woman in the compound a bowl full of rose petals. The instructions were that, before the start of the fast, we were to first take a bath, Indonesian style—scooping water from a water tank in the bathroom and pouring it over ourselves—and then, in the last rinse of water, to add the fragrant rose petals.

A vital part of Ibu's femininity was the close companionship she gave Bapak. I saw it when they stayed in our house in Briarcliff. Aminah was doing the cooking for the party, but sometimes Ibu would decide that she wanted to cook a special dish for Bapak. She would come to the kitchen and take over completely, mobilising everyone to help. By all reports her cooking was delicious.

Ibu supported Bapak in other ways behind the scenes. In 1970 on Bapak's round-the-world journey, she had a routine. After she was dressed and ready to attend a talk by Bapak, I would clean her spectacles. Then instead of putting them on, she would call for Usman the translator and ask him to clean her glasses.

'Ibu Is Within You'

While he did this meticulously, she chatted with him. Only then would we go to the talk. As the journey progressed, I realised that, in her subtle way, Ibu talked to Usman to quieten his feelings and give him a blessing before he went to translate for Bapak.

When there was a talk by Bapak, we would always see Ibu in a front-row seat. On one occasion, in Dublin, however, she nearly did not appear. She was tired at the end of a long day of air travel from the USA and Bapak had decided to give a talk that same night. Ibu thought she was going to rest instead of attending, but when Bapak came in and said gently, "Come on, there's work to be done!" Ibu immediately responded and started getting herself ready.

In his turn Bapak went out of his way to please Ibu. In Paris, while I was in my room writing a letter, Bapak came in with Ismana and sat down to talk. He told us that he had been out to the showrooms at the car factory because Ibu particularly wanted to have a Citroen.

Bapak's full schedule on a world journey left him and Ibu little privacy. They would take it when they could. At the airport in Kuala Lumpur, I was sitting a short distance away from Bapak and Ibu, waiting for the boarding call to depart for Jakarta. It was the end of the journey. I saw them chatting and laughing together, happily reminiscing about some event of their travels.

Ibu was the nearest of all the women I ever knew to a Great Mother figure. Women came to her with their problems, and she responded spontaneously, according to her insights of the moment, guided by her inner self. She was instinctively aware of the feelings of others. This acute awareness was active, even in small things. I remember once sitting with her and starting to feel weak. She looked at me suddenly and said, "Have you not been to the doctor lately?"

She gave enormous attention to the many women in Subud who felt the need to be near her, talk to her, ask her advice, laugh and sing with her. She would change someone's emotional state through loving care, a song, a story—fact or fantasy—or a shared secret. It was her spiritual condition that worked these wonders, but she used simple outer ways in the process.

In particular, Ibu would make others happy by singing. Here in Cilandak she had a favourite song, which she often wanted one of us to sing to her and at times with her. Was it called "The Rose in Her Hair?" ...

Chapter Nine

It was very romantic and I remember that part of it went like this:

> In her eyes there was moonlight
> And a rose in her hair;
> In my arms there was no one
> So I put her in there . . .

On a more serious level, she used song differently. She loved children and in the USA in 1959, she would call Cathy, who was six at the time, to visit in her bedroom. On one occasion she sat her on her lap and sang to her a beautiful melody. When she finished she said to me: "This is Cathy's inner song."

Again, I remember at one stage on the world trip, in Toronto, Lydia and I were unhappy because of something that had happened the day before. Our sensitivity, from continuous latihan, was heightened and the slightest roughness of feeling from someone was felt acutely. Ibu sensed this and said, "I know you two are sad. Ibu will sing you a song." Upon which she proceeded to chant a most melodious strain that came from her inner feeling. It was very difficult to hold back the tears. When she had finished, she said. "Now, you two go out and have fun, take the day off."

Ibu was always aware of the need for relaxation. There were times in Cilandak, in 1969, when she would ask some of the ladies to visit her in her house. On one occasion she took us to the second-floor living room, which is very spacious. She had music—waltzes—played, and we were told to dance with each other. There was lots of fun with much laughter, especially when she asked me to dance with her.

Sometimes the comfort Ibu could give had a more obvious spiritual origin. For instance, on our first day in Wolfsburg, we were all rather exhausted from constant travelling. I felt tired beyond endurance. Ismana was sick in bed for the first time on the trip. I was surprised when I came out of my bedroom at 10:00 A.M. to find Ibu sitting in an annexe nearby. She was together with Laura and Leonora, the German doctors, and another lady. She called me over and said:

"I have not yet had the time to tell you about something that will make you very happy. In Hamburg, I cannot remember if it was during the latihan, or during the testing, I suddenly saw you. You were standing in front of me, dressed in a very beautiful long white dress and you had a crown on your head. You were standing (she got up and showed me how) and looking here and there and I thought, *Why! This is Istimah!* and then you said to me, 'I am always near Ibu.' "

'Ibu Is Within You'

As Ibu told me this, I felt my exhaustion completely lifted. With Ismana sick and several hundred people waiting to meet us, this was an enormous help for the busy day ahead.

Because she was mother and spiritual helper, as well as companion to the Subud ladies, some of them became so attached to her that it was uncomfortable to watch. I once saw a woman become so obsessed with wanting to be near Ibu that she "lost herself." It was as if she needed something that only Ibu could supply.

In such cases Ibu would comply only up to a certain point. She had a presence that demanded that you not approach her carelessly or in any way unconsciously. When those around her did not control their excessive attachment, she could, at any moment, and in no uncertain terms, distance herself from them.

Ibu was first of all a very religious person. She was, in a Subud way, constantly occupied with the worship of God, remembering her latihan and responding to the guidance of her inner feeling.

In Oslo, we went out touring in large motor cruisers, which the members had rented. I was in one with Bapak, Ibu, Ismana, Mastuti, and my son David. For a long time, Ibu stayed below in the cabin and asked me to keep her company. She said to me that we must constantly be praying to God for forgiveness, because we are sinning all the time.

Like Bapak, she observed the Islamic daily prayers and this included the dawn prayer, which was always completed before 5:00 A.M. One day on the trip around the world, I was tucking in the blankets on Ibu's bed, getting her ready for sleep. Half jokingly I said, "Now, Ibu, you sleep until ten o'clock tomorrow!" "Oh, no!" she answered in her idiomatic English, "I am frightened to God!"

All this I remember so well. Now suddenly Ibu is gone. . . .

The chanting of the Koran has stopped. How quickly the time has passed. Several have left; I guess some have far to go. It feels cooler. . . . Perhaps it's raining again. . . .

Chapter Ten
The Spiritual and the Material

IBU'S DEATH changed many things for me. She had been the centre of women's activity in Wisma Subud and therefore of mine. She had introduced us to many traditional Javanese customs, both domestic and celebratory. We became, through Ibu, an extended family. The change for me was as much inner as outer. I became more aware of my own viewpoint. This was soon to bring up doubts about Bapak's increasing emphasis on the worldly activities of the Subud Brotherhood, particularly enterprises and projects.

After Ibu's death, Tuti, Ibu's grand-daughter asked me if I would help her to clear out Ibu's bedroom. Ibu had stacked away many things for use as gifts. Tuti and I spent several hours doing the job. We threw away things like market receipts from the maids. We put all the new batiks in a safe place and decided that a silver serving set should go to the grand-daughters. From what Tuti said, I realised that the family was going through a difficult adjustment to Ibu's passing. She triggered in me a deeper grief than I had so far acknowledged.

During this time Rahayu, Bapak's eldest daughter, moved out of Wisma Subud for a month. The story was that she had gone to her house in Jakarta to be alone. Later, it was said that she went through a strong spiritual experience and that this had prepared her for a more active role in Subud, taking on much of Ibu's work with the ladies. From that time, Rahayu also answered Bapak's correspondence, met people and gave names, things that only Bapak had done until then.

Subud was at this time changing rapidly all over the world. People were taking the inner life—awakened by the latihan—into their outer activity in business enterprises, human welfare ventures, culture and entertainment. Bapak confirmed this as the natural outcome of the latihan. "This is a latihan of life," he said. As he did with human welfare projects, so too he endorsed the cultural activity of Subud members:

Chapter Ten

In the past the arts found their origin in people who were filled in their hearts and minds with the power of God. Therefore people in the past had a higher culture than we have in our day. Now in your state you have found contact with this power of God. You will become pioneers to again fill this world with arts as they existed in times long ago. [35]

Members of Subud with common cultural interests now formed groups in Europe and America in drama and dance, music, literature, crafts, painting, sculpture, architecture, films and photography. Every International Subud Congress was an opportunity for new associations and an occasion for evenings of entertainment.

Varindra Vittachi was enthusiastic. He wrote at the time of Hamid (Hamilton) Camp and his band, The True Brethren, who were playing on Broadway in *Story Theatre*—an adaptation of Grimm's Fairy Tales: "Hamid has had rave reviews. All the New York critics have evidently been deeply touched. I wonder by what? They have found the tales—theme, acting, and production—'beguiling,' 'magical,' 'enchanting,' 'original.' The True Brethren are likely to be on Broadway for a long time but they are planning to get to the 1971 World Congress, because, as Hamid says, 'that's what it's all about.' "

At this time also Harold Hitchcock, a gentle mild-mannered English painter and Subud member, was enjoying some fame in the southern United States, receiving the freedom of Huntsville and Winston Salem. Rather surprised that his delicate inner-world paintings inspired the love and affection that they did in the Americans, he said, "It seems that my paintings aroused an awareness of the loss America had suffered in putting material things first." One of his mystical landscapes hung on the wall in the Big House where we had the women helpers' latihan.

I felt protective of the spiritual side of Subud. I shared Bapak's concern that the organisation should not crowd out the spiritual. I sensed the threat of "organisers" and found them not only on group committees but also amongst the cultural and welfare enthusiasts. I was also wary of emotional fervour about culture and welfare.

When promoting enterprises, Bapak was unambiguous. In work there was no danger to our latihan, he said. On the contrary, business enterprises were the way to bring our latihan into daily life:

The Spiritual and the Material

It is fortunate for us that, with the presence of the latihan kejiwaan, if we are vigilant, we will be able to act as it were enveloped by the guidance of the power of God. What is important in this case is for you to be able to be aware of your actions, those that are wrong and those that are right.

Bapak encourages you to take up some kind of enterprise so that, little by little, you begin to put to beneficial use the latihan kejiwaan you receive and follow. . . . Bapak has repeatedly tested to show you that while counting money, drawing, working at a craft, thinking about a task, in all this your movements and actions are truly accompanied by the force of a power that is free from the influence of nafsu (passions) —that cause you to be without the presence of your inner prayer to God. With the latihan present in you, your devotion to God does not lessen. [36]

I didn't disagree, I just felt that business enterprises were not for me.

Ibu was still very much in my feelings. I dreamed about her:

Bapak was giving a talk. The chairs were set towards the back of the room and I sat in the front row. The space between the chairs and Bapak was filled with a group of women, mostly Indonesians, sitting on the floor, as was often the way. Someone asked me to sing a song. I chose an old tango and the words went like this:

> An old love, you never forget and you never leave it,
> An old love from our soul may—yes—drift away,
> But it never says goodbye.

One of the women, sitting at the edge of the group in front, turned around smiling and nodding, and said, "Yes!" It was Ibu. After my dream, as morning came, Bapak's words on the day Ibu died softly awoke in my memory, "Ibu is within you."

By the fortieth day after Ibu's death, the community in Cilandak had begun to concentrate on the coming Fourth International World Congress, to be held in Indonesia in August 1971. Local members could be seen visiting the Big House to confer with Bapak. Subud in Indonesia had several members in high places, including senior diplomats and government officials, among them top-ranking police and immigration officers. There were also those who had connections with the President's palace and the governor's office. Rear Admiral Sutanto was Chairman of the Indonesian Subud National Committee and former Foreign Minister Achmad Subardjo was the Honorary Chairman of Subud Indonesia. Varindra Vittachi, Chairman of the Subud World Council, was a long-time friend of Adam Malik, the Foreign Minister.

Chapter Ten

All these contacts were mobilised, and those who held important positions in public life arranged the necessary permits for our visitors and support from the Indonesian Government. There was to be a significant influx of foreigners and all gatherings at that time had to have a security clearance.

President Suharto was invited to officially open the Congress. He was to be accompanied by ministers of the Central Government and the Acting Governor of Jakarta.

Building work in Wisma Subud was now a top priority. A contract was let to build a new latihan hall with a thin curved concrete roof. Two hundred workers were busy on the enormous scaffolding of timber. The talk in Subud was increasingly about fund-raising as the preparations progressed.

There were many other amenities required for the coming Congress. The architect Ramzi Winkler was given responsibility for providing the accommodation for more than thirteen hundred overseas visitors. As there were no large hotels or residential university colleges near Cilandak, he decided to build temporary dormitories and dining halls, using bamboo. His designs were spectacular and well-suited to the tropical climate—long, two-storey structures with large curved overhanging eaves for the dormitories, each for two hundred people, and round open-sided buildings with huge thatched conical roofs for the dining halls.

Meanwhile, the membership of Subud in Jakarta continued to grow and on Sundays, Wisma Subud was full of parked cars as several hundred men and women waited their turn for latihan in the old hall.

On Congress opening day, the foreign visitors put on their national costumes, the red carpet was rolled out from the entrance of the new gleaming white latihan hall, and Bapak, in traditional Javanese dress, greeted the President of Indonesia. It was a high point for Subud in Indonesia.

Indonesians are strong on protocol and seem to enjoy long and formal addresses. President Suharto welcomed the representatives of the seventy-nine countries attending. He spoke of the high regard in which spiritual values are held in Indonesian society, and he succeeded in capturing the friendly feeling of the occasion. He seemed very sincere. "Harmony and friendship are ideals which can only be realised after maturity of spirit has been achieved through various spiritual exercises," he said. "These in essence honour the value of man."

The Spiritual and the Material

Then: "If the latihan kejiwaan [of Subud] is able to stimulate the dynamics of society in a harmonious way, if it is able to stimulate people's effort towards progress with spiritual maturity, then this latihan kejiwaan has achieved its aim to honour the value of man."

All this was reported on government television, radio, and in the newspapers, bringing Subud to the attention of the whole nation.

In response Bapak's address was designed to give the President, his ministers, and the people of Indonesia some facts about Subud. It was also, as one Indonesian explained, a clarification for those who had mistakenly compared Subud with the many *kebatinan* (mystical and meditative inner ways) sects. Bapak emphasised Susila—right living:

We chose the name Subud because its meaning accords with the latihan kejiwaan through which we experience a change . . . to become human beings who are able to conduct themselves properly, to be of good character, to have a feeling of surrender with trustful acceptance and sincere submission to Almighty God. [37]

During the following days, Bapak compared this Subud World Congress to the hatching of an egg. He was referring to the Wayang story of the heroic birth of Bima, a prince who achieved much through his trusting and faithful nature. The egg from which Bima emerged was a hard one to crack. The analogy was that the pioneering period of Subud was now over. This use of a Wayang example was not part of Subud culture, but it served as a natural link between Bapak and the Indonesians, whose values often derived from these mythical stories.

It was also apparent that Bapak was preparing the organisation for a possible expansion of membership. The business of the Congress now established the institutions of Subud, both spiritual and material, for such a future. The International Congress was confirmed as the highest body of Subud—composed of the Kejiwaan Councillors (Spiritual Councillors) and Committee Councillors from each country. Within this there would be seven geographical zones. All this was not my area of interest; however the representation at Congress and zonal meetings of two Helper Councillors and one Committee Councillor appeared to me to provide the right emphasis of the spiritual over the material, which Bapak had always insisted upon.

Meantime the feeling of brotherhood at the Congress was overwhelming. It confirmed my long-held belief that the latihan was the hope for mankind.

Chapter Ten

Then into this extraordinary atmosphere of goodwill and optimism came for me a deeply troubling experience. It was Bapak's launching of a Subud bank.

One day I went to Bapak's house to translate for a South American group meeting with Rahayu. When I arrived, Rahayu told me there had been a change of plan. Bapak was to address a session of the World Congress in the latihan hall about the bank, and he had told his family to attend. I prepared to go home, but Hardiyati asked me to stay. When Bapak's family got up to leave for the latihan hall, one of them held my dress—as a friendly gesture to have my company—and said, "Walk with us to the hall." I once again tried to leave, but again they held on to my dress. I had little choice but to go to the meeting. I sat with them in the third row.

Bapak had been talking about a bank for some years, but now he saw it as a real possibility based on investments by members. He now introduced the idea and the Congress ratified it. I felt terrible about it and the pressure from the committee to participate that followed. In my view, Subud was all about the latihan—the gift of God. What did that have to do with banking? After hearing Bapak, something broke inside me. I had looked towards Bapak, as selected by God, to be the channel for the coming of the latihan, and now he was opening Subud to the material forces!

As if in answer to my concerns, Bapak's explanation of the place for the bank in the activities of Subud was straight to the point. He said:

A bank is a one hundred percent commercial undertaking, hence a one hundred percent worldly matter. Why should the spiritual Brotherhood of Subud need to set up a bank, when it was founded essentially on worship of God, and exists only for the practice of the latihan kejiwaan to the end that we may find the right way after we die?

The material world does indeed constitute a very great temptation for anyone who sincerely worships God. But, it has been lightened and made easier for us—and we have been fortunate—in that we have received an inner strength originating from the power of God. [38]

"The reason for setting up the bank," Bapak said, "is not to make money and profits in order to become rich. . . . The money will be channelled to members carrying on enterprises in their various countries. . . . We are setting up this bank in order to take care of the members."

The Spiritual and the Material

I was not convinced by what Bapak said. I felt wholly negative about the bank. I could find no reconciliation between the Bapak proposing this and the person I respected as the bringer of the latihan. I was sure the material level would influence the direction of Subud and that it would go wrong.

To make matters worse, I felt there was quite strong persuasion to invest. After his talk Bapak asked for investments. In front of the Congress assembly, he told his family to invest. He then asked me. I said that in matters of money it was always my husband who made the decisions. He accepted this. He asked for pledges to be made at a lectern set up in front. Again he asked his family and me. This time I could not say no, but I only collected the pledge form and made no commitment. After the meeting I went home and asked Erling if he wanted to invest in the bank. He said "No!" so I discarded the subscription paper.

This was not the end of it. My dismay at Bapak's new direction now turned to consternation. Even with his lucid explanations, I could not put it together with his spiritual mission.

It may seem that my reaction was exaggerated. By normal standards, it may have been. But it came on top of Ibu's death and being very 'open' after the spiritual experience of the world journey. Also something deeper was disturbed. Not only did I feel the dissension of the spiritual and material forces, but I began to feel let down. Righteousness flooded over me and threatened to overwhelm me. Here were echoes of my experience with the priest who asked for donations at Mass, all those years ago in Chile.

Whereas most other Subud members supported the bank with enthusiasm, many of them capable and good people, I was powerless to see the bank otherwise than as a mistake. As later became clear, I was in the midst of a dramatic purification* of my inability to handle the opposition of spiritual and material. It was my personal problem and it was finally to affect my health.

When the Congress ended and the visitors left Indonesia, committees took over the establishment of the bank. It was to be in Germany where there were Subud members with some banking experience. Bapak continued with its promotion.

From there on I was in extreme distress. I spoke to no one about it except my mother and Erling. However, some others were disturbed. One woman would come to see me and talk about it at length. I never answered her.

---

* Purification: In Subud this means a cleansing of faults in the inner feeling, which can often be observed outwardly as a changing of attitude or a temporary illness.

Chapter Ten

I did not want to have any part in the gossip. This kind of thing went on for months, until I became ill. At first my illness expressed itself in a very strange form. I began to feel pain on my left shoulder, near the neck. It grew into a large red inflammation. The Subud doctor was unable to help me. My psychological situation grew worse. I wept and did not want to see anybody. Finally I got influenza, so badly that I had to stay in bed, though in the heat of the tropics, this is an ordeal. My mother said I should have enough character to throw it off. For the first time in my life, I shouted back at her. As the weeks went by, I became worse.

A friend of mine, Stacey Mills, who lived in Hawaii, wrote inviting me to spend some time with her. Stacey was a Subud member and a Rolfing therapist —a method of body realignment through deep massage, which releases chronic muscle tension. I felt too sick even to get out of bed, but Erling insisted that I go.

I flew first to Hong Kong. Arriving late at night, I took a taxi to a hotel. At around 2:30 A.M. I was awake with pain, so I called Varindra Vittachi, who was running *The Asian* newspaper. I told him I was on my way to Honolulu and why. He was very kind. He called one of the Subud women to keep me company and arranged for us to go to his apartment the next morning while waiting for the plane. On the flight to Honolulu, we encountered the most violent storm I had ever experienced in a plane. It was thrown all over the place, dropping at times uncontrollably in air pockets. The flight attendants were also strapped in their seats the whole way.

In Honolulu, Stacey made me very comfortable in her elegant apartment. The next day she began her Rolfing, which was to be my salvation. She and I were about the same age and shared similar interests—as well as Subud, nutrition, and health foods.

Soon after my arrival, her toaster exploded. "This has never happened to me before." she exclaimed. I remembered that when I was at Varindra's a gadget in the kitchen had similarly fused with a bang. Two days later I went to see a doctor. As he picked up one of the instruments from his steriliser, it short-circuited. I was at the point of exploding inside, and all these incidents had a strange feeling of coincidence. I felt as if there were some connection between my deep psychological distress and these material happenings. Later I read C.G. Jung's observations of such acausal events, which he called synchronicity.[*]

---

[*] Jung observed that coincidental events which partook of both physical and mental realms were often connected by meaning. In this case, I was so stressed that I was likely to 'blow my fuse,' meaning, I could die.

The Spiritual and the Material

One day Stacey invited me to lunch together with a famous astrologer. He asked me if I wanted him to make up my horoscope. I wasn't interested. Later, Stacey told me that he had said, "I do not know what is happening to that lady, but if she doesn't get over it soon, she will be dead in a year."

A few weeks later, I heard that Bapak was to visit Honolulu. It was a big event for the group. I did not want to go to his talk because he was on a world tour to promote the bank. My rejection meant that I also lost the psychological support my relationship with Bapak had provided. This showed itself in a most unexpected way. I am a very law-abiding person, yet I found myself jaywalking at the traffic lights, causing a near accident. The police picked me up and took me to the station. Fortunately I was let off after explaining that I was under stress. Nevertheless, it was a very shaking experience. My doctor suggested that I had become so vulnerable that, without the stabilising help of Erling's or Bapak's authority, I had turned to the symbolic authority of the police.

My stay in Hawaii was physically very healing. I had many Rolfing treatments by Stacey, and we went regularly to latihan. I became relaxed, made new friends, and went swimming. Now I gradually began to see that my trouble had arisen from my own rigidity. I had a problem in dealing with opposites—not only the issue of material versus spiritual, as with the bank, but a much more fundamental problem of handling opposition in myself. My judgement, that the material world was in opposition to the spiritual, may have been born of my Catholic upbringing, but my intensity about the matter went deeper.

With this understanding the trauma began to lift. From now on I was more able to take responsibility for my opinions, my judgements, and my reactions. I stayed in Hawaii for three months, and by the end, I felt stronger and healthy. I was more at peace with myself and Bapak.

When I returned to Cilandak in early July 1972, I had an impulse to visit Bapak in his office. This was around 10:00 A.M. His office was downstairs in the Big House next to the garden and separated from the family area. The entrance was along a short closed-in verandah on the compound side of the house where visitors could sit and wait.

The office was cool and light. It was air-conditioned, and morning sunlight filtered through translucent curtains along the tall side windows. It was a medium-sized room with wall-to-wall carpet. Bapak sat at a large polished teak desk on which there was a telephone and a few neatly placed writing accessories. I sat across the desk from him with my back to the door.

Chapter Ten

Like a gentle father, he welcomed me. We spoke in Indonesian. He was, as always, completely in harmony with himself and I felt the room was permeated by the lightness of his presence. I stayed about forty-five minutes and returned each day for a number of weeks. I used to go feeling confident and with great respect for Bapak.

We talked about his hopes that the latihan would spread and his plans for this. Sometimes we discussed the world situation, at other times simple things, like how he felt the heat of Jakarta. His voice was very kind, yet powerful. The conversation was always easy, at a normal level, with no high spirituality. I never talked about personal concerns, either about myself or about the Subud bank.

His attitude towards me was always friendly and kind, not in the least remote. He was genuinely interested in having a chat. He was a man with a life to live in this world and was happy to share his conversation with me. I felt very relaxed, as between two people who were totally committed to the latihan and the knowledge of its importance to mankind.

Bapak seemed strong in those days. On one visit he was eating a sweet, which was very unusual. He told me that his doctor had advised him to stop smoking. It did not take him long to follow this advice. After a few visits, I noticed that he dispensed with the substitute sweets as well.

I used my own inner guidance as to how long to stay. I visited Bapak in this informal way many times. Then, just as I had spontaneously started visiting him, one day I stopped. From this I learnt something very important—that the impulse to be near someone who is sensitive and caring like Bapak must come from one's inner perception. If it comes from the heart, things can go very wrong. I also learnt that Bapak was like a mirror. If I were to see him, I had to be separated from myself—meaning my emotions—which otherwise only reflected myself back to me.

Towards the end of 1972, I was walking in the compound one evening when I noticed several overseas visitors, Richard Engels from Germany, Francis von Kahler from the USA, Edward van Hien from England, and one or two others. I told Erling about this. "Why this unannounced arrival?"

"Because the bank will be moved from Germany to Indonesia," he said.

This was such a preposterous idea that I was incredulous. I had seen how money could be mismanaged in Indonesia. In a few days, it was announced that the bank would be moved to Jakarta.

The Spiritual and the Material

In February 1973, we were surprised when Bapak's family told us that Bapak had the "flu"—his good health was legendary. Bapak's son Haryono with his wife, Ismana, who had been staying in England, suddenly appeared in Wisma Subud. Days went by until finally we learnt that Bapak had been attending a meeting about the bank in the house of one of the Indonesian members in the compound when he became ill and had to leave. He had had a severe heart attack.

I remember one of the residents saying to me that she was quite angry because the truth had been kept a secret. However, I could understand that it was better for this to be kept quiet for a while until the prognosis was clear.

The attending doctors were amazed at Bapak's recovery. He carried on without complaint or concern. As his condition improved, he would go for morning walks and often ended up at the secretariat office. One Tuesday morning I was the rostered duty helper for the 11:00 A.M. women's latihan and went to unlock the hall. I had been told that Tuti had the key and that she was in the secretariat. I found one door of the hall unlocked and entered. As I approached the inner door that led to the secretariat, I could hear Bapak talking inside.

To avoid disturbing him, I opened the door very slightly and called to Tuti to give me the key. Bapak heard me and asked me to come in and sit down. He proceeded with his talk, now directing himself to me. He talked about his Ascension experience. Sjarif was translating but I could also understand what Bapak was saying in Indonesian. He then said to me, "Very few people know who Bapak really is. Haryadi, Bapak's son who died, he knew. Rochanawati, she knew. Rahayu, yes, but only since Ibu's death. And the other one who knows is your daughter, Sandra."

Although Bapak was less active during the year following his heart attack, the momentum continued in the Brotherhood. Subud Brotherhood International Foundation (SBIF), set up to hold donations and legacies in trust for the support of Subud activities, was incorporated in Switzerland. National and Zonal Congresses were held. Members all over the world started business enterprises and welfare projects—schools, homes for the aged, refuges for orphans, medical supplies to under-developed countries, and others.

David was opened on the eighteenth of April 1973, Palm Sunday, by Erling. He was seventeen. In June he graduated from high school and in August he left for the University of California at Berkeley, to study architecture.

Chapter Ten

Bapak meanwhile initiated a project to build a large office building on one of Jakarta's principal avenues. This commercial venture was also to provide space on its ground floor for the Subud bank. Like all of Bapak's projects, it seemed at first far beyond our means, but members all over the world invested and it was able to slowly proceed. IDC, the Subud architects and engineers in Wisma Subud, at this time enjoyed some success in designing schools and factories and a township in Sulawesi, expanding its staff to more than sixty employees. They were able to take on the engineering of the office building which, when completed, was to be a prestige twelve-storey tower, with the Shell Oil Company, the British Council and other important tenants.

Whilst this emphasis on business occupied many people, the latihan and Bapak's talks continued to be my reason for being in Indonesia.

Cathy was opened on the sixteenth of January 1975, a few months before her eighteenth birthday. Aminah and Mrs Irman, both long-time helpers living in Wisma Subud, conducted the opening. I stood well apart, following my guidance not to get my heart involved. Her opening meant that Mayko, Cathy, and I were now all doing the latihan.

I remember one morning, perhaps the first time we went together to the 11:00 A.M. latihan, the three of us in long skirts ascending the wide gradual stairs to the hall. Keeping my eyes averted from other things, I measured my pace to harmonise with Cathy, acutely aware of the importance of the occasion. It had for me a special quality—the feeling of continuity of three generations, fulfilled and enhanced with the ultimate dimension of sharing in the worship of God.

Erling spent six years as Chairman of the Buildings and Grounds Committee of the Board of the Joint Embassy School of Jakarta, responsible for building a high school for almost two thousand students. This school was not only the place of education for foreign children, including ours, but it also provided work for a number of Subud members as teachers. Through their employment in the school, they were able to get visas to stay in Indonesia and be near Bapak.

Erling was meticulous about justice and honesty in business dealings and was a champion of those in difficulty. As a result he often attracted people who felt that they had been wrongly treated. Their problems included matters ranging from obtaining visas to investment conditions for Subud projects. In his contacts with the business community he enjoyed considerable respect, and was the representative in Jakarta, on a part-time basis, for a large American bank.

The Spiritual and the Material

Now Erling began to consider leaving Indonesia. When a chance came for us to sell our house in Wisma Subud, he took it and we moved to a rented house in Jakarta to settle our affairs. We travelled back and forth to Wisma Subud for latihan and Bapak's talks and to visit Mayko, who did not want to leave the compound. My brother came from Chile to keep Mayko company.

Our maid, Clementina, meantime had met and married an Indonesian. He was a driver for the American Embassy, taking children to the same school that Sandra attended. He was a very nice man and agreed that Clementina continue to live with us and take care of Sandra up to the time when we would leave. She insisted on remaining Catholic although he was Muslim. Later the combination of Chilean and Indonesian produced three most beautiful children.

During this time I had a strange experience which connected me to the unconscious processes of my psyche. It happened after buying bulk wheat from the flour mill. Noticing that they sold off the wheat-germ cheaply with the bran, a friend suggested that I package it for the local supermarket. The discussion became suddenly charged when, after considering the abbreviation of Istimah's—Is's—as a label, we came to the name Isis. I immediately felt that there was something significant about this name although to my knowledge I had never heard of the Egyptian goddess or of her consort Osiris and the birth of Horus. A strange excitement overcame me as I read the myth in the encyclopedia. This was my first indication of a contact with my unconscious through symbolism such as is contained in myth. Later I would be going through very intense inner experiences, which had, to my mind, symbolic parallels with the Isis story. Already I felt strangely moved by forces that indicated inner changes that were beyond my understanding. My dreams were to become more symbolic as they became deeper. It was the beginning of a long period of encounter with the unconscious depths of myself.

In September 1975 we decided it was time for us to leave Indonesia.

What lay below the water-line of my consciousness was the development of my individuality through the confrontation of opposing principles and conflicts of duty. My process was to be no picnic. A prayer awoke me in the night: 'Almighty God, have mercy on me in the days of my dole.'

Chapter Eleven
Helpers and Being Helped

At the end of my stay in Indonesia, an inner locution had started which repeatedly said, "Christ is in Heaven." It would come and go of its own accord. With this I later found it unbearable to look at Christ crucified. Although this had to do with my inner process, it was real enough outside. When I went to church, I chose not to look at Christ on the Cross. If I accidentally saw a crucifix, it would bring me to tears. Perhaps this was the development of something that had started as early as 1969, when I had a half-awake vision of seeing the top of a hill and on it Christ crucified. Next I saw him off the cross and in the arms of Mary.

I knew that "Christ is in Heaven" meant the Christ within. Therefore the feeling I had, that the crucifixion should not be prolonged and that Christ had come down from the Cross, referred to my own inner process.

It was with great interest that I later read C.G. Jung's view that the reconciliation with the divine self, represented by Christ, would in our era be no longer after death. The new psychological status of our age is, he said, " ... that man will be essentially God and God man." * Here was a re-phrasing of Bapak's startling statement, "Now God has come Himself."

Now I went with Sandra to Hawaii to await Erling, who still had business to settle in Jakarta. Mayko stayed in Wisma Subud, and Cathy returned to the farm in New Zealand.

One day I was doing latihan with two women in our rented apartment in Honolulu when the words started to come, "Christ is in Heaven ..." but this time it continued, "... and the Devil ..." I stopped my latihan; I did not want the Devil in my latihan. I started to do latihan again, and the same words repeated. Immediately I stopped as before, leaving the sentence unfinished. Then a voice inside me said, "You must let it come." I obeyed and the message and the words came, "Christ is in Heaven and the Devil is in the darkness of systems."

---
* C.G. Jung, letter to Father Victor White in 1954.

Chapter Eleven

As this was happening, I was given to understand that the completion of the inner locution was arising because one of the helpers present was a symbol of a systematic person.

This interior message stayed and on many occasions afterwards helped me to understand the forces at work in human relationships.

OUR DECISION to leave Indonesia was something that had been arrived at gradually. As well as spending many hours a week on the construction of the Joint Embassy School, Erling had been a consultant to an Indonesian firm negotiating joint ventures with foreign companies. By 1975 the school was substantially complete and the inflow of new projects to the Indonesian company had slowed down due to Indonesia's financial recession the year before when world oil prices collapsed. Erling felt his time in Indonesia was coming to a logical close.

On the other hand, I had become totally integrated into life in Indonesia. I could have continued to live there happily, but I also identified with Erling's situation. In retrospect it was right on many levels for us to leave. My contribution to Subud and Bapak's mission had become limited, since Indonesian helpers looked after Indonesian members. Outside of Indonesia I could share my experience, gained by living near Bapak. Nevertheless I found leaving Indonesia very difficult, and I was especially sad to be leaving Bapak.

We returned to New Zealand in January 1976 and found a house to rent in Howick, south of Auckland. We joined in the activities of the Auckland Subud group, and after three months or so, I was asked to join the helpers group. We were seven women helpers and met once a week for a latihan at the Subud House in Sandringham. We became very close. Everyone was dedicated to carrying out their helper's duties as well as possible. At our meetings there was a conscious commitment to our inner state. We did not socialise, or break for tea, until our spiritual work was done. In this way, and by testing together, trust grew between us and we gained the respect of the members when they needed help with their problems.

As the year went on, I found myself concerned with the question of choice in the human condition. I observed that often we did not exercise free choice—our actions were mostly reactions. Meantime in the helpers' group, we began testing more questions arising from our own needs. With time, the questions became deeper and more personal.

Suddenly I had a breakthrough. In testing how to handle one of my emotions, I experienced a state of clear separation between myself and my reaction. This state showed me the possibility of choice.

I had tested (to re-experience my emotion) : 'What was my reaction?' Then immediately tested again: 'How is the feeling of being inwardly separated from both the forces outside (coming from the situation) and the forces inside (coming from my own reaction to the problem)?'

The clarity of the resulting separated state was remarkably different. In the first test, I was emotional. In the second test, I was inwardly separated from the emotion. After the test I felt free of the problem and at peace.

Bapak had mentioned separation when I was leaving Indonesia. I had asked him about Mayko's situation. I said, "Bapak, I am leaving Mayko here, but I am worried. She has many problems."

"Ah," Bapak answered, "Bapak is the same. Bapak has all sorts of problems. The difference is that Bapak can *separate* but Mayko cannot. Not yet!"

Now I understood from my own experience what he had meant.

In our helpers' group, we began to talk and test about it, seeking to understand. We asked to be shown, in the latihan, how it affects our feelings and consequently our soul to live in a state of inner separation, versus being caught by our emotions, thoughts, fixed ideas, and so on. We were able to experience how liberating it was to separate inwardly, and that our normal state was an unconscious condition where we had no choices—only actions and reactions in continuous motion. This insight was to have an important influence on my life and to be a recurring theme in all my succeeding helper's work. I saw that this condition was inherent in the latihan. Bapak had described it in terms of life forces:

That is why in the latihan one really feels that one's inner self is no longer influenced by the passions, heart and mind, which means that in the latihan the inner feeling has truly been separated from their influence.

Why should the passions, heart and mind be separated from the inner feeling, when these are man's most important equipment for his life in this world, which can be used to increase and broaden his knowledge? It is because, unless the passions, heart and mind are separated from the inner feeling, it will not be able to be in a pure state in receiving the latihan, so that it will be impossible for the inner feeling to receive the contact from the Great Life Force which, in fact, has permeated it inwardly and outwardly.

Chapter Eleven

This is the reason why the influence of the passions, heart and mind must be separated from the inner feeling. In such a state the inner feeling will awaken and be able to recognise the existence of the various kinds of life forces which flow in and out and move it.

Eventually it will be able to distinguish between the good and the bad, namely, between the life force that originates from the true human self and the life forces that come from the sub-human forces. i.e., the material, vegetable and animal life forces and the life force of man.

In receiving the latihan, the one who receives is truly guided by the power of Almighty God towards the attainment of an ability to distinguish between the various kinds of life forces in man (chemistry in the spiritual realm) and this will eventually lead to the realisation of his true self and elimination of the false one. [39]

Like many members I had come to live in a less reactive way as a consequence of the latihan, without defining it as separation. Now, my testing had heightened the experience so that I could see it much more clearly. Bapak explained in a later talk why there were degrees of awareness of separation:

Bapak wants to explain to you about the word 'I'. The word 'I' is a very important thing to have and use. But if you misunderstand it or misuse it, or if you are not clear about it, then it can also be very dangerous, because we say all the time, "I do this" or "I do that" or "I know that." But who is 'I'?

The nature of a human being embraces what we call the lower forces. These are elements of life in this world which participate in our being and through which we are able to live here. They start with the material force. If we were oblivious to this force, we would be unable to create our houses, clothes, transport and so on. Then there is the vegetable life force, which we get from eating and so makes up our physical body. The animal force comes to us through the meat and microscopic organisms.

Then there is the life force of human beings. All these and higher forces co-inhabit our being. These are our friends. So we have to be aware of them, and we have to live with them and know how to deal with them. If we really knew it, God has been incredibly wise, kind and perfect in what he has created for us in this world. But these life forces are only for this world. They accompany us only to the threshold of death, because beyond that we no longer need them and we no longer can share our life with them.

Helpers and Being Helped

To repeat, our being is filled with life forces, each of which is vying for influence within our being. [We feel them as our needs, wishes and desires.] So when we say 'I', it's not at all easy to be clear who is 'I' and who is influencing 'I' at that moment.*

The purpose and significance of the latihan kejiwaan is to enable us to experience the separation of 'I' from all the lower forces which manifest within us through the nafsu (passions). The latihan trains us to constantly experience the separation of 'I', or our real 'I', from all these lower forces so that gradually we get to know who is 'I' when 'I' is no longer influenced by the material, vegetable, animal and the human.

It is this distinction, this separation, that is the significance of the latihan kejiwaan in our life.

To do this [separation], you have been given something that you are aware of as being alive within your life. ... This life-within-your-life is the action of the power of Almighty God. It is something that God has placed within your being.

The power of God is in everything he has created. ... The only difference is: Which of His creatures are aware of this presence of the power of God and which of them is not aware of it? This is the distinction which becomes apparent in the latihan kejiwaan. [40]

We had tested separation as an action to be applied to a particular problem. We soon realised that ideally it should be our natural condition all the time—and one which we can progress towards, even though most of us may never fully achieve it.

Meantime our small helpers group settled down to work well together. We were using testing the way Bapak had done—to show a possibility that already existed in our latihan. We were not getting ahead of the person's progress, and we were not introducing a teaching or a method.

When testing a question with a member, we would start out by agreeing that she should try to receive the answer for herself, rather than rely on us (the helpers). We would simply stand by as witnesses—receiving the answer in our latihan.

---

* C.G. Jung describes the same dilemma in psychological terms: "We have got accustomed to saying ... 'I have such a desire or habit or feeling of resentment,' instead of the more veracious 'Such and such a desire or habit or feeling of resentment *has me*.' " *Collected Works 11*, pars. 138-49.

Mary Watkins in referring to Gurdjieff's claim that we spend most of our lives in a state of waking sleep also puts it clearly. "As our thoughts, feelings, and actions come to the edge of our conscious field, our awareness goes out to meet them and merges with them. As our awareness becomes absorbed and attached to the emotion, thought or action, *we become it.*" *Waking Dreams*, 1971.

Chapter Eleven

After the test the member would (voluntarily) describe her experience and only then would we, if requested, state our receiving. In this way the member had the opportunity to clarify her own experience without any overt influence from the helpers.

We found that this was desirable for two reasons. The member's own receiving, if clear, carried more conviction than someone else's, and secondly, the member remained responsible for her own guidance.

A helper, however, sometimes made the mistake of giving an interpretation or an explanation instead of describing her own receiving. The helper would start thinking and give an opinion, so losing touch with the immediacy of the test. This was due to the helper's lack of experience and could confuse the member and the other helpers.

A common form of interpretation was the use of examples. I found that examples were unnecessary and distracting to a person (with the latihan) who was trying to find her inner guidance. Examples come from the heart and mind and draw our awareness away from the inner feeling and into the realm of emotion and thought.

There were many signs that someone in a testing session had lost touch with her inner feeling: an irrelevant discussion would start up, a helper would attempt to console someone with kind words or a hug, another would begin to weep while giving an explanation—tears were sometimes a sign (of the error) that someone was using her heart to try to solve a spiritual question—and so on.

We also practised Bapak's suggested testing to experience various parts of the body being moved by the life force of the latihan. One form was simply for the helper to ask the member to show: "What is it like when you walk in the ordinary way?" . . . After that to ask, by contrast: "What is it like when your legs walk from the latihan?" They would then move from the latihan. This might be followed by similar tests for the hands and so on.

Later as a National Helper, I found that testing movement of the body, could be helpful before starting testing for guidance. I started by asking: "Show how the legs move from the latihan?" then continued up the body to the arms and head, and finally requested: "Now, do the latihan moving all parts of the body." * The latihan of the participants deepened, and their receiving in the testing that followed became more clear.

---

* When Bapak did this testing with us he often added the voice and the eyes, and sometimes the feeling and the awareness.

Helpers and Being Helped

Bapak had from time to time approached our experience of the latihan from a new point of view. I realised that we in turn had to avoid the tendency to turn his tests or explanations into methods or systems.

In our helpers' work, we came across the misunderstanding that surrender in Subud—in confronting problems in daily life—was the same as just giving up. Even a helper might be heard to say to someone with a problem, "Just surrender it" (meaning, put the concern out of your mind). Such acts of empty abandonment led to nothing. If however the problem could be made clear and conscious by testing in the latihan, then the surrender could be with direction.

Later, Bapak gave a talk in Melbourne which addressed this important issue. He said:

This matter of testing applies not only to external questions, but actually applies to everything, including your own nature, including your own latihan. Bapak wants to explain to you that you should never be apathetic. Yes, it is true, you have to surrender in the latihan, we surrender to Almighty God, but surrendering does not mean being apathetic, it does not mean accepting just whatever happens, without wanting to understand why. [41]

As time went on, I found that this attentiveness was also a prerequisite for bringing the latihan into daily life, in particular when pausing before acting. When, in this pause, I became aware of my inner feeling, I experienced the benefit of being inwardly separated. I called it making space for inner guidance, or contacting my inner self, or simply being more conscious. If I didn't forget my latihan, things went better. If I was forgetful or careless in what I did, I was often reminded by something going wrong. Learning this didn't happen quickly, but the more I practised pausing and getting in touch with my inner feeling, the more it became a way of life.

In early 1979, I was selected to become one of the three National Helpers. This meant that although my main activity was still attending the local helpers' group, I was to represent them nationally and keep in touch with the New Zealand membership through travel and correspondence. I became active in making arrangements for national weekend helpers' gatherings held in the major cities. In parallel with the outer preparation, I could feel each time an inner preparation take place. On one occasion, a few days before a meeting of women helpers from all over New Zealand in Christchurch, I received: *'El corazon que esta empapado con la dicha de Dios no puede pecar'.* ('The heart that is drenched with the Joy of God cannot sin.')

Chapter Eleven

The meeting was typical of our twice-a-year helpers' gatherings, starting Friday evening and finishing Sunday afternoon, with the time totally devoted to latihan and to testing. There were twenty or so women. It was lovely to see them all at their best, feminine in their dress and sincere in their commitment. Some who had been burdened by problems already started to look relaxed and free and those who were full-time housewives and mothers with big families were able to step out of their roles and be themselves.

We tested to find the obstacles to progress in our latihan. Each helper was tested in turn, with the person being tested reporting first on her receiving. The other helpers then related their receiving, usually giving similar results but from different viewpoints. This was very helpful and left us with a close feeling for each other.

Some of the women had brought marital problems to be tested. Out of this came a great deal of understanding about the masculine and feminine. By testing how it is when she acts from her feminine nature and alternatively from her masculine nature, a woman was able to come to a new understanding about herself. This did not mean that all problems were resolved. It was often like planting a seed.

Testing with a woman to find out how her husband felt when she acted from her feminine nature and alternatively from her masculine nature, often enabled her to understand her partner's reactions. In this way she became responsible for herself. This feminine-masculine testing also showed how the impulse of women to be themselves, very evident in the world today, could be used by the unconscious masculine—resulting in an unbecoming aggressiveness and loss of feminine relatedness.

The women helpers were interested to know when they were acting from their feminine, and when they were acting from their masculine side. By further testing we found that if we could "observe" in a state of separation, we could function either from our feminine or from our masculine side, without being caught up unconsciously. Then, if we could do this, we could act from the masculine side, without losing touch with our femininity.

Being a helper had its occasional trials. During one of our national gatherings, a member, who was very antagonistic towards the helpers, decided to take the opportunity to tell us all the reasons why helpers were no good.

Helpers and Being Helped

We listened to everything that she had to say and then asked her to join us in a latihan. As a result, she became very quiet and her attitude changed completely. The latihan had resolved what we could not.

In April 1981, the New Zealand National Helpers were invited to attend the Australian Congress in Brisbane. There, we shared with our Australian counterparts much of what we had been doing in our women's meetings. This led, some weeks later, to the Australians arranging their own national gathering at St. John's College in Sydney, and inviting New Zealand helpers.

This and subsequent gatherings of helpers and members from the two countries, devoted entirely to the spiritual, were very successful. They gave helpers the opportunity to widen their experience and members the chance to have prolonged periods of latihan and testing together, as only helpers had done up until that time. It became clear that there was a place in Subud for national gatherings devoted entirely to the spiritual—as distinct from National Congresses where organisational matters dominated the agenda.

From that time on, efforts were made in New Zealand and Australia to hold a helpers' gathering over several days as a prelude to each National Congress. This way of 'putting the latihan first' resulted in the succeeding Congress being more fruitful and harmonious. Helpers had become active (where they had been passive) in contributing to the tone and environment in which the committee side carried out its work.

In parallel with the helpers' work, my own process of purification accelerated. Although I became more aware of the needs and feelings of others, sometimes my own process was difficult to resolve. My dreams seemed to show that I was purifying my ancestral traits and the effects of my childhood. I experienced at times extreme inner affliction. In my reading of C. G. Jung, I found confirmation when he described individuation as a process marked by inner conflict.

During this time, Sandra's spiritual capacity was becoming more evident. One day soon after our arrival in New Zealand, when she was ten, I was giving her breakfast before school. As I stood nearby wondering to myself about a dream that I had had that morning, she said, "Mum, I just saw something. It was right in front of me on top of the table. I saw with my eyes open, a vision." She described a man with a long white beard and his house. He had seven white doves.[*]

---

[*] Seven white doves symbolise the seven gifts of the Holy Spirit. *Ad de Vries*. In Catholicism these are Wisdom, Understanding, Counsel, Fortitude, Knowledge, Piety, and Fear of the Lord.

Chapter Eleven

The man with the long white beard (whom Sandra called 'the magician') was the wise old man—an archetypal character symbolising a source of wisdom.* This vision signalled the beginning of a process by which Sandra could respond to another person's need by seeing a vision containing the necessary insight. My unspoken concern about my dream had been the trigger in this case.

At the time, because the experience was so new, it didn't occur to me that the imagery in the vision was connected with my dream. Subsequent visions showed that the appearance of "the white magician" symbolised the arrival of archetypal wisdom, which was then conveyed either by what he said or by the associated images. Over the next fifteen years, Sandra saw hundreds of visions, drawing many into my diaries as she accompanied me through my process of purification.

Sandra's visions** included many new and recurring figures. As an example, one evening in January 1977 just before dark, she and I were out for a bike ride when suddenly she said, "Mummy, I saw a vision where I was riding my bicycle in the sky. There was a fire and I rode through it without thinking. Past the fire I saw all those figures that appear in my visions: Moses, Jesus, The White Magician, Santa Teresa (of Avila), Mary (the mother of Jesus), and the beautiful woman with the two-coloured dress who holds the round ball full of spikes."†

Sometimes Sandra had a vision about herself, like the following when she was fourteen. I was driving her home from school when she suddenly said, "Mum, I just saw a large white eagle. It was above the car when it swooped down. It came inside me and turned around to face the direction I was facing. It had hazel eyes that possessed a majestic and intuitive power. The eyes seemed to be able to see through someone and penetrate into their soul. Also through them, I seemed to see beyond our world into other and unknown worlds."

In May 1977, in partnership with another Subud family, we bought a four-hectare property in Whitford, south of Howick, on the waterfront. Cathy meanwhile continued to live independently on Waiheke Island. She wrote to Bapak saying she wanted to change her name. She asked Bapak to give her the complete name, not an initial. He gave her the name Erica.

* C.G. Jung, *Archetypes of the Collective Unconscious and Four Archetypes,* par. 398

** Sandra's visions were always in a waking and conscious state, as distinct from dreams.

† Sandra's visions contained universal (archetypal) symbolism, so it was often possible to make interpretations in the context of the situation. However, after some time Sandra began to simultaneously receive the meaning with the vision.

Helpers and Being Helped

In June, Bapak set out on a world journey and suggested Mayko stay with us in New Zealand while he was away.

THE THIRTY-DAY Ramadhan fast in 1977 ended on September 15, and in accordance with custom, we celebrated with a selamatan at Auckland Subud House. The following morning I awoke after a striking dream:

I had heard that Bapak had, on his previous trip, tested some very strong things—frightening things, experiences in the body. I had not been there, but now Bapak would test again. Bapak appeared as an ancient Oriental sage wearing a robe, not at all in appearance like the Bapak I knew. He was old, very wise, and very powerful. He stood in front of the audience, and I was in about the fourth row. We sat on benches and in front of us were wooden rails like the backs of pews where we could rest our hands.

To my right sat another Bapak quite different from the one in front but equally respected and powerful. It was as if the Bapak in front were directing the spiritual life and the Bapak sitting next to me was more of this world. It was an honour that he sat next to me. Everyone knew this.

When the testing started, it was to do with smelling an acrid smell. The ceremony was unique. I put my hands on the wooden rail as if in prayer and the Bapak next to me did the same, following my movement. Another test began and the same thing was repeated. Again this was an honour.

There was much expectation among the people that the third test would be very difficult. Something happened in the ceremony which was not clear to me, but then the Bapak in front directed his attention to me and said, "You will be given a task." He spoke as if he knew all about my future. He handed me a long, narrow book which opened as he did so. He then said, "My daughter, you will be given the task of repairing Indonesia." Someone sitting to my left asked, "Will this happen in Indonesia?" "No," the answer came, "She will work outside." I felt slightly disappointed, for I liked being in Indonesia.

Then I turned to the Bapak on my right and said, "I heard every word of the instruction he gave to me except for one word and that made me miss the entire meaning. What is it?"

The Bapak next to me replied, "You must not listen to every word, you must . . . ." "Get the feeling?" I asked. "Yes, get the feeling," he said.

That was the end of the dream.

Chapter Eleven

On September 26, a Monday, my neighbour drove me to Howick to do some shopping, with the understanding that Erling and Mayko would pick me up later. In the car Erling said to me casually, "There was a phone call for you from Sjarif Horthy (Bapak's translator) in Canada. Bapak asks if Istimah can join him in Latin America to help with the translations, travelling from Argentina to Mexico. I asked him to call you back later." When Sjarif called again, he said that Bapak had been prompting him to call me sooner, but he had allowed other activities to interfere and delay him. He then gave me the schedule for the stops in South America and Mexico and the flight numbers.

I deduced from what Sjarif said about his delay in calling me, that Bapak's first request to him to contact me had occurred close to the time of my dream. I understood that the dream had explained to me the right way to translate Bapak's talks—to get the "feeling" of what he was saying. If I tried to get the single words, I would, as it said in the dream, "miss the entire meaning." I was to find this advice very helpful.

As for "the task of repairing Indonesia," I had left Indonesia in accordance with the needs of the family. However, Indonesia was for me as least as much a state of feeling as a place and leaving for New Zealand broke my connection with that state. Bapak, in his intuitive wisdom, or as the channel for God's grace, was now offering me a chance to repair that state of feeling, which was so fundamental to my connection with my true nature and purpose in life. What was in the dream "an honour," to be with the living Bapak to translate, was shown to have a deeper purpose. I was to be given, by the wise and ancient spiritual Bapak, the task of repairing my feeling of connection with Bapak's mission.

The arrangements went well. Erling was able to get me a seat on every one of the flights on Bapak's itinerary. I decided to go earlier and spend some time in Chile.

I left for Santiago on my birthday, October 6, 1977. As the plane flew above the snow-covered Andes, I felt a surge of exhilaration and realised how I had missed my country. I entered the city in the evening and checked myself into one of the hotels that I remembered. How nice it was to see that nothing had changed. I left my luggage and immediately went to the church that I had so often attended. In the morning I phoned Toti Davanzo, whom I had last seen in Indonesia. "Recognise my voice?" I teased, provoking a Chilean scream of excitement.

Helpers and Being Helped

In no time her husband Fernando came to pick me up and invited me to stay in their house. When he heard the reason for my appearance he joked, "You are Bapak's favourite!" I laughed. I knew from my dream, that there was more to it than that.

I had been away from Chile for fifteen years. Now I realised how much I had missed hearing my language. Chilean Spanish is unique and my emotions delighted in its nuances. It awakened subtle memories like long-forgotten fragrances. I met my brother, still full of his masculine ideas. "How could Bapak use a woman as his translator?" he said . . . but as always with his huge laugh! Toti drove me to see the house where I had lived when I was single, to complete the nostalgia.

I flew to Buenos Aires to await Bapak. He was arriving from Rio de Janeiro and was in the fifth month of an eight-month round-the-world tour. I heard that since he brought the latihan to the West in 1957 he had travelled almost a million kilometres visiting Subud groups, equivalent to twenty-one times around the globe. He arrived on October 20. My first impression was how well he looked. Wearing a light coloured gaberdine suit and his black petji hat, he stood straight and walked at his usual easy pace, relaxed and smiling. He appeared more in his sixties than seventy-six. With him were Rahayu, Mastuti, Tuti and Muti, and Sjarif as English translator.

Over the next five weeks, we were to travel from Buenos Aires to visit Subud groups in Santiago in Chile, Lima in Peru, Quito in Equador, Cali and Bogota in Colombia, and Mexico City, all Spanish-speaking groups.

Bapak immediately held latihans, conducted testing, and gave talks. I noticed that he brought an increased frankness to what he said. The openness of Latin peoples may have encouraged this directness, but this was also to be one of Bapak's last major world journeys. There was a new urgency I had not detected before. He spelled out the world's need for the latihan and our obligation to take care of it. He gave nineteen full-length talks and numerous short ones during these seven stops.

Without any preparation, beyond the instructions given to me in my dream, I proceeded to translate Bapak's talks into Spanish from Sjarif's English translation. This included attending the men's latihans where Bapak did testing. I also translated for Rahayu and Sjarif in their conversations with members and helpers. It all went very smoothly.

Chapter Eleven

In many of these talks, Bapak used a mythical story about two sons of Adam to illustrate the difference between Subud and other spiritual groups who follow a way of study with the mind. He re-emphasised that the latihan kejiwaan of Subud is a receiving of the Power of God. You don't have to study, he said, because the kejiwaan is in the hands of God:

It is told that after Adam was created, he had many sons. . . . In this story two are particularly mentioned, whose names were Sajid Anwar and Sajid Anwas.

Now Sajid Anwar followed completely in the footsteps of his father—in other words, in the way of life and the attitude of his father, which meant that in his life he surrendered himself completely to the will of God and patiently followed and received whatever God willed for him. So that the way that was followed by Adam, and also by Sajid Anwar, is actually the same as that which we have received in the latihan kejiwaan. This is also the way that was received by all the Prophets and Messengers of God—for example by Abraham, Moses, Jesus Christ, and Muhammad. It is said that all the Prophets and the Messengers of God were actually descended from Sajid Anwar.

But Sajid Anwas was different because he did not agree with the way that was followed by his father and by his brother. Maybe he felt that this way did not require enough work, or that it was too easy, or that it didn't make sufficient use of man's intelligence, or maybe he felt that the way that they followed was too slow. So he set to work by way of meditation, by way of samadi [concentration of thought], by way of emptying and negating the self through practising asceticism, through reducing food and sleep, through giving up all the pleasures of life, and by isolating himself far from society and other people.

God is all-loving, God is all-giving to his creatures, so whatever man desires, whatever man hopes for, God will give him in the measure of his strength. And indeed the strength of Sajid Anwas was very great, so that when he practiced asceticism, when he refrained from sleep and from food, he did not do it for one or two days, or one or two weeks, he did it for years. So that finally God gave Sajid Anwas that which he wished for. Sajid Anwas became a being whose life could not be measured. . . . He indeed became a very powerful being and from him descended all the dewas [gods]. He changed his name from Sajid Anwas to Sang Hyang Sis [which has the same root as Zeus, the Greek god]. Later he changed his name again to Sang Hyang Nur Chakior [which means brilliant (like a light)].

Helpers and Being Helped

Brothers and sisters, with this background, it's not surprising that in the world today people still follow this way. Of course, they do not do it with the strength or the same power that was possessed by Sajid Anwas, but still they try to follow the same way. That is why Bapak leaves it to you, if you wish to choose that way. . . . [42]

"This latihan," Bapak said, "is not the way of Sajid Anwas [meditation or self denial], but is the way of Sajid Anwar [surrender to Almighty God]."

In Bapak's comments on helper's responsibility, he explained why he had had to make this journey. Addressing the helpers in Buenos Aires, he said:

Bapak has heard that there are members who are opened and after a short time leave. Also that among the people in Subud there are still those who don't really feel very much in their latihan. Bapak regrets this, for it shows that the helpers do not really act in a responsible way. It is true that the One who guides is only God Almighty but the helpers have to feel responsible for those they open. They must watch and be aware if a member doesn't receive, and take an attitude of making sure that this person will be able to receive.

Bapak is an example. He is already old and to come to Argentina is a long way, but Bapak forces himself to make the journey because he knows that through Bapak you have all joined Subud and it is Bapak's responsibility to give you explanations which are clear about your duties as helpers. [43]

Bapak went over the purpose of the procedure of opening new members—the need for explanation during the three-month waiting period and for an expression of faith by the new member. He particularly emphasised the basic tenet of the Subud opening—that the helper should do only his own latihan, surrendering himself to the power of God.

When the talks were finished, Bapak visited the home of Mariano Caballero, relaxing in the garden with his family and the members. He received and sang songs. Tuti and I translated. They were like prayers. One that was very beautiful was in Arabic.

I was so used to being entirely with Subud members, that what happened on our arrival in Santiago caught me by surprise. Florencia, a Subud sister who worked at the airport, had arranged for the arrival procedures—immigration, customs, etc.—to be streamlined. As we went through the formalities, I put myself at the end of the line. When it came to my turn, the police on duty in the immigration hall, noticing that I had a Chilean passport, asked me, "Who are these people?" I replied politely that they were my friends.

This didn't satisfy them. The senior one, with a mixture of Latin charm and authority, insisted: "We are the police, Señora, and we want to know who are these people!" I didn't want to get left behind, so I countered by saying "Why do you ask about them in particular?" "Ah!" he said, "The quietness and peace that has come over this place since they arrived is unmistakable. They have something special."

I didn't know what to do. How could I start explaining about Subud to the police? Florencia, who was known to them, appeared and I suggested that she would have time to talk to them later. But they again insisted, so I explained a little about the latihan and they let me go.

Although Bapak repeated his story of Sajid Anwar and Sajid Anwas at several stops, he varied his talks as we travelled from group to group, responding to the situation that he found in each place.

In Lima, he spoke about the place of the latihan in the world situation today. What is sure, he said, is that we are seeing the end of belief. "Intellectuals and intelligent people nowadays find it very difficult to believe in God. They ask, 'What faculty can I use to prove to myself the reality of the Power of God?' It is for this reason that God has given mankind the latihan kejiwaan. Through this latihan we can know the soul." . . .

The heart and mind are the field of man and are limited, while the soul is the field of God and is not localised and can go anywhere. . . . This was proved by the Ascension of Jesus Christ and Prophet Muhammad. . . . [44]

Later I read that Bapak had talked about this in more detail two weeks earlier in Rio de Janeiro:

When the Messengers experienced their Ascension, when they were there, they were able to know and understand everything that happened to them here. . . . And it is quite clear that what went up to heaven and came back again was not the physical body, but the jiwa [soul]. Some ask, "If it was their jiwa [soul], how come that they could still remember—how could they still think and understand?" . . .

This is exactly what we are looking for—to be able to leave this world with our jiwa [soul] and still remember everything that happened to us here. . . . This is what we experience in the latihan, which is when we feel our jiwa [soul]. Are we unconscious? We know very well we are not, because if we are in the latihan [state] and someone taps us on the shoulder, we can immediately turn around and say: "Who is it?" [45]

Helpers and Being Helped

As we boarded the plane for Cali, Tuti laughed and repeated an earlier warning, "Just wait until you get to Colombia, you are in for a surprise!" She wouldn't tell me why. When we got off the plane, I certainly was surprised. The people were so effusive. A crowd pressed around us with a great show of affection and emotion. I remember one lady patting Bapak's cheeks with both her hands and saying to him, "Bapak, you are beautiful!" Bapak just laughed and put his arms in the air. We were almost carried along by the excited members and put into waiting cars. I suddenly found myself separated from the party with no idea where I was going. For a moment I was concerned, but I ended up in the right place. It was arranged that we stay in the large house of Marcos Garces, overlooking the city.

After the first night's talk, Bapak asked the committee to find another place for latihan without a stage, so he could be down among the members during testing. To my amazement they rented the Catholic church. Apparently they were able to arrange it because the land had been donated by our host's grandmother many years ago. It was huge, as large as a cathedral. The benches had been taken out, but nothing else was changed. The altar was there with the crucified Christ, and Bapak's chair was just underneath it.

The latihans were in large groups, two hundred and thirty women in one and two hundred and seventy men in the other. It was here that Bapak had most to say about the conduct of the latihan. With the women, he sat watching them as they followed their spontaneous receiving—making all kinds of movements and sounds. Bapak sent me amongst them to find those who could not feel the latihan. There were seven, and I took them to do latihan later with Rahayu.

Bapak also told Rahayu and me to advise women when things were not right. For example, Bapak said to me, "Look at those two women, hugging each other. Go and separate them!" We were kept very busy.

The next session was latihan with the men, with Bapak, Sjarif, and myself sitting out in front. There were several hundred men and as soon as Bapak said: "Begin!" they broke into a very strong and active latihan. The surge of their loud voices reverberated in the Gothic arches of the church and filled the space around. The latihan went on for a long time. At one point Bapak left for the bathroom and Sjarif went with him, leaving me alone. I thought to myself, *What a strange situation. Here I am, a woman, alone in this large and vigorous men's latihan, moreover inside a Catholic church!*

Chapter Eleven

That morning a young man had come to Bapak to say that he didn't feel anything in the latihan. Now, Bapak observed him in the latihan not far from where we were sitting. Bapak got up and stood in front of the young man to do latihan with him. Nothing happened. Bapak took him by the shoulders and shook him saying, in English, "Move! move!" [meaning, relax, let yourself be moved]. But still he couldn't move. Bapak then went behind him and pushed the back of his knees so his legs collapsed. I knew that only Bapak had the right to do this. The guidelines remained—do not interfere with another person in the latihan!

(Later, in 1983, this same man, when testing with Bapak in Cilandak, moved like the wind. Bapak laughed and said, "And this was the one who could not move in the latihan in Colombia.")

On the Sunday morning we were to leave, Bapak gave a short talk on the verandah overlooking the garden. Afterwards there was a party. Members played guitars and other instruments and sang. Someone asked for a Chilean song, and with it the members called for me to dance. One of the men came and asked me. I was still reluctant, but Bapak said, "Go on, dance with him!" Luckily it was a slow waltz. Bapak and the latihan had brought out the best and the most joyous in us all.

In Mexico the group organised a police escort from the airport. With the aid of wailing sirens, our cars sped non-stop through the world's worst city traffic, arriving in no time at the hotel.

Here, as in Bogota, Bapak talked about talents.

"The fruit of the latihan," he said, "is that it leads us towards our own individuality, towards the development of our own nature and our own talent—that is, what we are really best suited for and which we can do well in this world." We are guided in the latihan as to how to do things in accordance with the soul, he said. For example, how to draw, how to write, and other various forms of work. Bapak followed his talks by testing several people's right work.

Frequently on the trip, Bapak's talks about talents led on to an explanation about business enterprises. He said:

What Bapak means by enterprise is to get yourself used to working in this world in the normal way of working, but at the same time not forgetting the guidance and closeness of the power of God. Although we are using the heart and mind, at the same time we are doing the latihan. . . .

Helpers and Being Helped

If a person dies when they are in the midst of weaving a cloth, and in that weaving is contained the worship of God, then that person will be in the hands of God. This is why Bapak encourages you to do enterprises, because we don't know when we will die—it is essential that we learn, practise and get used to the fact that at every moment, in every action, we are guided by and in contact with the power of Almighty God. [46]

During the trip, Bapak said that he was working on his autobiography, to be published after his death. It included some of his early 1932 spiritual experiences, and he asked me to read from a Spanish translation to the group. One experience was of having a spear thrust into his chest by a robed man who then pulled it out together with a clot of blood. The stranger then placed a radiant object in the wound, and Bapak felt a wonderful freshness spread over his whole body. These experiences were told without interpretation of their symbolism.*

At Bapak's invitation, I continued with him to Los Angeles and San Francisco. At the end of November, I returned home.

Less than two months later, the Christchurch group called and asked me if I would come and help them to prepare for Bapak's visit. Since I had left him in San Francisco, Bapak had travelled to Seattle, Vancouver, Hawaii, and Japan.

Working with the local committee, which found and rented a large furnished house for the party, and I was able to give them details of Bapak's needs. I was joined by Erling, Mayko, David, and Sandra on the day before Bapak's arrival.

I stayed at the house, supervising last-minute preparations, while Bapak and his party were brought from the airport. I first saw him already seated in the living room. In all the years I had known Bapak, I had never seen him look so exhausted. I realised what a stress this long trip around the world, now in its eighth month, must have been.

Bapak was incredibly resilient, and in two days he was looking well again. When Bapak saw Mayko, his face lit up with pleasure. He came across to her and, taking off his ring so as not to cause her any discomfort, he took her hand in both of his and said, "You are going back to Cilandak." Then turning to me he said, "And you take her back." I was deeply touched by his concern for Mayko.

---

* Bapak made no effort to interpret the meaning of the symbolism of any of his experiences.

Chapter Eleven

Bapak's party was the same as in South America: Rahayu, Mastuti, Tuti, Muti, and Sjarif. I was at the house every morning, seeing to Bapak's breakfast, and there I would meet Rahayu and talk about her plans with the women.

Personal questions that had been left unresolved by helpers, were part of every visit. On this occasion I asked Rahayu about a woman who had been married for some time but who could not have children because her husband was infertile. The woman was obsessed with it and was considering alternatives. I explained that it wasn't a question of adoption; she yearned to experience a baby inside herself and was planning artificial insemination.

Rahayu told me of a Subud woman in Indonesia who had had this need—to feel pregnant and to have a baby, and could not. Her problem had been solved when one day she was able to surrender it with complete sincerity. She then went through the experience of the conception, the pregnancy, and the birth of a baby. It took a whole night, and she was left completely satisfied. Regarding artificial insemination, she said she had never had to answer such a question, but she felt, "No, the baby would have no direction." She asked Bapak and he confirmed it, simply saying, "No, it is not right spiritually."

In a talk Bapak mentioned Sandra. He said she was a Subud child who had been able to feel the latihan since infancy. "When she is eighteen," Bapak said, "it will not actually be necessary to open her, but she should go through the formality."

The next time I saw Bapak was at the Subud World Congress in Toronto in August 1979. Four weeks before, as I prepared to sleep, I was experiencing a beautiful latihan, and in this state I slept and dreamed:

I came to a place where Bapak and his family were on tour. Tuti, Muti, and Sjarif were there. Bapak came to talk to us, on stage. Suddenly his heart failed. Those close to him rushed to help him. He was revived. He started talking again. His heart failed again. At this point, while half alive, he gave instructions that some of his heart blood be injected into the white rose in my hands. The rose was mine. It turned pink from the blood that flowed into it. I am not sure if Bapak was revived, but when his heart failed again, he was gone forever.

Next, I was sitting on a bench with the pink rose in my hands. The colour was not solid pink; it was made up of little red veins or lines in the white petals. The stem of the rose was attached to a glass tube containing Bapak's heart blood, which fed the rose.

Helpers and Being Helped

I looked over my left shoulder at my close friend, a Subud member, sitting nearby. I offered him a petal or two as a keepsake. I offered it without cutting it off, because I was not sure if he would want it. I also had a dog on my lap. It had belonged to Bapak and therefore was used to a special life. I was caring for it, but I felt as if its future was now uncertain.

This was a landmark dream. My interpretation of it was that my dependency on Bapak was ending. I was right. Through the latihan, I was now consciously accepting responsibility for myself.

In Toronto at the Fifth Subud International Congress, Bapak's party included Rahayu, Mastuti, Tuti, Muti, and Sjarif. Bapak spoke of his illness. He said he had what was normally considered a dangerous heart condition. For six days and nights, his pulse rate had accelerated to one hundred and sixty. The doctors had said people normally would not survive this condition, so when the heart specialist suggested that Bapak go into hospital, he agreed. Bapak said there had been some trouble with the equipment, but somehow the treatment was successful and his pulse rate returned to seventy-two. From there on, he recovered.

I asked myself why did Bapak have to go through this heart problem if in the end he was given the strength to survive it and was helped to get well? I understood that it was a purification of the heart and Bapak had to go through it for all of us. With the latihan he could go through intense heart activity and survive because it was by the will of God. His experience was symbolic of the unequivocal need for Subud members to experience purification of the heart. Bapak once said:

The heart must change from being [like] earth to water, to air, to light. In earth, a hole can be made and can remain there, but in water although it can be touched, no hole can be made. In air, nothing can touch it and when finally the heart is like light, then all those around want to be near a person with such a heart.*

[Meaning if our heart feeling is solid like earth, we can feel hurt for a long time by what people say or do, whereas if our feeling is fluid, like water, we get over an attack straight away. As our heart becomes cleaner, we are, like air, not touched and finally a heart filled with the light of God gives out blessedness to everyone.]

The Toronto Congress was held during the Ramadhan fast, which gave our meetings a special lightness and harmony. Mayko and my brother (now renamed Latif) were there. Bapak had advised Latif to take Mayko back to Chile.

---

* Original translation not traced.

Chapter Eleven

The stress of living away from her family was becoming too much for Mayko. You are not alone in Cilandak, but you are isolated if you don't speak English or Indonesian. Now the three of us met every night for dinner and had long conversations. In the day Mayko went to Bapak's talks, not bothering with the translation into Spanish. She enjoyed the ambience of people in latihan and the sound of Bapak's voice; that was enough for her.

At the Congress, Bapak spoke about the state of the world:

... The advent of the latihan kejiwaan is connected with the present state of the world. ... At this time, it can be said that humanity is afflicted by a disease of mind and heart which gives rise to all sorts of ills. It has become common for clever people to be spun off their feet by their own cleverness. They amuse themselves by playing games with the lives of the ignorant and deceiving them, and the ignorant are easily influenced by anyone who can cause a stir in the community. Rich people are made giddy by their own riches. This is the sickness of the heart and mind, the sickness of the nafsu (passions). [47]

Bapak did testing with individual members, in front of the full assembly of some sixteen hundred people. It was a measure of the atmosphere of goodwill that people were not embarrassed to be tested individually in front of such a large gathering. He showed how the helpers should test with a member to find his or her talent. One of those he tested was a young South American man who had been unable to find work. Bapak first asked about his interests and capabilities and then tested question after question, persevering until the young man could recognise* his own talent, which was that of a mechanic. This whole episode was very moving, with Bapak showing much care and patience.

At a helpers' meeting called by Bapak to test for the appointment of the first International Helpers, he turned to me and said, "I want you to witness this, so you can see how it is done." Then he tested those National Helpers who were ending their four-year period, and from them nominated four International Helpers for the European Zone.

In December 1979, Erling, Sandra, and I flew to Jakarta to visit Bapak. He was looking well. However, we learned that a week before our arrival, he had again had an acceleration of his heart and was in fact in a delicate condition.

---

* He made movements and gestures.

Helpers and Being Helped

One day during our visit, Bapak sent for us to join him. He talked to us and a few other members about the danger of war. He told us that the situation with Iran was truly dangerous and that war could arise from it. "The world," he said, "is in a state where man can no longer put it in order, and at any moment anything can happen. While man has only personal interests and grabs everything for himself, there can be no order. Only when man can act from his humanity—that humanity that surpasses all barriers—can order come into the world."

Bapak said that even though all that is happening is an act of God Himself, Subud members should pray to God and ask for help, in order to avoid a calamity. Man cannot rely on himself to fix the world; he must turn to God.

Bapak then asked us if we had any questions. Prompted by his comment that man would have to turn to God, I said, "What can we do, as Subud people, to bring this about? For some time now, I have a feeling that there is something I have to do and I don't know what it is." Bapak answered, "In Subud we cannot plan ahead, but we must be aware, so that, when we are meant to act, we do."

Bapak then said, "In Christianity there is the belief that there will be a Second Coming. Bapak has been approached about this question and Bapak has answered that it is up to God." Then, looking directly at me, he said, "People believe the Second Coming to be another man; however this is not so. The Second Coming is . . . a . . . Waiting."

In the context of my question, I understood that Bapak meant the Second Coming would happen in a special inner state of waiting.

Two weeks later Bapak left for Tokyo. We farewelled him at the Big House. It moved me to watch him as he walked to his car. I could see that he could not spare the strength to look or talk to anyone. Brodjo told me later that Bapak said of this journey, "I am bound by my promise." In June 1981, we received an invitation from Bapak for either myself or Erling to join him on a trip around North America. We decided that Erling should go. He met Bapak in Hoboken, New Jersey, and followed him to Washington D.C., Vermont, Vancouver, and Los Angeles. Bapak gave a series of talks which showed the significant development that was taking place in Subud, seventeen of which were published under the title *All of Mankind*.

Chapter Eleven

In May of the following year, Bapak visited New Zealand and stayed at our house in Whitford. With him were Mastuti, Rahayu, Tuti, and Sjarif. People came from all over New Zealand, and from Australia and elsewhere. David was able to come from Papua New Guinea where he was working. Bapak gave seven talks in Auckland and held long latihan and testing sessions. On the last day of his stay, Bapak called for Erling and gave him a new name, Mark. "Mark means strong," Bapak said.

Meantime I had heard regularly about Mayko from Latif in Chile. My concern deepened with every letter. I knew, from having been with her in Cilandak, how painful her purification was. There she had suffered a kind of spiritual anguish. While for me, her affliction was intolerable, she herself never sought for outer help. She told me once that there sometimes spontaneously came to her such a powerful love from God and for God that she had to express it in some way. Without thinking, she would find herself kissing her own hands.

When it had come to my leaving Mayko in Cilandak, I had not been able to stand her suffering. I had gone to see Bapak again. "Bapak," I said, "could some of the helpers do latihan especially with Mayko?" He answered, "Oh no! Mayko's latihan is much higher than all the helpers here; it would only bring her down." There seemed no answer.

One evening just as I was about to go to sleep, an inner voice said, "The best seed is in Mayko Pio." *Pio* in Spanish means pious and devout. It confirmed to me Mayko's attitude to her suffering. This was again what Bapak had said, but because it came from my unconscious self, it brought—as I had often found with dreams—the power to reassure me and help me to accept.

Now that Mayko was in Chile, things became worse. Latif wrote to say she had had a fall. She subsequently had to have an operation on her head and from then on she had been confined to bed, often in a coma. Her situation was again unbearable. I needed to give her love, and I felt completely helpless at a distance.

On December 2, 1982, Mark, Sandra, and I flew to Chile.

I was glad to find that the clinic was in a quiet and pleasant area of Santiago, across the Rio Mapacho from the city centre where there was little traffic. It had been converted from an old residence of good quality with high ceilings. Mayko had a big room to herself on the main floor, neat but rather stark, her bed, one chair, and a small closet.

Helpers and Being Helped

The window shutters were drawn, and as I approached the bed in the dim light, Mayko seemed deeply asleep or perhaps unconscious. I stood at her bedside and wept uncontrollably. When I became composed, I began the latihan.

Day after day I returned alone to do latihan with her. I surrendered myself utterly to God. Even though Mayko was in deep sleep, her body would move about vigorously with her latihan. Each day the movements became finer and quieter, the feeling more delicate. I became increasingly sensitive to her state and mine. I felt as if her final ties to this world were loosening.

Latif and I visited Mayko with the doctor. This time she was conscious; maybe the nurses had not drugged her because the doctor was coming. Latif asked Mayko for a kiss and asked, "You do remember me?" She answered, "Hmm," and gave him a kiss. As she lay there awake, my connection with her made me acutely aware of her extreme sensitivity. I suffered, as even the sound of the doctor talking to Latif seemed to me loud. When they left I stayed, gently stroking her hair.

One day I asked a friend to join me. She said afterwards that her own latihan had changed. "It became," she said, "very deep, wide and filled with eternity." Later she told me that this deep latihan had stayed with her all day and kept her awake during the night. "It was like a bright light extending beyond my body. I could not turn it off."

After New Year, at the end of a latihan with her, I felt guided to say inwardly, "Mayko, when God calls you, don't be afraid to leave. There is nothing much more in this world for you." I then went with my friend to hear Mass at the Grotto of the Virgin of Lourdes, the church I used to go to as a teenager.

Mayko passed away early next morning, January 6, 1983. I went immediately to the clinic. I entered her room. I saw her body, yet I clearly felt that Mayko had gone, completely gone. I didn't cry. I felt relieved. At last, I thought, God has freed her from a sad and sick body. I did latihan once again. I was so grateful that I had been given the opportunity to do latihan with her these last weeks before she left this world. How extremely important it had been to make contact with her again.

That Mayko had left this world on the dawn of the day following my inner message felt to me like a confirmation that she had been waiting for me to come, to do latihan with her, and to assure her that it was all right to leave.

Chapter Eleven

Many relatives and friends came from all over Chile to the funeral. After Mayko was buried, I went back alone to the Subud hall where her wake had been held. As I stood in recollection, I said to her: "In this latihan hall, I can still feel the feeling that you left behind when you took the most important, the most sublime step of your life, the act of leaving this earth. You did it according to your nature, quietly, inconspicuously, with that way of yours—of not wanting to disturb." I found that I still wanted to go to the area where Mayko spent her last days. I went to the clinic and asked permission to enter her room. It was empty, impeccable, and profoundly still. The feeling of something special was still there.

Being with Mayko during the last weeks of her life had been a major experience for me. I had gone from despair at her illness and her suffering, and regrets for my failings towards her, to a closeness in which I thanked her for all she gave me in my life. For the first time, I was able to treat her *"de tú"* (a most familiar way in Spanish).

A FEW DAYS before Mayko's death, I had attended a latihan of helpers and committee members and was invited by the helpers to lead some testing. I began with tests of various parts of the body, and then proceeded to test about how to inwardly separate in the midst of stress or action. The testing was strong and clear. This led to testing again with them during the three weeks that followed Mayko's death, until the time of my departure. During four such sessions, the principal theme was that of experiencing how to inwardly separate from one's own reactions. The latihans were ethereal and near ecstatic, and the feeling among the helpers became increasingly harmonious. Also, I noticed that this spread to the group latihan, which gained a higher quality and strength. Many of the women helpers came or called me later to say how valuable the experience had been. They said they now understood that they could have an inner space, which could remain calm—between their talking, acting, feeling, and so on, and their inner self—in spite of the emotions involved.

In the high state arising from these latihans, I had a dream:

I go to Cilandak and enter a long room where there are people standing with their backs to me, suggesting the overflow at a Mass. I move on and go to the latihan hall. I see that it is full of church ornaments. The latihan hall has become a regular church, and there is no latihan. I cry desperately from deep inside.

Helpers and Being Helped

At first I could not see how this dream applied to me. It seemed more to relate to the outer situation in official Subud, which had long distressed me. It was some time before I understood its full meaning.

It was about myself. It showed how I was reacting to the official Subud enterprises and how extreme was my reaction. In the symbolic language of the dream, I was seeing the Subud brotherhood's absorption in many projects—such as the bank, which had contributed to my distress in 1970, an office building, a conference centre, and others—as having become like 'religious ornaments,' which had captured the attention of the members. It showed my concern that the official Subud project activity had eclipsed the latihan—"the latihan hall had become a church without latihan."

The desperate crying from deep inside with which the dream ended was my purification of this concern. Thanks to the grace of God, this burden on my inner feeling—my life-long problem of the conflict between the spiritual and the material—was at last being lifted.

Chapter Twelve
Bapak's Last Years

WE MOVED TO AUSTRALIA at a time when International Subud activity was concentrating in Sydney. The International Subud Committee (ISC) had its office there, and a number of people had come from other countries to help in trying to establish an International Subud Centre. Our decision was based on Bapak's advice that Sandra needed a different environment for her studies, and our testing confirmed that Sydney should be our new home.

The move opened up the opportunity for me to do more helper's work. On January 3, 1985, in response to a proposal put to Bapak by ISC that I should be Vice-Chairman, and another by the outgoing National Helper that I should be a National Helper, ISC received a telex:

Bapak approves the nomination of Istimah Week as Kejiwaan Councillor for Australia, not, repeat not, as Vice-Chairman of ISC. Signed for Bapak, Rahayu.

The role of Kejiwaan Councillor (Spiritual Councillor) was one of being active as a National Helper throughout Australia and to represent the country on the spiritual side at the World and Zonal Congresses. I was very happy with this decision, as it had come from Bapak without my solicitation.

Sandra was to go to Europe later, but in the meantime, she alternately worked and continued her studies. She was opened in December 1984, shortly after her eighteenth birthday. As Bapak had predicted, it was just a formality, for she already had had her own latihan for many years.

Over the next five years, I travelled to all the major groups in Australia: Sydney, Melbourne, Hobart, Adelaide, Canberra, Darwin, Perth, and Brisbane, having meetings, doing latihan, and testing with members and with helpers. I often returned to Sydney with new understanding. The amazing thing about the latihan was that I would listen to myself speak and would learn things that I never knew before. It was as Bapak said in 1969, "If you continue to do your latihan and surrender to God, you will be given the secrets of life."

Chapter Twelve

In this work I was often reminded of Bapak. I would think, "Ah! so this is how Bapak handled it." or "So this is what he meant." or "Now I know why he did it this way." I realised how he must have felt in similar circumstances.

There was no reason for members to expect anything extra from a visiting National Helper; everyone had the latihan and there were local helpers with whom to test. However, I found the role of National Helper carried a symbolic effect. With this came strong latihans, lasting sometimes up to an hour. This resulted in many women being able to go further into their latihan—into a deeper state of surrender. This was liberating and their faces shone with the experience.

The testing often revealed something hitherto unknown or long-standing. For example, during a visit to Melbourne, a woman found from the testing that her lifelong sense of duty to her church was too rigid. The latihan was moving her to give more to herself. As we drove to the airport, I thought, *Can she carry out her receiving when it requires such a big change in attitude?* The answer came, "Surrender the results, because the work is timeless." This reminded me that sometimes it would take years for a person to be able to follow, or fully understand, a test by Bapak.

National Helpers' visits were spent principally meeting and doing latihan with the local helpers group. After this we had latihan with all the members. This often led to testing members' questions, which the local helpers had not yet resolved. The questions were about spiritual matters arising from the latihan process, such as finding the right attitude to a difficulty. We were not there to test ordinary life questions like, "Where should I invest my money?" or "How can I find a husband?" These were decisions for the heart and mind.

Some ordinary life problems could have an outer and inner aspect, and the helpers would often have to decide whether to test or not. Marriage difficulties illustrated the point. These were problems of behaviour, but they also had a spiritual dimension—reflected in the person's attitude. This was sensitive territory and was amongst the most difficult for helpers, especially if the person wanted the helpers to take sides. By dealing with the problem inside the person—as their responsibility—it was often possible to find a solution. We would test with the woman, to find the way for her to bring the latihan into her daily life and into her handling of the situation. She could also test to find her right attitude to her husband. This was strengthening for the woman.

Bapak's Last Years

As a result of this work, I came to understand something of the difference between feminine and masculine perception. Women often had a natural capacity to be sensitive to things being wrong or unresolved in a situation, without necessarily knowing exactly what the problem was. Men on the other hand were good at solving problems, but often did not notice that a problem existed. When a couple were aware of these differences as complementary strengths, the man could often grasp and understand what the woman had vaguely sensed.

The work of the helpers was by now of great assistance to Bapak. It relieved him of many questions previously directed to him by mail. At the same time, he was kept informed by reports sent to him by National Helpers all over the world.

Meantime in August 1983, before moving to Australia, I had gone with Mark to the Seventh Subud World Congress in England. We rented a house in Windsor for a month and were joined by David, Erica and Sandra. Mark and I visited Bapak and his family to pay our respects, but didn't stay long. Bapak looked somewhat frail. For some time he had been saying that he was handing over the affairs of Subud to the membership, but he still never seemed to say "no" to anyone. The family were doing their best to see he wasn't imposed upon.

The Congress was held at the Anugraha Conference Centre, which the brotherhood had built as an International Subud Centre. It was a converted manor house on nine hectares of beautiful English parkland in Windsor. The architects had retained the elegant exterior and remodelled the interior with meeting halls and first-class hotel rooms. Because it was not yet finished, the Congress sessions and latihans were held in a huge tent erected in the grounds nearby. There were almost two thousand participants.

When it came to the testing in a plenary session to select International Helpers for the next four-year period, I was disturbed to see that it was not arranged as Bapak had shown at the previous Congress in Toronto. Instead of testing those National Helpers who were ending their four-year period, it was announced that only Kejiwaan Councillors would be tested. Since Bapak had asked me in Toronto to specifically witness the way it was to be done, I was left with the feeling that Bapak's wish had not been carried out.

Chapter Twelve

Now, in 1985 in Australia, although I had adjusted to the concept of enterprises in Subud, I was confronted with the major Subud projects and the bank beginning to fail financially. As Bapak had promoted them, I found it was important for me to understand why this was happening. The first thing I perceived was my own attitude to these failures—I was deeply concerned that the foolishness and incompetence of people could jeopardise the Gift of God. I needed to first become inwardly separated from my own concern. I was then able to do this when others brought the same question to me for testing.

I understood that the failures could only have been avoided if the people involved in the enterprises had been able to inwardly separate. As Subud was young—we were pioneers—people were often not using the project to find their worship in life, as Bapak had intended. The impulses to be over-clever with money or self-indulgent with ideas were natural. The error was to give in to these impulses. These were opportunities for people to change. Had they inwardly separated, these forces could have gone to the right place. Bapak put it this way:

Once we know that God is accompanying us [in the latihan] . . . and we make a mistake, that is our mistake. If we admit our mistakes and are willing to take the consequences, the bad effect of our actions will not follow. [48]

In June 1986, I attended an Asian Zone Conference in Jakarta. Then in October, Mark went to a meeting in London, appointed by the Australian and New Zealand National Committees to represent the interests of the membership's investors in the S'Widjojo Centre, the Subud office building enterprise in Jakarta. While he was there, Bapak invited Mark, Sandra, and me to come to Cilandak in November, to attend Bapak's Eleventh Windu* (Bapak's eighty-eighth birthday on the Javanese calendar).

We went and Bapak's joy in seeing Sandra was obvious. The Windu celebration was a big occasion with hundreds of guests and a *wayang kulit* (Javanese shadow puppet play) performance. Bapak gave two talks. He emphasised the importance of practising our religion (religious observances) at the same time as following the latihan. They go together. "The helpers should not mislead people by saying, 'The latihan is enough, you don't have to practise your religion.'" he said.

---
* Windu: Javanese eight year cycle. Bapak was eighty-five on the Gregorian calendar.

Two days after the Windu and while a number of the visitors were still in Cilandak, Bapak had all the women in the compound do latihan in his presence in the latihan hall. At the end he had us test: "Show your attitude to Almighty God?" He was very stern and repeated the test. I felt such a strong vibration of life force that I had to lean against the wall for support. Afterwards it kept me awake throughout the night. I didn't understand why Bapak had appeared so stern. I can only assume that his severity was appropriate to the help he was moved to give.

In Subud, the relationship between men and women followed the normal cultural mode of each country. In the West, for example, men and women mixed freely and enjoyed relative equality. The one important exception was that men only did latihan with men and women only with women. Men helpers only assisted men members and women helpers only women members (opening, testing, and so on).* It was therefore not within my role as a woman helper to discuss problems or spiritual experiences with men. This was in the guidelines, and it felt right. As a result, talking with men about spiritual matters was rare for me.

At the same time, I felt free about it. If I was in a situation with friends where the conversation led to a discussion with a man, I had no problem. There was one particular exception, if a man became highfalutin'. By that I mean if he became inflated with imaginary ideas—for example, explaining his situation in terms of past lives, or giving spiritual meaning to current world events. In that case, I became an unwilling listener and usually found a polite way out of the conversation.

The most common situation would be for a man to start spontaneously talking about a genuine experience which had touched his feelings. I respected that as it was natural that a man who had something unresolved arising from his feminine side would feel comfortable talking to a woman about it.

A good friend of ours was an expert in computer science. He was a member of an American think-tank and worked on the mathematics of missile guidance systems. After six years in Subud, he had a strange experience in which he found in his office a gold replica of what the Roman Catholics call the Miraculous Medal, wrapped in a paper with a written message from Catherine Laboure, a French Catholic saint of the nineteenth century. This inexplicable episode coincided with a strong awakening of religious feelings. But it was to be some time before he recognised that these feelings were a quality of the feminine side of his nature.

---

* Men and women helpers had joint group meetings (not latihans) at the local, national, and international levels.

Chapter Twelve

Years later, as I was accompanying Sandra to London, I stopped in New York and met this friend at lunch. He began talking enthusiastically about a "saintly woman" he knew in Paris, whom he believed had exceptional spiritual sensitivity. I felt that he was attributing to this woman a special sensitivity of his own feminine side. I suggested that his exaggerated reverence for this woman arose from a quality in himself and that he was therefore wasting it by projecting it on to someone else. His initial reaction was to disagree, but before I left New York, I spoke to him again on the telephone to thank him for his hospitality. He said with touching sincerity that he felt that our meeting had been timely and what I had said to him at lunch was profoundly important to him. "I am very happy with this understanding," he said.

After I arrived in London, I was talking with a friend of Mark's, also a Subud member. He told me that, to his immense sorrow, his daughter had been taking drugs. One day he asked God, "What can I do for my daughter?" and heard a voice say, "Ask her forgiveness." He was surprised at this, but he obeyed the guidance and she got over her problem. I was very moved by this account and I understood that, because the sins of the parents are passed on to the children, by asking forgiveness, he broke the cycle of (otherwise unavoidable) inheritance. His daughter was then freed of the cause of her need for drugs.

I FOUND that working as a helper, doing extra latihans, and testing all manner of personal problems and experiences can accelerate the process of change in oneself. In my case, as the process touched on my ancestral problems, I discovered a special need to understand my tendency to polarise. It was not just the spiritual versus the material. People were to me high or low, right or wrong, and I was either enthusiastic or totally disinterested.

Years earlier I had received in a latihan: "You must eliminate Claudius-Claudia from yourself and your family line!" This referred to a disposition in my ancestry—two contrary qualities, the one masculine, rigid, old, and infirm (represented by Claudius) and the other feminine, adaptable, young, and healthy (represented by Claudia). I now saw that it was not the qualities, but the tension between them, which had to be eliminated.

However purification in Subud was something that had to be lived through in its own time and in its own way. Two visits I made back to Chile at different times showed that something could happen when I least expected it or in a way that I had not foreseen.

On the first trip, I went with Erica and, leaving her with friends in Santiago, I flew north to visit Antofagasta where I had spent much of my childhood. The plaza, the church, and the houses in my old neighbourhood were little changed. I had heard of some curative thermal waters in the hinterland, so I travelled north to Iquique and took a bus up into the high Andes. The winding narrow dirt road was cut into the mountain side and was so steep that I dared not look back at the plain below. I arrived at night at Mamiña, one of the highest of the old towns built by the Spanish Conquistadors and stayed at a simple rest-house with thermal baths. The place was stark but clean, and I was the only guest. I came to breakfast in the dining room with deep feelings of distress. I could hardly stand myself. Suddenly emotion overcame me as I heard on a cassette recorder a Chilean song from a happy time of my adult life. Tears poured from my eyes. The dichotomy between the barrenness, the loneliness, and the nostalgia of the song was overpowering. It felt as if God had showed he cared. In this unexpected way, I was brought to feel and release some of the hidden anxiety of my childhood.

On the second occasion, much later, I went to Punta Arenas, especially to confront the events of my early childhood. I wanted to know about my father's behaviour. He was torn by opposition in himself—he could be so kind and also so violent. I wanted to unravel the Claudius-Claudia inheritance. When I got there, my aunt Fanny was seriously ill with cancer. Pepe, her poet husband, had died several years before. Fanny was only ten years older than I and had been my close friend when we were young. She had been asking for me and recognised me immediately. She was very clear minded. "You came!" she said.

I immediately did latihan with her. I felt it was not necessary to explain to her about Subud. I knew that to give her the latihan was the greatest gift possible. I could see that she was receiving. That was the beginning of her changing in front of my eyes. She became more quiet and peaceful. She told me about my father's outbursts, things I didn't know. I assimilated it all without distress—I was now there for Fanny. I did the latihan with her twice a day for a week, and when it came time to leave, she said, "You have brought me great peace." A few days later she died.

I knew I had come all this way to pass her the latihan before she died. I was immensely grateful, and only later I realised that in this unexpected way I was helping to resolve the problem of my family line. Bapak's words were never far away: "It is very important to receive the latihan before you die."

Chapter Twelve

I noticed my inner locution "Christ is in Heaven" had changed. It now was "Christ is *contigo*" (*contigo* means, with you). I thought, *How strange, half English and half Spanish!* Yet how right, *contigo* is more intimate than 'with you.' " Still later it became a gentle repetition "Christ . . . Christ . . . Christ . . ."

In June 1987, an Asian Zone Conference was scheduled in Cilandak. I was to attend as Kejiwaan Councillor for Australia. Michele, a close friend living in Sydney, was also going to Cilandak to attend an International Helper meeting and had been invited to visit the Subud group in Kuala Lumpur on the way. We decided to travel together and that I would go with her to Malaysia for five days.

Michele organised the itinerary for us to leave Sydney on June 11 and return from Cilandak on June 23. When I showed the plans to Mark, he agreed to everything but suggested that I extend my stay in Cilandak for three or four days—he said he didn't know why, but he felt quite certain that I should. This was to be one of my most important visits to Cilandak and, as it turned out, staying the extra time was crucial.

Before leaving Sydney I had an impressive dream:

I had just arrived in Cilandak. It was night. Suddenly I saw the moon—only a few metres away from me. It was so close that I could see only a part of it. It was a rich amber colour and its nearness was amazing. . . . I awoke with the latihan and lay there for some time still looking at the surface of the moon.

The experience affected me strongly. I was left in a state of inner separation in which the latihan and the image of the moon continued together.

On our way to Malaysia, the plane touched down briefly at Jakarta airport just as the sun was setting. Having recently dreamed of the moon, I was struck to see through the cabin window a large full moon, glowing on the horizon.

We stayed in Kuala Lumpur with the Alphonsos, a very hospitable Subud family, attending latihans with the helpers and meeting with individual members. The visit went well. By using testing, many personal and group questions were answered to the members' satisfaction.

On June 16 we flew to Indonesia. The beauty of the atolls was breathtaking as the plane cruised low over the Java Sea. In Wisma Subud, I was put in the guesthouse on the second floor where Bapak lived with Ibu during our first visit in 1965. Each time I came back, I noticed how much the trees had grown. The flame-tree I had planted at our house years ago as a twig was now an enormous size and a mass of red and yellow flowers.

Bapak's Last Years

By coincidence, Ilaina Bartok (now named Maria) had also arrived, just a few days before. It was her first visit since she had lived in Wisma Subud eighteen years earlier. I was very happy to see her again; she and I had been the closest of friends in this place.

The first news I had of Bapak was the morning after my arrival. I met Harlinah Longcroft, who still lived in the compound. She said that Bapak was quite weak and had trouble breathing. Oxygen had to be available for him at all times. "Nevertheless," she said, "Bapak has been saying that the International meeting should go ahead and take place near him and maybe the Zonal Conference too!" She also told me that Bapak had said in his last talk that he now lived between life and death—in both worlds at the same time. "For a long time now," he said, "Bapak does not sleep."

In spite of Bapak's condition, the delegation, from the thirteen countries of the Asian Zone, from Japan to Saudi Arabia, was invited to hold the opening session of the Conference at Bapak's house on the morning of Friday June 19. We went there in private cars and small buses. Many people from other parts of the world were there as observers.

Since the last time I had been in Indonesia, Bapak had, at the behest of his family, built a new house at Pamulang, about thirty minutes farther south from Cilandak. It was designed with elements of an almost forgotten Javanese architectural tradition, which graded the living areas in terms of privacy from a large *pendopo* (outer reception area) in the front, to intimate family areas far back in the interior of the house. The *pendopo* was an elegant glazed-in hall about twenty metres square, with a gentle sloping roof supported in the middle on four carved teak pillars. The house behind was two storeys with a staircase immediately inside the front doors leading up to a balcony. It was a beautiful building and appropriate to Bapak's needs as an aged person.

When we arrived, the atmosphere was quiet and relaxed. People talked little and moved quietly, out of reverence for Bapak. Latin American music was being played softly through a speaker system. The opening speeches of the conference were simple and friendly. When this was over, we returned to Wisma Subud.

Our first working meeting began at 2:00 P.M. in the Latihan Hall, and soon after it started, I quite unexpectedly began to feel ill. There was nothing to explain it, and I couldn't describe the symptoms. I stayed in the meeting, believing the condition would pass. However it got worse until I finally had to leave.

Chapter Twelve

I found I didn't have the strength to walk to my room. All I could do was to go to the nearby house of Maryam Kibble, a long-time resident and friend. I cried for a long time, beyond consolation, and the strange thing was that I couldn't hold my head up. Maryam called a visitor from Malaysia who was a homoeopathic doctor. Her medicine calmed me a little, then the three of us did latihan together. Maryam insisted I sleep in her house that night. It was twenty-four hours before I started to feel a little better.

That night, when Bapak was being treated by Ibu Widarbo, his physiotherapist, he said, to allay her fear of his dying, "It's not right now." He then put his fingers first over one eye and then over the other, as if to shut out the light of the room, and said, "No, it's not yet, for I can still see the moon." [The waning moon had two days to go].

During the following days, I felt very fragile, but I returned to the meetings. At night I slept in my own room. The second night, I awoke feeling sick. Again I could not describe it as a normal sickness. I was in agony—a kind of anguish, the most uncomfortable sensation I had ever known. I felt I was going to die. In the end I came to terms with myself. I simply gave my affirmation to God, "Yes, I accept that I will die now and that I will be buried in Indonesia." What I did not know was that this was happening just a short time before Bapak's death.

The next day was Bapak's birthday, June 22. In the morning we did latihan in the Wisma Subud hall. It was very quiet when I came in, but soon it became very strong. During the day, we heard that Bapak was unwell, but that the selamatan for his birthday would still be held at his house.

In the evening, we were driven to the *pendopo*. I sat with Ilaina and Michele, three old-timers together—we had each been in Subud thirty years. How right it was that Ilaina was there. I felt it was no coincidence.

Haryono gave a short talk in Indonesian and English. He then suggested that we walk from the *pendopo* into Bapak's house singing 'Panjang Umurnya' (the Indonesian birthday song) and 'Happy Birthday' in English. I thought the idea was that Bapak would be able to hear us from his sickbed. But as I looked up, I saw Bapak, in a formal Indonesian batik shirt, sitting near a small table on the balcony, with his family around him. I found myself choking as I tried to keep singing while tears rolled down my face. Others around were also weeping.

Bapak's Last Years

When the singing finished, Bapak stood up and cut his traditional rice-mountain birthday cake. He turned to us and waved and continued to wave as he walked away. I would have liked to stop weeping, but my tears came from such a deep place, I had no power to stop them. I didn't know that Bapak had pneumonia, but inside I knew this was the last farewell.

The following morning at 5:00 A.M. there was a knock on my door. It was Ilaina. She simply said, "He's gone!" Bapak had died at 4.05 A.M., at the time of the dawn prayer, Subuh.

I called Mark in Sydney and at the same time asked him to notify the International Subud Committee office, which would inform the rest of the Subud world. I went to Bapak's house to attend the Islamic ceremonies. The body was bathed by the men, privately inside a special enclosure created by hanging batiks, then wrapped by an Imam and placed in the coffin in the centre of the living room. The Imam then led prayers, and hundreds of members came to pay their homage. The following morning I was fortunate to be given a seat in a car in the funeral cortege. I saw Bapak buried next to his mother in the family tomb at Karet Cemetery in Jakarta. That evening I attended the first of the traditional *selamatans* at the house.

At the second *selamatan* (on the third day), my latihan became very strong—blissful and conscious—as the Imam recited the Islamic verses, La-illaha Illalah (There is no God but God). This was the latihan kejiwaan of Subud that Bapak had brought to mankind.

TWO YEARS LATER in Sydney on June 22, 1989, the anniversary of Bapak's birthday, I had this early morning dream:

I was outdoors standing alone. I could see groups of Subud people chatting and enjoying themselves as if on a picnic. I turned around and found I was facing the ocean, although I couldn't see it. From there, Bapak came straight towards me, smiling. He was more like a wise old man, tallish and slim. He handed me some colour photographs and told me that they would be shown at some significant event. I looked at them and saw that they were of different groups of Subud people. In one group sitting on the ground outdoors, I recognised a friend from Chile. Bapak said it was very important that these photographs be shown at this event and that I had something to do with it. He was happy about this. He then returned to where he had come from.

Chapter Twelve

The Subud people in the area started coming towards me to see what Bapak had given me. I asked them to keep back because by gathering near me they were obscuring the sunlight, without which I could not see the photographs. As I awoke I was left with the words *"gotong royong"* (working together).

I felt that the dream was a message of trust in myself—trust in my experience with Bapak and its possible contribution to the spread of Subud—a trust which contributed to the writing of this book.

SOMETIME BEFORE Bapak's death, he had started to prepare us to stand on our own feet. He explained how he saw Subud would be later when he was no longer with us:

Bapak is only a pioneer in Subud. Bapak is not the one with authority. The only one with authority in your lives is God Almighty.

Bapak is here with you now to give you advice and so on. But you have to understand that Bapak is a human being [and already eighty years old] and one of these days will no longer be with you. And if by that time you have still not learned to stand on your own feet—how to receive for yourselves and how to express in reality what you have received from Almighty God—then Subud will be limited to Bapak's own life span.

But that is not the will of Almighty God. The will of Almighty God is only that Bapak should be a pioneer, that Bapak should bring to us something which will bring us into contact with God's power. And once we have received this, then we can carry it on ourselves. So if the helpers can carry out their duties and put into practice what Bapak has told them, then Bapak has received that Subud will last for eight hundred years. And only after eight hundred years will there be some change, will it turn in some different direction.

So, brothers and sisters, what you have to realise and to feel from your own experience of the latihan—which Bapak has brought to you and which is now your possession—is that God is actually closer to you than anything else you possess. Closer to you than your own seeing, your own hearing, your own thinking. The power of God is always there accompanying you in everything you do. . . .

Bapak would like to explain about the impression that when Bapak dies he will be far away. It is not like that. Because Bapak is enveloped by the power of God, actually [already] there is nothing left of Pak Subuh; everything belongs to God. [49]

Epilogue

Pak Subuh said "Bapak is Subud and Subud is Bapak." I believe the Bapak he referred to was the one who brought a message—the latihan kejiwaan of Subud. This was the spiritual Bapak that came back from his Ascension in 1932 with a task to be performed and the means of carrying it out.

Among those who encouraged me to write this memoir of Pak Subuh was a religious historian. She said I should write about him for history's sake, because of my unique experience. "Within a generation," she said, "Pak Subuh the man will have been overtaken by Bapak the image and by the message that he brought and lived. What can we say of the historical Jesus? Our experience of Christ within has overtaken the man."

My intention, however, has not been to be an historian, although I have tried to give an accurate account of my experiences. I wanted to present Bapak the Messenger as I knew him. In this I have been sincere. In doing so I trust that I have at the same time described Pak Subuh the man.

Appendix
The Meaning of Subud

*S*UBUD *is an abbreviation of the words Susila Budhi Dharma. Subud is not a new religion, or a sect of any religion, nor is it a teaching. Subud is a symbol of the possibility for man to follow the right way of living:*

Susila denotes those qualities which give rise to character, conduct and actions which are truly human, and in accordance with the will of God.

Budhi indicates that in all creatures, including man, there is divine power that works within him as well as outside him.

Dharma signifies sincerity, surrender and submission to the Will of Almighty God.

Susila Budhi Dharma means to follow the will of God with the help of the divine power that works both within us and without, by the way of surrendering oneself to the Will of Almighty God. [1]

Glossary

Bapak	Indonesian word for Father—used for a respected older man. In this book it refers to Pak Subuh.
Pak Subuh	Bapak Muhammad Subuh Sumohadiwidjojo.
Subuh	Indonesian word meaning dawn. Also the Islamic dawn prayer, Subuh. Bapak was given the name Subuh because he was born at dawn. The word *Subuh* has no direct connection with the word *Subud*.
Ibu	Indonesian word for Mother in Indonesian and a term of respect. In this book it refers to Bapak's wife, Siti Sumari.
Subud	An abbreviation of Susila Budhi Dharma. The possibility of right living through the grace of God received in the latihan kejiwaan of Subud.
Susila	Right living in accordance with the Will of God.
Budhi	The divine power residing in the nature of man himself.
Dharma	Submission with patience, trust and sincerity to the Will of God.
Latihan	Indonesian word which literally translates as training or exercise. Here it means the spiritual exercise of Subud.
Kejiwaan	Indonesian word meaning spiritual.
Contact	In Subud means the initial receiving of the latihan, also known as the *Opening*.
Jiwa	The spiritual content of the self, usually translated as soul.
Nafsu	The passions that animate feeling and thinking.
Helpers	Those who according to Bapak had enough experience of the latihan kejiwaan of Subud to be able to pass on the contact to others.
Cilandak	The suburb of Jakarta where Pak Subuh established his home and the first International Subud Centre.
Testing	The name given to receiving answers to questions in the latihan state. Its function is to check the progress of the latihan in oneself or to gain insight into a problem.

References

Talks by Bapak Muhammad Subuh
Copyright held by the Subud World Association

Appendix

[1] The Meaning of Subud, London 1959, and
     A General Talk to Applicants, Singapore 1960

Introduction

[2] London, August 11, 1959

Chapter One

[3] London, August 11, 1959
[4] Coombe Springs, August 19, 1957

Chapter Two

[5]   New York, May 3, 1959
[6]   New York, May 3, 1959
[7]   New York, May 9, 1959
[8]   Leicester, July 8, 1970
[9]   Leicester, July 8, 1970
[10] Quito, November 6, 1977
[11] Bristol, UK, June 26, 1977

Chapter Three

[12] New York, May 3, 1959
[13] New York, May 6, 1959
[14] New York, May 13, 1959
[15] Briarcliff, July 8, 1963
[16] Briarcliff, July 9, 1963
[17] Briarcliff, July 16, 1963
[18] Autobiography, Bapak Muhammad Subuh

Chapter Five

[19] SIS Bulletin Vol 2, No 6, 1965

Chapter Six

[20] Letter 1033/69, Pewarta, Vol VII No 5
[21] Cilandak, December 3, 1969

Chapter Seven

- [22] Poona, June 30, 1970
- [23] Leicester, July 11, 1970
- [24] Oslo, July 16, 1970
- [25] Hamburg, July 18, 1970
- [26] Poona, July 1970
- [27] Skymont, August 17, 1970
- [28] Skymont, August 19, 1970
- [29] Skymont, August 19, 1970
- [30] Manchester, August 28, 1970
- [31] London, September 1, 1970
- [32] Melbourne, September 19, 1970

Chapter Eight

- [33] Cilandak, December 5, 1970
- [34] New York, July 15, 1963

Chapter Ten

- [35] Wolfsburg, August 1964
- [36] Cilandak, December 5, 1970
- [37] Cilandak, August 5, 1971
- [38] Cilandak, August 26, 1971

Chapter Eleven

- [39] The Basis and Aim of Subud, 1969
- [40] Vancouver, July 11, 1981
- [41] Melbourne, May 7, 1982
- [42] Mexico, November 22, 1977
- [43] Buenos Aires, October 22, 1977
- [44] Lima, November 1, 1977
- [45] Rio de Janeiro, October 16, 1977
- [46] Mexico, November 20, 1977
- [47] Toronto, August 14, 1979

Chapter Twelve

- [48] Cilandak, January 7, 1979
- [49] Cilandak, January 7, 1979

Personae

Bapak's family:

Bapak [means Father] Muhammad Subuh Sumohadiwidjojo, born 1901, died 1987. Name abbreviated to Bapak Muhammad Subuh or simply Pak Subuh. Bapak had a younger brother and sister.

Eyang [means Grandmother] Kursinah, Bapak's mother, died 1974 aged 97 years.

Chasidi (Bapak's father), son of Kiai [religious teacher] Abubakar.

Rumindah, Bapak's first wife, died 1936.
Rahayu, Bapak's eldest daughter, born 1928.
Haryono, Bapak's son, born 1930, married Ismana.
Haryadi, Bapak's son, born 1931, died 1954.
Suharyo, Bapak's son, born 1933, died 1935.
Hardiyati, Bapak's daughter, born 1935, married Sjafrudin, who died in 1967.

Ibu [means Mother] Siti Sumari, Bapak's second wife as widow with two children, married to Bapak 1941, died 1971.

Rochanawati, Ibu's daughter, died 1966.
Tuti, Muti, Indra, Tina (short names), daughters of Rochanawati (Bapak's grand-daughters).
Adji, son of Rochanawati (Bapak's grandson).
Mastuti, Bapak's third wife, married to Bapak 1974.

Istimah's family:

Istimah Week, name originally Irma.
Mark Week, Istimah's husband (name originally Erling).

Mayko [means Mother] Anastasia, Istimah's mother.
Guido Petric, Istimah's father.
Latif Petric, Istimah's younger brother (name originally Guido).
David Week, Istimah's son.
Erica Week, Istimah's elder daughter (name originally Catherine).
Sandra Week, Istimah's younger daughter.
Clementina, Mayko's maid, then companion, then Sandra's nurse.
Fanny, Mayko's younger sister, married to Pepe Jose Grimaldi.

Istimah Week
PO Box 134   Oneroa
Waiheke Island
New Zealand